A Plum Jam

Cenarth Fox

For
Mel de Bono
Lifelong supporter of the performing arts

'Set Europe ablaze.'
Winston Churchill

Chapter 1

September 1900, Staffordshire England

'Get out! Get out!' screamed the terrified miner. He saw, smelt and heard the start of the cave-in and ran. Rock, timber, dust and death roared into the shaft giving the men and boys no chance.

In that instant, every miner wants freedom or instant death. Being trapped with gashes, blindness and smashed limbs, likely unable to move is agony. Dirt tastes terrible. You have no cyanide pill, just choking, groans and silence. It could be hours before rescue arrives if at all, and if it does, you may die before you get to hospital. Nah, sod that for a game of soldiers; die quick, my son, go now.

Clara didn't know her dad. She was all of six weeks when he went down the mine and never came home. Thank God he died quick like. The collieries in England in 1900 were dangerous; maiming and killing men, boys and pit ponies. Charlie Richards was just another statistic.

'You'll have to leave cottage, Missus,' said the landlord. Clara's mother, Dorothea, known as Dottie, feared the worst; no money, no breadwinner and a babe in arms. The Poorhouse beckoned.

Dottie struggled to pay for hubby's funeral. She clung to the memory of kissing Charlie on that fateful morning. 'And that's from wee Clara,' said Dottie as the man of the house set off. Then came the news and Dottie's howl was heard all the way to *The Gresley Arms*.

But luck's a fortune and Dottie and Clara fell on their feet. A wealthy family in the local manor house needed a housekeeper. The vicar of St Johns, Alsagers Bank, fresh from burying Dottie's old man at Audley, heard of the domestic vacancy at Apedale Hall and recommended the widow Richards. Well done, Padre, and Dottie accepted with a huge sigh of relief.

The stately home was a massive mansion with turrets and towers, and stunning grounds where lawns and trees gave pleasure to all. Once she could walk, wee Clara helped her mama with cooking tasks and later took to needlework like a duck to water. She went to the local school and Sunday school and life was grand.

September 1900, Dublin Ireland

Michael O'Donovan was the son of Brendan and Mary and nephew of John Doyle. The Doyles and O'Donovans were staunch Catholics and Irish nationalists. They knew all about British rule in Ireland. In homes and pubs when talking politics, the O'Donovans and Doyles joined anyone with a passion for Irish independence.

The Penal Laws and Potato Famine were well remembered. No need for books as oral history thrived. Wee Michael grew up hating the British.

His Uncle John taught him to clean, load and fire a rifle, and his father told him tales of great men who resisted the Brits. His mother tried to steer him from violent thoughts but even she longed for an independent homeland.

Michael's schooldays were full of nationalistic pride.

September 1908, Apedale Hall, Staffordshire

Clara ran into the kitchen, her eyes wide, and her rosy cheeks ablaze. 'Mama, there's a new boy.'

'Hush, Clara, remember your manners.'

She kept bubbling. 'I seen him, Mama, I seen him.'

'I saw him,' corrected her mother, who was the last person to be giving grammar lessons.

'His black hair is like the coal in the bucket, and thin legs and eyes make him look like a ghost.'

'Enough, Clara; you mustn't gossip about people, and especially not your betters.'

The young girl wondered about the word. 'What are betters, Mama?'

'Important people what own houses with pots of money.'

Clara took it all in. 'Can I play with my betters?'

'No you cannot.'

'But we're both children, Mama.'

'We are domestics, and in society, people mix with their equals. You play with children of your own class.'

Clara didn't like society's rules. 'Will he live here forever?'

'I don't know. His name is Oswald and he's Sir Oswald's grandson and Mrs Edwards-Heathcote's little boy.'

'You could ask Sir Oswald if his grandson would like to play.'

Dottie put down her rolling pin and wiped her hands on her apron. 'Clara, come and sit here.' The child did and was given a polite explanation of the class system in Edwardian England.

Clara respected her mother's instructions and never played with the future Member of Parliament but remained interested in the new boy who came to Apedale Hall. He took no interest in her, in any of the domestics or lower classes but reckoned the cakes made by Clara's mother were rather jolly good.

Young Oswald was the sporting type, and the spacious Hall with its rooms and grounds were ideal for the energetic lad. Given an epée, he was as happy as a sandboy and fenced with passion.

April 1916, Dublin Ireland

You couldn't call it a war. The Irish crouched behind barrels—yes, barrels! Bullets whizzed overhead. The amateur soldiers dressed in everyday clothes armed with rifles and courage. They were rebels in their own country. Michael O'Donovan was one; a kid, all of 16, who fought like a tiger. His father and uncle were frontline troops. He scampered around carrying ammunition and relaying messages but all to no avail. The rebels were smashed. Their planning was ordinary and their lines of communication a joke. They were Irish amateurs fighting British professionals.

On the sixth day, not long before the rebels surrendered, Michael saw his family members shot. His uncle, John Doyle, mercifully died instantly when a bullet smashed into his brain. Michael's father, Brendan, suffered a far worse fate. His wounds were to his abdomen with blood gushing free. They dragged the wounded man from the line of fire. Michael heard his father was lying near Boland's Bakery and, caring not for the bullets and exploding shells, ran to his Da.

'I'm here, Father, I'm here,' he said clasping his old man's hand. Brendan coughed blood.

'Take care of your mother, me boy. Take ...'

He coughed more blood. 'Oh Jesus,' cried Michael and pushed a handkerchief against his father's stomach. It was a pathetic effort and Michael saw the light fade in his father's eyes as he breathed his last.

Both his father and uncle died fighting for their passionate cause—Irish independence. Michael hated the British.

Giving his mother the news heaped more pain on Michael's grief. His brave mother screamed when told both her husband and brother were dead. Worse, it was within an hour of the ceasefire. Michael did what he could to help his mother and sisters then told them he must visit his friend, Patrick McKnee, who'd been wounded the day before.

'No, Michael,' begged his mother. 'Stay here. It's too dangerous.'

'The fighting's over, Ma. I won't be long, I promise. And I'll tell Father Kelly to come and see you.'

His friend lived nearby. Michael knocked. 'It's me, Michael.'

In the sitting room, lying on the settee, Patrick McKnee lay wounded, his family and friends around. Michael knelt. The room was packed, the mood depressing, and anger bubbled. Defeat and death brought misery. Could life ever be worse? Indeed it could.

Over the six days, British soldiers saw their comrades killed and deemed it murder by ignorant, Irish scum. Some Brits craved revenge.

Without warning, British soldiers burst in from the rear of the house, screaming abuse. 'Fenian bastards,' roared the officer and drove his sword into one of Patrick's friends. Screams exploded, gunfire flashed and bayonets lunged. These were professional soldiers venting their fury on anyone Irish. War crimes got busy in Dublin.

Michael scrambled on all fours heading towards the front door trying to flee the carnage. Blood spurted. Anyone became a target. He reached the door and stood to escape. The officer saw him, raised his revolver and fired. Shooting an unarmed man in the back was justified to the enraged British soldiers. One of Patrick's mates stood and copped the bullet destined for Michael. He fled.

Bursting inside the family home, his face screamed terror. Not wanting to alarm his mother and sisters, he made a dramatic recovery and invented a story about sporadic fighting still happening despite the surrender. He'd forgotten Father Kelly. Who wouldn't?

Would the British come to murder him and his family? No but Michael never forgot the deaths of his family and friends. His hatred of British soldiers lived on and he vowed to one day make them pay.

But the ceasefire heralded official atrocities as the British began their court cases and a steady stream of executions. One wounded rebel was unable to stand so the considerate Brits tied him to a chair before the firing party did their business; talk about a soft target.

And after these bitter "legal" reprisals, came mass arrests with Michael O'Donovan one of nearly 2000 imprisoned. Many never faced a trial, were shipped across the Irish Sea and imprisoned in an old whisky distillery. It was the middle of WW1 and German POWS were shipped out and the Irish shipped in at Frognoch, North Wales.

Is it any wonder Michael grew up hating the British?

But did the Brits shoot themselves in the foot? By placing so many Irishmen in the same POW camp, experienced rebels taught inexperienced rebels like Michael O'Donovan the skills of guerrilla warfare. It would be years before the instruction and inspiration of men like Michael Collins would inspire Irish men to bite the British but bite they did. Michael O'Donovan was the perfect student.

July 1916, the Somme France

Oswald Mosley, the young lad from Apedale Hall, choose a military career. He went to Sandhurst only to be expelled for riotous behavior. When war broke out he was commissioned and fought in France where his actions were described as reckless. Wounded, he retired to recover, returned, was wounded again and, as a result, walked with a limp for the rest of life.

He became a pen-pusher in Blighty but a lowly job never appealed. With his father a baronet, Oswald was entitled to affix the appellation Sir to his name, and Sir Oswald's interest now turned to politics.

1916 Apedale Hall Staffordshire

Dottie died leaving Clara heartbroken, an orphan and without a home. Her mother's sister lived in Newcastle-under-Lyme, and Clara again fell on her feet. Thanks to Dottie's tuition, Clara was an expert cook, dressmaker and soon became darn good at millinery. Wealthy ladies paid Clara to whip up a new hat for church and the odd mayoral function. Clara's future looked bright.

Chapter 2

November 1918, London England

Oswald Mosley's dashing good looks and superb oratory skills helped him climb the political ladder. He stood as the Conservative candidate for Harrow becoming a very young Member of Parliament. He set tongues wagging with his ability to speak off the cuff and with passion, and many saw him as a potential leader; hail Mosley, the future PM.

Being born in Mayfair and part of an aristocratic family, Sir Oswald reinforced his silver spoon heritage by marrying the daughter of the wealthy Guinness brewing family. Oswald and Cynthia tied the knot with King George V and Queen Mary as guests. Between them, the newlyweds boasted prestige and wealth. But Mosley wanted more; he wanted power.

He became good at swapping. He swapped political parties and lovers. He disagreed with the Conservatives on their Anglo-Irish policies—Michael O'Donovan appreciated that—and so resigned from the Tories and eventually joined the Labor Party.

He swapped women too, well, unofficially. He sired two children with wife Cynthia but enjoyed—a euphemism if ever there was one— his wife's sister as well as her step-mother, his mother-in-law; surely a rare achievement. He and Henry VIII had something in common.

As a Labor politician, he won the seat of Midlands and became pals with the Prime Minister, Alex Baldwin. Oswald fancied a senior role in government and was given the task of tackling unemployment. He prepared a powerful dossier, so powerful politicians spoke highly of it decades later. But the cabinet rejected it which got right up Oswald's nose and so he rejected Labor. Another party, another resignation.

Back in Staffordshire, Miss Clara Richards made dresses and hats and read the local newspaper. She remembered the black-haired boy who lived, on and off, at Apedale Hall. Did she ever? Now look at him; the youngest MP, a brilliant public speaker, a title, and all over the newspapers at his own society wedding. Clara read with interest.

Goodness, she thought, *who would have believed young Tom* (his family's nickname for Oswald) *would become so famous?*

But he did and Clara didn't. Apart from her sewing, she faced one important decision; spinsterhood or marriage. She chose the single life—not much choice really—and settled into genteel poverty while her former Apedale Hall resident did exactly the opposite.

1921, Westminster London

The 1916 Easter Rising—a dreadful military disaster for the Irish— finally produced a result. The British government gave Ireland its freedom, well, a version thereof. Six of the counties wanted to remain a part of the United Kingdom but the other 26 became a sovereign state, an independent and free Ireland.

Michael O'Donovan read the news and rejoiced. Hundreds of Irish POWs in North Wales had been released. Many went home but not Michael. Having seen his father and uncle killed and his friends massacred, he turned his back on Ireland. It broke his mother's heart but he reckoned employment prospects were much better in England.

So in the land of his hated enemy, he moved to London, found work on the docks, and mixed with other Irish men and women, each with a singular hatred of everything British.

1931 England

Oswald won elections as a Conservative and later as a member of the Labor Party. But when he formed his own, the New Party, life turned sour. The New Party began the race from a long way back. With no traditional supporter base, he stood for parliament and lost.

His philandering proved less of a distraction when his wife died of peritonitis. Oswald travelled to Italy, saw the work of Signor Mussolini and fell in love with fascism. Hitler's activities appealed and Mosley returned to England with fire in his belly.

In Staffordshire, Clara was drifting towards life on the shelf. One of her cousins played matchmaker introducing Clara to the brother of a friend. At the local dance, Clara took to the floor with one, Victor Rackett, allowing him to walk her home. They were both lonely and, hoping being lonely with someone else was better than being lonely alone, opted to wed. Oh dear. Still, we all make mistakes.

Victor worked in the mines as did his deceased father-in-law. The newlyweds rented a cottage and got on like a house in February with no heating. Victor spent his time and money in the pub. Wherever their marriage was made, it definitely wasn't in heaven.

Back in England, Oswald promoted fascism. At first people, newspapers and politicians liked his ideas. The British Union of Fascists was born and boasted 50,000 members. Their rallies were lively. Plenty came to protest and others to sticky beak. Michael O'Donovan, living in London, became a curious onlooker.

Many protestors were Communists and Jews, the people Mosley blamed for the ills of society. They hurled abuse at the former Apedale Hall resident.

To protect himself and to give protestors a taste of their own medicine, Oswald formed a private army, dressed them in black and called them his Blackshirts. They dealt with protesters by punching first and delivering expletives later. Bones broke and blood spilt.

All this violence produced headlines and Clara Richards, now Mrs Victor Rackett, shook her head in wonder at the derring-do of her former neighbour.

Even Michael O'Donovan, earning his living in London, followed the rise of the fascists with interest. He held no truck with their politics but Mosley's attack on Britain's policies in Ireland, piqued the former Dubliner's interest.

July 1936, Newcastle-under-Lyme England

Clara put her husband's supper on the table. He arrived via the pub. He couldn't spell *affection* let alone show any. Victor burped and slurped his sausages and mash then dropped a bombshell.

'I'm quitting the mine.'

The shock left Clara speechless. His next sentence left her cold.

'We're moving to London.'

'London!' exclaimed Clara finally finding her voice. She'd never been out of Staffordshire.

'There's plenty of work, and we can rent a terrace near the docks. You can take in washing or do your sewing.'

Clara shook her head. The discussion—what discussion?—was over. London, here we come.

'We go next week,' said Victor and they did.

They settled in Poplar in the East End, and Victor found work in a rope factory by the docks. They rented a terrace in Driffield Road, and with the Great Depression stalking the world, life was tough.

Having children was not discussed. Either or both failed in the reproductive organ department leading to Victor turning even more to the grog. Clara used her sewing skills to make a few bob.

Coming home with the little shopping she could afford, she picked up a discarded newspaper because a photo caught her eye.

There was the boy from Apedale Hall, dressed in a black shirt and sporting a splendid moustache. She read about him.

My, how young Oswald has come up in the world.

Look at him directing his hordes of black-shirted followers. The newspaper carried details of a meeting of the British Union of Fascists at Olympia, a London building housing 12,000 people.

Who are these Fascists?

Young Tom, or rather Sir Oswald, would be speaking. Victor would be in the pub or collapsed on the settee having staggered home drunk. Alone, Clara went to the rally.

It was packed. Clara worried she'd be the only woman but plenty of females were there and many were keen to have their say.

Then the man himself took to the stage to both cheers and jeers. No notes needed for Oswald who whipped the meeting into a frenzy. He urged Europe to unite. He railed against talk of war, against Communism and the Jews. His followers lapped up his rhetoric. Clara, fascinated to see how the boy had become a man, agreed with parts of his rhetoric. She became a closet fascist.

She couldn't discuss her new found religion with Victor. She couldn't discuss anything with the brute. As war grew ever more likely, Clara's passion for the Fascists grew stronger; Victor drank more and turned to physical violence.

The Fascists were handy with their fists, and Victor copied their thuggery by using his wife as a punching bag. She wanted out; out of the East End, her marriage and her misery but know not how.

And speaking of marriage, as Clara suffered, her former house mate, the widower Sir Oswald Mosley, decided to embark on a second marital journey this time choosing one of the well-known Mitford sisters, Diana. Clara didn't receive a wedding invitation as the nuptials were celebrated in Germany in the home of fancy talker Joseph Goebbels, where the guest of honour was that chap from Austria, Adolf Hitler.

1936, East End, London

Mosley and his mates fumed. Their meetings kept being interrupted by violent protestors, mainly Communists and Jews. The BUF decided to make a stand. They would defy their opponents and march through the heart of London's East End, with its large Jewish population. Talk about asking for trouble.

People petitioned the police to forbid the march. The Chief Constable refused. People built barricades to block the march. There was enormous publicity and the inevitable happened; a riot.

Mosley led his 2000 plus followers. 20,000 protestors lined the streets. 5,000 police fought a losing battle to keep the BUF and protestors apart. Threats became actions and violence erupted. It became known as the Battle of Cable Street.

Michael O'Donovan was there; so too Clara Rackett. She wanted to see her former neighbour in the street in the flesh. Michael wanted to see how the British fought one another.

Nearby hospitals were kept busy treating the wounded. Both sides suffered including police on horseback. The Blackshirts kept marching. Protesters screamed abuse and lunged at BUF marchers. People opened upstairs windows of terraced houses and hurled abuse, rotten fruit and vegetables. Lumps of coal and pieces of broken furniture became frightening weapons.

The onlookers were too busy shouting at the Fascists to worry about the ammunition from above; much of it became friendly fire.

Clara caught a glimpse of young Tom. *Did he look at me?* It was as if a member of royalty passed by and glanced in Clara's direction. A mad thought flashed in her brain.

Did he recognize me? Does he remember the housekeeper's daughter from Apedale Hall? Not a chance but as she reminisced, a sharp pain on her shoulder broke her reverie. In an upstairs terrace, a chair was smashed and one of its legs thrown, badly, from a first-floor window missing the target of any Blackshirt. Instead, Clara copped the flying furniture and it bloody well hurt.

She grabbed her shoulder and screamed. It wasn't a loud scream and could have been ten times louder and still not been heard over the boisterous protestors.

In the throng, Michael O'Donovan, the former POW from Dublin, stood behind Clara and to one side. Like Mosley, he didn't know her from Adam but saw the missile land and the women's reaction.

He pushed past people to reach her. 'Are you all right, madam?'

Clara couldn't remember when she was last called madam, but it was never by a man with a certain lilt to his voice.

'I think so,' she replied.

He indicated the front door of the nearest terrace. 'If you move back, you might be safer.'

She saw the sense in his suggestion and did so. He joined her and just as they reached the front of the house, both copped the contents of a chamber pot which joined the fruit and furniture as part of the barrage from above.

Never trust an Irishman.

Clara was lucky as she copped only the liquid contents. Michael's cap became a bullseye for liquid with an added bonus of solid waste.

'Feckin' shite!' he exclaimed.

Clara couldn't speak. Her throbbing shoulder pain disappeared as she realized what happened. For a second she thought his suggestion was a trap to place her in the line of fire but looking at the equally annoyed and decorated gent, she knew he too was a victim.

The stench was revolting and the thought even worse. 'There's a horse trough around the corner,' he said.

He led the way. It was not the usual method of meeting someone and may well have been a first. Dung dating or shit socials were not widely advertised. At the horse trough, they cleaned up as best they could, introduced one another and discovered they lived only two streets apart.

'If you like, Clara, I can walk you home,' he said.

She thanked him, and although smelling awful, they set off discussing Sir Oswald, his supporters and policies. Clara kept schtum about living in the same mansion as wee Tom, and Michael breathed not a word of his role in the Easter Rising of 1916. Apart from the beliefs of Sir Oswald and raw sewage, they shared nothing in common. They reached Clara's house. She thanked him and they shook hands just as the front door opened and a belligerent Victor Rackett glared at the couple.

'Where have you been?' he demanded of his wife. He went to grab her but froze. 'Christ, you stink, woman.' He glared at Michael. 'And who the hell are you?'

Living in England, Michael knew when not to speak. His accent announced his nationality, and if an enraged and intoxicated English bully demanded an answer, the best, the only reply was silence.

Victor grabbed Carla and dragged her inside tempting Michael to smash his fist into the brute's exposed belly. He paused trying to look past the man to see the woman, his eyes asking if she needed help but she was gone.

The man snarled at Michael. 'If I ever see you again, I'll kill you.'

The door slammed. Michael wasn't sure who he hated more—the British or a wife-beater.

He walked the short distance to his home making a mental note of the address of the woman he met at the Battle of Cable Street.

May 1940, London England

Mosley vehemently opposed any hint of war in the 1930s. When the balloon went up, he remained as vocal as ever. He wanted Britain and Germany to sign a truce. His cry of *No War* became *End the War*.

Oswald knew Adolf. They met when Mosley and his second wife were hitched in Joseph Goebbels lounge-room. Mosley, Hitler and Goebbels hated Jews and Communists. So if Britain threw in the towel and the Nazis added Britain to its list of conquered countries, no prize for guessing who would become the puppet PM in Downing Street; Churchill out, Mosley in.

When Churchill became PM, he ignored the ravings of the rabid rabble-rouser but members of his government reckoned Mosley was bad for morale. Lord Haw Haw on the radio and Mosley on the streets were British citizens they didn't need. Hitler's plan to bomb the people could destroy morale. Mosley's plan to support the Führer from inside Britain further eroded British hopes.

Enough was enough. Mosley and wife were escorted to Holloway Prison in London where life wasn't too bad for the toffs. There was a house within the prison and there they spent the best part of World War 2.

Clara Racket wondered why young Tom from Apedale Hall had become so quiet. She found out and wasn't happy. No anti-Semite, although she hated the Commies, Clara wanted Sir Oswald free to push his case for peace.

Chapter 3

June 1940, Cambridge England

Louise Beatrice Wellesley, a.k.a. Juliette Beauchamp, a.k.a. Plum, flew from France to England in the dead of night. For a year she worked as a sleeper for the Secret Intelligence Service (SIS). Her life as a French citizen was never boring. Boring?

In gay Paree she performed semi-naked on stage at the Folies Bergère. At an after-show party in Montmartre she was arrested holding a smoking revolver with a murdered playboy draped across her body. The French Resistance kidnapped her believing she was collaborating with the Nazis. She escaped thanks to a Wehrmacht tank commander and, as he lay dying, she shot and killed a leading Gestapo agent. Her rescuer, a British spy in Paris, was a double agent working for the Germans.

At midnight, she ran through the empty streets of Paris with the double-agent firing, shooting to kill. She escaped and hid in a brothel beneath Edith Piaf's apartment where she kidnapped a German General. They fled Paris only to be captured by a Resistance group convinced she was the officer's mistress and thus a collaborator. Only a fellow Brit, a wounded pilot, Pongo Singleton, her brother Henry's best friend, saved Louise from a brutal rape and being murdered. She squeezed aboard a Lysander flying Pongo back to Blighty and her secret life working for the Secret Intelligence Service ended.

So no, her life in France was never boring. But now it was over and, at last, she was home.

None of her family knew of this other life; none of her friends or fellow students knew. They all thought she was an actress in a troupe of Shakespearean performers staging the Bard's plays Down Under. She didn't tell a soul about her life as a sleeper in Nazi-occupied France and couldn't because she signed the Official Secrets Act.

Back home she pondered the question; *what the hell do I do now?*

From the small aerodrome just outside Cambridge, she made a discreet telephone call to Major Ralph "Bunty" Bunting of the SIS announcing her unexpected arrival in Blighty.

'Welcome home, Miss Wellesley. Come and see me tomorrow.'

It was late and having just heard the heartbreaking news about Pongo, her brother's friend, Louise despaired. She needed a bed for the night. She owned nothing but the clothes on her back. She had no money, identity papers, toothbrush, comb or spare knickers.

At 2am, she sat in the mess, wrapped in a blanket, and sipped a steaming mug of tea. A former WW1 officer came and sat beside her.

'Good morning, Miss.' She studied the warmest smile she'd seen in an age. 'Wing Commander Wilfred Summer, RAF, retired. Now, how can we help?'

Louise burst into tears; not gallons or gushing but simply relief and emotional release. Wilf patted her arm.

'May I ask your name, young lady? Any name will do if you're worried about something you may have signed.'

Louise smiled for the first time in a long time. 'Louise,' she said, 'Louise Wellesley.'

'Well I'm delighted to meet you, Louise Wellesley.' He held out his hand and she shook it. 'See that lady pouring tea. She's my better half and will soon sort your billet. Sit tight, my dear, you're among friends.'

He squeezed her arm and nodded to his wife. She arrived.

'Hello, dear, I'm Winifred although everyone calls me Winnie.'

And so began Louise's first night back in England. She slept in the smallest bedroom she'd ever seen in Wilfred and Winifred's cottage in the largest nightie she'd ever seen; any paisley port in a storm.

Sleep was wonderful. She woke and panicked before realizing where she was. Winnie tapped gently on her door.

'There's a bath for you, dear. You soak for as long as you like.' She did and it was lovely, even better than one in the luxurious Mercure Hotel in Paris. Her fellow guest then was a Wehrmacht officer, a tank commander no less. This morning she stayed with loyal folk from the land of her birth, in the country she loved and wanted to defend with all her might. Bloody Adolf. She hopped out of the bath, and delighted in discovering a new "old" dress, underwear and shoes on the chair in her tiny room.

Over breakfast, Louise found a way to start her life again.

'So how can we help, Miss Wellesley?' asked Wilfred. 'Your wish is our command.'

Louise struggled to stop more tears as Winnie popped fresh toast on the table.

'Homemade marmalade, dear, although I'm sorry about the missing butter; come on, help yourself.' She did. She remembered how her brothers used to tease her at breakfast when she was little. 'Oh boy,' they'd say, 'there goes Plum and her jam.' She missed them, wondering where they were and if they were all right let alone alive. This was her first war although Wilf and Winnie survived the last one.

'I can't thank you enough, Mr and Mrs Summer. I need to go up to London today. I'm afraid all my identity papers and money are lost.'

'Don't worry, leave everything to me,' said the retired Wing Commander. 'I'll make a call or two.' He left to telephone.

Winnie studied Louise making her feel a little uncomfortable. 'My eyes aren't what they used to be, dear, but I can't help thinking I've seen you before. Have we met?'

Louise stared at the old lady. 'I'm sorry but I don't think so.'

'We've lived here since Wilf retired, and we only go into Cambridge. Still, don't you mind the musings of a silly old woman.'

Louise wondered about opening up to reveal anything of her life. She gave them her real name. *Should I have done that? Would Major Bunting be annoyed? Have I broken any SIS rules?*

Louise drowned in tea and loved the taste of homemade English jam, something she missed so much. Winnie knew not to pry and Louise knew how to be polite while giving away nothing.

Wilfred returned. 'All set, Miss Wellesley. The trains are a bit unreliable so I've arranged transport with an RAF courier.'

'Oh thank you,' said Louise delighted to have a plan. She thought about ringing her mother and her Cambridge friends, the Vestys. But London called and her news about Godfrey Quisling Silsbury needed to be explained.

'We need to be back at Teverton in an hour,' said Wilfred.

Winnie hopped up in a tizz. 'An hour!' she exclaimed. 'I'll make sandwiches for the trip, and I want you to try on these other shoes, Miss Wellesley. Those ones look a little tight.' They were.

Louise didn't object. Her hosts wanted to help and took pleasure in doing so. Mothering was an intrinsic part of Winnie's soul and fuss she did. Wilf left his Morris 8 in the garage with petrol rationing restricting travel. He took Louise's new bag, another gift, with her meagre belongings and set off to the front gate. Louise gave Winnie a hug to end all hugs. The old woman grabbed a coat and pressed it against Louise.

'You might need this.'

Louise was overcome but hurried to catch up with the Wing Commander. He set a cracking pace and twenty minutes later she saw in daylight the place where she landed a few hours earlier.

She pictured Pongo squeezed in the rear cockpit of the Lysander with her. She remembered his expressions of undying love, and then the ground crew officer telling her the brave pilot was dead.

She looked around for the RAF car which would whisk her up to London. Nothing. Then a roar from behind made her turn. A man with helmet and goggles astride a motorcycle pulled up and grinned.

'Taxi for London, Miss,' he said and Louise shook her head. Thank goodness for Winnie's gift of a coat.

The Wing Commander placed her bag inside the sidecar and offered his hand. She settled, excited. The motorcyclist handed her a leather helmet and pair of goggles. She looked the part. Wilfred stood back and saluted as the machine roared off to London.

When Wilf returned home, Winnie remarked. 'I'm getting a bit funny in the head. I was sure I'd met that young girl before.'

'You're not potty, my dear. We've both met her at the St Peter's Players in Cambridge.'

Winnie sighed. 'Of course, she's that brilliant actress.'

It was no use chatting en route; you couldn't hear a thing above the roar of the motorcycle. Louise spent the time tugging her coat closer and admiring the green and pleasant land she'd missed for the last 12 months. The roads were clear. Summer in England in 1940 was not your regular holiday season. There was little traffic on the roads, children were sent to the country, women worked the farms and men went overseas to fight.

The outer suburbs of London gave Louise a sense of excitement. She would soon make her report of life in Paris, about the Resistance, the Gestapo, the Parisian police and a certain double-crossing Englishman. She decided to omit the times she spent in a fashionable hotel suite with a leading Wehrmacht officer, the one who died in her arms.

The motorcycle stopped at the first crossroads in London.

'Where can I drop you, miss,' shouted the rider.

'Baker Street will be fine,' shouted Louise in reply.

'Whereabouts? Baker Street was extended about ten years ago.'

'Number 64 please but anywhere will do, thank you.'

Like the countryside, London was different. Sandbags were piled high on footpaths. Windows were taped. Nobody dawdled. Everyone stepped it out, head down, off to somewhere. Traffic sounds continued but laughter and greetings were in short supply.

The motorcycle pulled up against the curb in Baker Street. Louise removed the helmet and googles and handed them to her driver. Getting out was no easy task. She was dressed in hand-me-down clothes and shoes, with a racing heart to match. She clutched her bag.

'Thank you so much,' she said and held out her hand. The rider's gloves were enormous and swallowed Louise's hand.

He saluted. 'Good luck, Miss,' he said and roared off to deliver his important documents.

Louise looked up and down Baker Street and at faces. No eye contact from anyone. It began raining so she entered the building where her secret life working for the SIS once began. The most important part of her assignment was to survive and survive she did.

She climbed the stairs and stopped outside Major Bunting's office at the door marked *Accountant*. She experienced a flashback and her previous life came alive in her mind. *This is where it all began.* She paused then knocked. No response. She waited then knocked again.

A man came up the stairs, saw her and barked. 'Who are you?'

Once she would have answered immediately and correctly. Now she knew better.

'I have an appointment with Major Bunting.'

The man moved to her. 'That's not what I asked. Who are you?'

He was dressed in a suit and Louise wondered if he was an SIS officer testing her. In a calm, polite voice she replied. 'I could ask you the same question.'

The man stopped. He stared at her. 'Wait there,' he ordered and called down the stairs. A squaddie bounded up and saluted.

'Sir.'

The man pointed at Louise. 'Place this woman under arrest.'

The squaddie set off towards Louise then stopped. He gasped. 'Mademoiselle? Is that you?'

Louise recognized him. He was on the training camp in Scotland before she left for France. Neither knew the other's real name and had even forgotten their SIS name.

The man in the suit watched all this with rising anger. He shouted. 'I gave you an order, soldier!'

Reluctantly the squaddie moved to Louise and spoke softly. 'Sorry, Miss. I'm sure this can be sorted.'

Before he could make another move, a door opened at the far end of the corridor and Major Ralph Bunting appeared. 'Oh there you are, Miss Wellesley. Do come through.'

Louise smiled at the soldier then set off having to walk past the man in the suit. He fumed which she countered with a beaming smile. 'Good morning, sir,' she said to the bumptious bully then entered Major Bunting's new office. He'd been moved and now it appeared worked in a broom cupboard.

He was full of praise and thanks making Louise feel proud and alive. She was bursting to share her story about the traitorous Godfrey Silsbury but her balloon was soon pricked.

'Oh Miss Wellesley I'm awfully keen to hear all your tales but we got word about our friend Silsbury before you landed. Those resourceful Resistance chaps found a radio and gave us the news.'

Oh dear, what a disappointment. Still, her news and loads of information would be welcome. And so for the next half an hour, Louise told her sleeper stories except the ones which involved sharing a hotel room with a certain Herr Oberst, and being arrested in the bedroom of a Parisian playboy. Bunty was seriously impressed with Louise on a high.

She put it straight. 'Well Major, I do hope you have another task for me. I'd like time to visit my family but whenever you're ready, so am I.'

A silence settled in the broom cupboard. Louise slumped. *Where is his enthusiasm, his gratitude? Where is my next assignment?*

Bunty couldn't hide his sadness. 'Alas, Miss Wellesley, life has changed of late. As you can see, my palatial surrounds reveal my current status. I'm told it's not a demotion, more a sideways move. Alas I regret the SIS is not what it once was. The new PM, Mr Churchill, has taken a shine to a new organization and I'm unable to offer you another assignment. As I'm sure you know, this damn war has flipped the world upside down.'

Louise's face said it all. To do what she did and survive was a mighty achievement. She didn't want a medal or a speech. But to be shown the door, and emptyhanded, was a real kick in the guts.

She spoke without thinking. 'But what am I to do?'

Bunty mused. 'Have you contacted Dickie Graves?'

Louise gasped. 'You think I should go back to acting?'

'My dear Miss Wellesley, judging by reports of your adventures in France, it's clear you have never stopped acting.'

If he intended to compliment her, Louise remained disappointed, distressed. The thought of a life upon the stage was once her fervent dream. But now, with a war raging and having tasted life as a secret agent dicing with death, the theatre somehow lost its allure. Real life acting sure beat the pants off acting on stage.

'Far be it from me to tell you what to do,' said Bunting, 'but I believe you were a great success on stage at the Folies Bergère, I hear the Windmill theatre is boasting they never close.'

She knew of this venue and its fame for nude models. His comment added insult to injury. She studied his face and sensed he was joking. Whatever, his remark was in appalling taste.

I put my life on the line, killed a prominent Gestapo agent, uncovered a British spy and my reward is to disrobe in public in a seedy West End theatre. If that's a joke, Major, I do not find it in the least bit funny! No wonder you've been demoted.

Before she could explode with anger and disappointment or both, the Major handed her an envelope.

'In there you'll find your passport, ration cards, identity papers, a glowing testimonial and your banking details. I've added a little cash as well but your wages have accumulated since you've been away giving you a nice little nest egg.'

Louise recovered a tad. 'Thank you, Major. May I ask about this new organization you said was supported by the Prime Minister?'

'Not my department, I'm afraid. It's called the SOE, the Special Operations Executive. They're housed here in Baker Street and elsewhere in London and in stately homes around the country. The charming gentleman you encountered before is "researching" for the SOE. I think he's spying on the spies.'

'Could I work for the SOE?'

'From what I've heard, it's very much a hands-on operation; lots of dynamite, daggers and derailments. The Prime Minster has been quoted as saying he wants the SOE to set Europe ablaze. I don't think they have much call for Shakespeare and chorus girls.'

Louise wanted to cry. She withdrew into herself, shoved the envelope in her coat pocket and clenched her hands, ready to snap. Her farewell handshake with the Major lacked any warmth; cold fish would best describe her grip.

'If you see Dickie Graves, please give him my best,' he said. She watched him. He lost a leg in the last war and now she decided he'd become a bitter man.

She gave a lukewarm smile and left. The squaddie in Reception stood to attention and gave her a cracking smile. She smiled in return, stepped into Baker Street and pondered the burning question.

What the hell do I do now?

Chapter 4

Louise had cash and a healthy bank balance but no bed, no change of clothes and no job. There was a war on. German bombers were due at any time and standing on a London street was potentially suicidal. *Come on, Plum old girl, this won't buy the baby a bonnet.*

It was time to tell her family and friends she was back in Blighty; no easy task. When she left, she supposedly set off to the Southern Hemisphere. Pre-written cards posted by SIS contacts Down Under reinforced her lie. Now, without warning, and as the Germans prepared to bring devastation to Britain, she was back. The Official Secrets Act meant her French adventure was never to be mentioned. But being home and saying nothing seemed, well, wrong and unfair.

She found a small hotel, booked a room, and paid to use the telephone. A sign in the booth was clear. *Be careful, the enemy is listening.* She made her first call.

'Hello,' said a well-known voice.

'Hello Mummy,' was all she needed to say. Her mother shrieked and the cook rushed into the hallway expecting to find the lady of the house on the floor, dying. Louise's mother, a widow, married her first husband's good friend, Sir Anthony Wilding. His magnificent home in Wiltshire oozed class.

Victoria gathered herself. 'Louise, my darling, is it really you?'

'I'm home, Mummy. I'm ringing from London. How are you?'

With help from her sister-in-law and the cook, Lady Wilding managed a proper conversation with her long-lost daughter.

'So where are you staying? Are you all right? When did you get back? *How* did you get back?'

The questions would have continued had Louise not interrupted. 'I'm staying with a lovely family at present but will need to find somewhere and preferably not in London.' Her lying came naturally.

'Not London, Louise, you can't stay there. You must come here. Are you all right for money?'

'Yes, Mummy, I'm okay. How are Sir Anthony and the boys?'

Louise dreaded bad news. Her brothers meant the world to her and having seen the ravages of war in France, she knew how war was no respecter of persons.

'We're all well here and the latest I've heard about the boys is they're okay. Edmund joined the BEF and was rescued at Dunkirk. He's on leave and staying at home in Surrey.'

Louise flushed with happiness. 'So the house hasn't been sold?'

'No and Henry's in the country on a special training course.'

'That's wonderful.'

'Now you sound all right but darling, you will tell me if you're not won't you? I've been so worried about you. How was the tour? Did you enjoy Australia?' She was off again with a barrage of questions.

Louise swallowed. Her brilliant acting convinced so many people but somehow, lying to her mother proved tricky. If anyone could tell she was lying, it was her mother.

'Oh I've so much to tell you, Mummy. I think I'll go down to Farnham and stay with Eddie for a few days. Then when I've settled, I'll ring and make arrangements to come to Wiltshire.'

'As you wish, my darling and it's so lovely to hear your voice.'

'And yours, Mummy. I must fly. Oh, and please don't tell the boys. I'd like to surprise them.'

'Of course. And speaking of surprises, Henry has one for you. Goodbye my darling, goodbye.'

Sir Anthony came out of his study to see what all the fuss was about. Louise put down the receiver and spoke to herself.

'Oh no, don't tell me I'm going to be Auntie Plum.'

Her list of people to contact was short. There were only two with the Vestys next. She felt bad not having called on them when her plane landed only a few miles from their Cambridge home.

She made the call and found herself shaking.

Why am I nervous talking to friends?

'The Vesty house,' said Louise's former teacher, mentor and dear friend Elizabeth.

'Good morning Miss Vesty. This is your favourite actress speaking.'

Another shrieking response burst from the phone. Louise was better prepared this time.

'I've just arrived back in London. How are you and your family?'

'Oh dear,' muttered Elizabeth, sitting to steady her nerves. There was no cook in the Vesty abode. 'Is it really you, Louise? I mean, Miss Wellesley?'

There was a 40 year age difference between these women but they chose to call each other Miss rather than use their Christian names. It was a sort of in-joke which reinforced their love for one another.

'After my mother, you are the first person I've telephoned, and it's so lovely to hear your voice.'

'I'm sitting down,' gasped Elizabeth, 'but I think I need a brandy.'

'Goodness, Miss Vesty; drinking before luncheon?'

They laughed. 'When can you come and see us? Are you going back to Cambridge? How was the tour in Australia? Where are you living? What's your next role?'

Again Louise was forced to stop the flow of questions. 'I'm resting at the moment then off to Surrey to stay with my brother Edmund. As soon as I'm settled I'll write and give you all my news.'

'We'd love to see you and you know you're welcome to stay as long as you wish. Oh I'm so excited.'

'I must go, Miss Vesty. Please give my love to the Professor and Molly, and I'll be in touch soon. Bye.'

'Goodbye,' said Elizabeth and kept saying it even after the line went dead. She forgot the brandy as she skipped back to the kitchen.

In her hotel room, Louise collapsed on the bed. Her spinning mind kept spinning. Only now did recent memories roar back to life.

Godfrey Silsbury tried to seduce and murder me. The Gestapo and Wehrmacht officers and several Resistance fighters came very close to invading my body with one being welcomed with open arms. I was framed for murder. I performed at the Folies Bergère.

Then reality kicked in and she groaned. Sadness filled her heart as she pondered the muted response from Major Bunting and the SIS. Her high hopes for another appointment with a thrilling mission in which she would play a challenging role were dashed. As far as the SIS was concerned, it was clearly a case of "don't call us, we'll call you".

Now she wanted to go home, sleep in her own bed and find out all about her mother and brothers. Where could she find a train time table?

But first she would call on her theatrical agent, the man who gave her the self-belief to try for a professional acting career, and recommended her to the Secret Intelligence Service. She admired him greatly and would welcome any suggestions he might have.

Without phoning Dickie Graves, she walked to his London address where he stood in the outer office explaining a letter to his secretary. He looked up and smiled as Louise entered.

'So it *is* true. Miss Louise Wellesley has returned from her acting triumph Down Under.' He stepped forward and he and Louise shook hands. Her heart beat faster. He spoke to his secretary. 'Jane, you remember our most talented actress.'

After greetings, Louise sat in her agent's office.

'I apologise for not making an appointment, Mr Graves.'

He waved a hand dismissing the matter. 'Bunty rang when he heard from you last night. It's wonderful to have you back home and looking so well, Miss Wellesley.'

'Thank you and I'm glad to be back.'

'I understand your overseas venture was a triumph.'

Of course he knows everything.

Louise was reluctant to discuss France even though it was Richard Graves who asked her to sign the Official Secrets Act and introduced her to the SIS. 'Do you know Major Bunting's department seems to have been somewhat downgraded?'

'Not downgraded, I'd say less popular with those in power.'

'And I have no idea what's happened to the theatres. Are they still running? And are you still finding work for your clients?'

'Yes I am, within reason. But many actors are simply no longer looking for work. They've signed a new contract to fight for King and country in the theatre of war; just like you.'

'Alas no more as I fear my SIS days are over. Do you know anything about this new organization, the SOE?'

'I'm afraid not. Being pals with Bunty from the first war, I had an in with the Secret Intelligence Service. Alas Mr Churchill and the chaps running the SOE are strangers to me.'

Louise grimaced. The news was bad. 'So the theatres are closed?'

They were when war was announced but gradually the government has agreed to allow them to re-open.'

'And it's safe to attend?'

He shrugged. 'Hardly safe because there is talk of the Germans invading and I think they will only do so if they can destroy the RAF and bomb our ships and ports.'

'And cities?'

He nodded and grimaced. 'And cities, and if Herr Hitler sends his planes, we may have no theatres in which to perform.'

Louise's eyes spoke volumes of sadness. 'That's terrible.'

He smiled to brighten the mood. 'So what are your plans, Miss Wellesley? Will you return to Cambridge and complete your studies?'

'I'm not sure I want to. The lure of the stage appeals but then so does the work I did when I went overseas.'

'To Australia you mean?'

His sparkling eyes gave the true meaning. 'Yes, to Australia.'

'Well there is another possibility. You might consider joining ENSA, the Entertainments National Service Association.'

'ENSA?'

'You'd be helping the war effort while performing on stage.'

Louise was both excited and curious. 'I've never heard of it.'

'ENSA provides entertainment for our troops, here at home and overseas. They have singers, dancers, actors, bands, comedians, jugglers, even Mantovani and his orchestra. They'd be delighted to welcome an actress with your immense talent. Why don't you audition?'

Louise's eyes lit up. 'It sounds interesting.' Her pulse raced. 'Are you able to recommend me to ENSA?'

'There's no need. They're always keen to recruit willing and able performers. Do you know the Theatre Royal in Drury Lane?'

She tingled. 'My parents took me there for my 12th birthday.'

'Then try knocking on the stage door. In next to no time you could be helping our troops while doing what you love so much.'

He stood and walked Louise out of his office.

'I can't thank you enough, Mr Graves. And I hope you'll keep me in mind for roles in the future.'

He raised her hand and kissed it. 'Nothing would give me greater pleasure, Miss Wellesley. And please, do keep in touch. Goodbye.'

In borrowed clothes and shoes, with her passport, cash and identity papers in her hand-me-down coat, she stood in the street outside the famous Drury Lane theatre. A chill skipped down her spine. Would she ever perform professionally in the West End of London? Apparently she could audition at the famous Theatre Royal.

As a child, from the stalls, she remembered the stage being huge, ideal for a big cast show, an opera or musical comedy. Now, standing alone outside in the street, preparing to audition in that mighty venue, her butterflies fluttered like mad.

She opened the stage door and was hit by noise, action, colour and lights. She entered and squeezed past props and people towards the stage—the vast stage—and stopped dead. The huge performing space was now tiny. Her memory failed.

What has happened to this wonderful old theatre?

World War Two had happened and the Theatre Royal became the HQ of ENSA with the stage subdivided. There were rooms for costumiers sewing costumes, carpenters building sets and props, clerks arranging travel permits, accountants sorting wages, and downstage in front of the orchestra pit sat one simple box set. Anyone auditioning stood in this tiny space and tried to impress the producers seated in the auditorium. The orchestra was a pianist and while performers auditioned, people called and chatted, hammers banged, and people carried on killing one another in Europe, Asia, Africa and elsewhere. This was entertainment in time of war.

'Hello Love,' said a middle-aged gent. 'Can I help?'

'Is this where you audition for ENSA?'

He pointed. 'Just follow your nose and ask for Mr Bertie Parsons.'

'Thank you,' said Louise and made her way towards the wings. She stood next to a girl in a costume which appeared to have been in storage since the last war. 'I'm next,' she said to Louise. 'What do you think; is my dress all right?'

Before Louise could reply, a loud voice was heard from the stalls.

'Next!'

The auditionee in the costume once weighed down with moth balls, set off to audition for ENSA. Louise tried to observe but was interrupted.

'You here for an audition, Miss?' She was and gave her name and answered questions. Her details were listed. 'Wait here.' She did.

The girl wearing the dress with an acre of tulle burst off the stage, breathless. She'd been successful. 'I'm going to be a fairy in Cardiff,' she buzzed, hugged Louise and left.

Louise worried. What she saw of the Cardiff Fairy did not fill her with awe. The young woman was overweight, off key and unlikely to win a role even with the "Everyone-Gets-a-Part" St Peter's Players in Cambridge. No, not true, *every*one got a part at St Peter's.

On the way to the audition, she bumped into a friend of Beauford Nightingale, her beloved former drama coach. She met this chap during her Am Dram days in Cambridge. When she told him she was to audition for ENSA, he laughed and said, 'Oh you mean Every Night Something Awful.' *Does he know the Cardiff Fairy?*

'Next!' came the cry from the stalls and Louise walked onto a tiny part of the stage of the Theatre Royal, Drury Lane. She removed her coat with all her worldly wealth and draped it over a chair. The person who called *Next* was Basil Dean, one of the co-founders of ENSA. He read the sheet with Louise's details.

'So Miss Wellesley, you're an actress?'

'Yes sir, I am.'

'You've been in school plays, the St Peter's Players, and played a small role at the Cambridge Arts Theatre.'

'Yes sir.' There was no mention of her Parisian nightclub success even sharing the bill with Edith Piaf.

'Can you dance and sing?'

Well, thought Louise, *I've paraded semi naked on stage at the Folies Bergère and entertained high-flying Nazis at the One Two Two Club in Paris.*

'A little but playing a role is what I love to do.'

She wondered if she was talking herself out of ENSA.

'Then please give us a sample of your wares.'

She walked in a small circle taking a deep breath and finished downstage centre front. She remembered the advice of one Beauford "Nightie" Nightingale, paused to lift the expectation of those in the theatre seats then gave her favourite Shakespearean speech.

O Romeo, Romeo! Wherefore art thou Romeo?

As she performed, the backstage babble and sounds faded. People moved into the wings to see who this person, this woman; this actress was producing such a clear, striking and moving audition.

Louise finished with:

> *Without that title. Romeo, doff thy name,*
> *And for that name which is no part of thee*
> *Take all myself.*

She finished and waited. Those watching from the wings spoke in whispers. Soon the work chatter and hammering resumed. Two men walked down the aisle towards the stage.

'Thank you, Miss Wellesley,' said the first man. 'I'm Basil Dean and this is my colleague, Leslie Henson.'

'How do you do, gentlemen,' said the auditionee wondering if they too wanted her to be a fairy in Cardiff.

'We were delighted with your audition,' said Henson.

'Our problem being we can't decide which company will best display your outstanding talent.'

Her toes tapped easily in her rather large hand-me-down shoes. 'Thank you,' she said, 'you're most kind.'

'Are you available to start immediately, Miss Wellesley?' asked Dean.

Louise hesitated. 'I've been away and not seen my family for ages.'

'Oh you've been touring, Miss Wellesley?' said Henson. 'Which company and which roles did you play?'

Louise worked hard to hide her panic. Of course she couldn't mention her Folies Bergère episode or the upper-class brothel or the Club Paradiso. But nor could she mention the Shakespearean roles Down Under, the ones she never performed. They might ask for the names of the leading actors, the producer or manager. They didn't exist. *Why didn't I prepare for this situation?*

She scrambled a reply. 'No, I've been staying with friends who moved from London to avoid the war.'

The gents were satisfied. 'Ah, very sensible,' said Dean and his colleague agreed.

'Well we'd definitely love to have you performing with ENSA, Miss Wellesley,' said Henson. 'We suggest you fill in the employment paperwork, pop in to see the ladies in the costume room, and then let us know when you're available. From there we can place you in a company where your skill will thrill.'

The men found the rhyme amusing. Louise smiled. 'Thank you, gentlemen; that sounds most satisfactory.' She put on her coat checking the pockets for certain items.

'No, thank *you*, Miss Wellesley,' said Dean and pointed. 'Please go with the Stage Manager and we look forward to seeing you soon.'

She smiled and walked to the SM who ushered her to a temporary office on the stage. Here she filled out the necessary forms, signed her life away, and was shown to the costume office.

The Cardiff fairy was trying on a new costume 'How did you go, Love?' she said to Louise. 'Did they give you a part?'

'I think so,' said Louise.

'Good for you. Now this lady will take care of you.'

This lady had been sewing since she was a child and many years ago once lived with her mother in Apedale Hall, a stately home in Staffordshire.

She held up a tape measure. 'Hello,' she said to Louise, 'I'm Clara.'

Chapter 5

July 1940, Surrey England

Louise sat alone in a compartment as the train chuffed towards Surrey. Years ago, her brothers would have noted the number of the locomotive. She didn't care for such details but did for her brothers. At last she would spend time with at least one of them.

Apart from childhood travel, she made this trip many times before going to and from London en route to the all-female Girton College, Cambridge. In those days, her parents insisted one of her older brothers would chaperone her. Now she travelled alone.

Her country was at war, her father dead, her mother re-married, her brothers enlisted, and none of her family knew her SIS history.

Going home stirred emotions. She was close to her family and being able to see brother Edmund and catch up on all his news pushed tears to the corners of her eyes. She chose not to tell him she was coming although her mother may well have done so.

The walk from the station on a summer's afternoon was wonderful. Trees boasted about their foliage, and birds flitted about asking her where she'd been these past four seasons. It was hard to believe people were being arrested, tortured and killed only a few miles away across the Channel.

She stopped outside her family home. The garden needed a little attention but otherwise it looked exactly the same. Here she grew up, played in the grounds, held birthday parties, and left to go to school and then university. There were so many memories in this place.

Not having keys, she walked to the back door for her first surprise.

'Horatio!' she cried as the elderly black Labrador hobbled towards her. His legs were no longer sprightly but his tail wagged like never before. Around his mouth, his black fur was white. He barked a greeting, just the one, and nuzzled into Louise as she knelt and embraced the loving family pet.

The back door opened and a woman stood there stunned. 'Miss Louise? Is that you?'

Louise smiled. 'Hello Mrs Crossley. Am I in time for supper?'

There was time, plenty of time for another hug and all three moved into the spacious country kitchen.

'It's wonderful to see you, my dear,' said the woman who'd cooked and cleaned for the Wellesley family since before the last war. 'Your brother will be delighted to see you.'

'As I him,' said Louise. 'Where is the scallywag?'

'Scallywag?' said a voice in the hallway. 'Who dares speak such frivolity in this house?'

Louise's smile was never wider. She strode to the kitchen door, flung it open and prepared for yet another hug.

Edmund opened his arms and Louise fainted.

'Smelling salts, Mrs C,' said Edmund pushing his wheelchair towards his prostrate sister. Luckily she missed striking her head on the solid side table against the wall.

Horatio pushed his way towards the victim and gave his first-aid routine of neck and face licking.

'Horatio,' bellowed Edmund and the dog moved back allowing the cook to give Louise a sniff which brought her round. She helped the new arrival to her feet and into the nearest sitting room. Louise slumped on the settee and Edmund wheeled himself in front of his sister.

'My fault, Plum, old girl,' he said, 'bloody bad manners. But I have to say it's absolutely fabulous to see you and looking so fit and well.'

'I'll fetch tea,' said Mrs C and called Horatio who followed her.

Louise produced a steady stream of tears. Her shock was not so much seeing her brother sitting in the same wheelchair their father used in the last months of his life but rather Edmund's changed appearance.

His right leg was heavily bandaged and the obvious reason for his new mode of transport. But her fainting fit came when she saw her brother's seriously disfigured face. It frightened the life out of her.

The right side of his face suffered serious trauma. His right eye worked although his skull was compressed and that side of his face suffered what must have been serious burns.

'Oh Eddie,' she said and moved to kneel beside him on his right side, his worst side. 'I'm so, so sorry to see you like this.'

He told his tale in as gentle a way as he could. 'I was in the BEF in France and copped a bullet in my knee. Bloody painful it was and I knew immediately my ballroom dancing days were gone.'

She smiled. 'You hate dancing.'

'So I hitched a ride in an ambulance all the way to Dunkirk. You being Down Under probably wouldn't know about the war in France.'

I know a darn sight more than you will ever know, brother dear. 'Go on,' she said.

'I was on a hospital ship with all the other poor beggars. The ship was painted white with these giant Red Cross signs everywhere when a Jerry swoops in and drops his cargo. I was on the deck on a stretcher when the bomb hit. Huge fire and I was silly enough to not cover my face.' He gingerly touched his face.

'Eddie,' was all she could say before tears killed her speech.

'God, I was one of the lucky ones. There were dozens of blokes below deck and as the ship went down, many were trapped and drowned in the hold; not in the sea, in the bloody ship.'

He studied his sister. The siblings were caught in the blood-is-thicker-than-water trap, but were friends too. She knew he didn't care for dancing because he didn't care for girls, at least not in a romantic way. It made not a jot of difference to her love and respect for him.

'Oh Eddie, I don't know what to say,' she blubbed, shedding even more tears.

'Silly me, old girl; I forgot to duck. But anyway, enough about me; tell me your news. How big a raging success were you in the colonies? Are you married and if not, why not?'

The mood changed. 'I'm staying, Edmund. I'm staying here to help you for as long as it takes.'

'No, Louise,' he spoke with defiance.

She sensed his anger. He hardly ever called her Louise.

'But you'll need to go to medical appointments. You'll have correspondence with the Army. And you can't take Horatio for walks pushing yourself in that old wheelchair. I'll push you.'

They both fell silent. Louise broke the ice.

'Does Mummy know?'

Edmund's ire kicked in again. 'No, and you must never tell her.'

'Never? But she would want to know. If you think she'll be upset at your injuries, she'll be more upset by you not telling her.'

'All right,' sighed Edmund and the atmosphere settled. 'I will tell her after my next operation.'

'Your *next* operation? How many have you had?'

'I haven't started yet but there is a light at the end of the tunnel, old girl. A wonderful surgeon in East Grinstead, a Doctor Archibald McIndoe, performs miracles for chaps like me, restoring faces, and has agreed to let me join his group of guinea pigs.'

'Guinea pigs?'

'RAF chaps who were shot down and copped terrible burns. I'm told Doctor McIndoe will have me looking like Douglas Fairbanks in his prime.'

Louise wanted to smile if only to encourage her brother but she was serious. 'Okay, but I'm staying to care for you and that's final.'

Edmund looked at his sister. 'You always were the bossy type.'

They studied one another. He opened his arms and they hugged as warmly as they could in such difficult circumstances. They broke the embrace when Mrs Crossley entered with a tray of tea.

After supper when Mrs Crossley retired, the siblings drank coffee in the snug. Louise wanted to ask Edmund more about his wounds but feared stirring up what must have been an horrific event; events. He sensed her reluctance.

'Well, Plum, life certainly has its ups and downs.'

'It seems only yesterday Mummy and Daddy lived here with the three of us.' Silence joined the discussion.

Their conversation was unhurried. Both didn't hesitate to say whatever they thought.

'You've hardly told me a thing about your trip to Australia.'

She shrugged. 'There's nothing much to say, brother dear.'

He sniffed. 'Assuming you actually went Down Under.' She studied him and he saw concern, even a touch of fear in her eyes.

'How is your friend, Alastair?'

'Nice change of topic, Plum, and his name is Alexander.'

'Is he well?'

'He is, thank you, and he's another reason why you don't have to stay and mollycoddle the invalid.' She stared at him not knowing if he wanted to continue the conversation.

'Oh?'

'C'mon Plum, we've been over this ground before. We both know I'm queer. Mother and Henry know, even Mrs Crossley. God, you're an actress. The theatre must have chaps who bat for the other side.'

'What's that got to do with me staying here to care for you?'

'Everything and nothing. Alex is medically unfit to enlist. He's a law clerk working as a hospital orderly. He can be assigned to help in my recovery leaving a hospital bed free for a poor blighter who needs it. I love you, Plum, but I'll love you even more if you go and do what *you* love.' He paused. 'Why don't you audition for ENSA? They'll snap you up on the spot. Have you heard of them?'

'I auditioned this morning.'

Edmund rejoiced. 'Well there you are. When do you start?'

'I told them I wanted to see my family first.'

'Then pop down to Wiltshire and see Mummy and Sir Anthony. There's no need to call on Henry's missus unless you want to suggest she name the brat Plum.'

He smiled, as best he could with a chunk of his face in dry dock. Louise nodded and her smile became a laugh. 'Will I be Auntie Louise or Auntie Plum?'

Their laughter petered out as both sensed it was time to retire.

'And you don't know what Henry's doing?'

'Special training, all hush hush,' said Edmund. 'Oh, and I nearly forgot.' He pushed himself to a desk, removed a key and offered it to his sister. 'This is for you.'

'What's it for?'

'I bought a flat in London in Maida Vale, only a short trip on the Tube to the West End. It's empty and no use to me. Make it your base when you're in town. It'll be a bolt-hole between all those tours you make with ENSA.'

'Eddie, I can't.'

He shook his head. 'Louise, for Christ's sake stop being such a bloody martyr.' He shocked himself with his language and tone of voice. He whispered. 'Sorry.'

She grimaced. 'My fault.'

He persisted. 'If you don't mind me saying, you can be damn annoying at times always so kind and polite, refusing any help, even from your brother.' He held out the key. 'Now please, take the key and don't have too many wild parties.'

She took the key, kissed his forehead, and pushed his wheelchair to the hallway.

'I'm okay from here,' he said. 'I'm in the downstairs boudoir.' He threw in sarcasm. 'Do you know the way to your old room?'

'If I get lost, I'll sing out.' She stopped on the stairs. 'Goodnight, brother dear, and thanks again for the flat.'

'Goodnight to you, actress and star.'

Louise stayed at home in Surrey for a couple of days. Edmund's friend, Alexander arrived, and he and Louise got on famously. She experienced deep happiness knowing her brother would be cared for by someone who loved him.

She raided her wardrobe and chest of drawers, packed a case and took the train up to London, then the Tube on the Bakerloo line to Maida Vale. She walked to the block of red brick flats. They were tucked away on a side street. She climbed the stairs, opened the door and bubbled with delight at the interior. It was ideal; a sitting room, bed room, kitchen and bath; perfect.

In her new hidey hole she unpacked her belongings. Nothing from her life in Paris remained. Now she was to report to ENSA and start another chapter in her life as an actress. But first, tomorrow she was off to Wiltshire.

Chapter 6

August 1940, London England

As the ancient proverb goes, the enemy of my enemy is my friend. The Irish Republican Army, the IRA, formed before the First World War, was alive and well during the Second. Germany didn't fancy Ireland, and the IRA didn't fancy Germany but both regarded the other as possible allies. The enemy of my enemy is my friend.

If the IRA could help Germany defeat Britain, it might bring about a united Ireland. So an IRA bombing campaign in London was their first salvo in helping the Nazis win the war.

Michael O'Donovan never joined the IRA back in his homeland. He knew men who were in and decades later, ensconced in England, he drank with fellow Irishmen who wanted to shorten the war.

'You should join us, Michael,' said Seamus from Belfast.

'You boast about fighting in the Easter Rising, Mick, but where are your true colours now, hey?' asked Daniel from Derry.

For ages, Michael pondered his IRA position. 'I'm not a grand one for killing women and children,' he said. 'I saw Brits kill me family and slaughter me friends. Those Brits I'll fight. But blowing up buildings with kids inside is not for me.'

'What if you could help the cause without killing women and children?' asked Orin from Armagh.

Michael's ears pricked. 'How?' he asked.

'Have you heard of the Abwehr?' Michael shook his head. 'It's the German spy network. They run spies here sending intelligence back to Germany.'

'I can't speak feckin' German,' said Michael.

'They all speak English you Eejit,' replied Daniel.

Pause. Silence. 'So? What are you saying?' asked Michael.

'You could help the Abwehr. No bombs, no killing women and kids, and you'll be doing the Army a great service.' The IRA men stared at

Michael. He remembered his father and uncle being shot by the British and his friend and their family being butchered. He decided.

'What do I have to do?'

Seamus slapped Michael's arm and Daniel raised his glass. 'Welcome to the Army, Michael. Here's to a united Ireland.'

They toasted and Michael wondered if he'd made the right decision. *What would me Ma and Da think?*

The IRA men reckoned Michael O'Donovan was a patriot but wanted to test him first. They gave him a safe task. He was to contact an Abwehr agent, here in England, and give him details of a fuel dump the IRA discovered. The Abwehr agent was to send the co-ordinates to Berlin and leave the Luftwaffe to do the rest. If the fuel was destroyed, Michael was in.

The Abwehr agent was a woman, Elsa Grayling, formerly Ratzinger. She married her English husband when he lectured at Leipzig University in 1932. The couple moved to England in 1936 and the authorities failed to note her nationality.

When Mr Grayling, a supporter of Oswald Mosley, was detained by Special Branch in 1938, Elsa contacted her cousin in the German Embassy in London offering her services. The Abwehr recruited Elsa.

She lived in a quiet Kent village and was pottering in her garden when Michael O'Donovan stood outside her front gate and spoke with his best Dublin accent.

'Good day to you, Missus. Would I have the pleasure of addressing Mrs Elsa Grayling?'

He convinced her from the start and they drank tea in her kitchen. 'I have information,' said Michael and handed her a piece of paper.

She snatched the paper. 'Gott im Himmel,' she exclaimed and Michael froze. 'What are you doing carrying this around with you?' Michael spluttered. 'If the police stop you, how would you explain it?'

'I'm sorry.' Michael reckoned his days as an IRA man were over.

She continued to fuss then became less angry. 'All right, I'll see the Abwehr get this information tonight. But for God's sake, man, never ever have incriminating material on your person.' She paused. He nodded. 'Thank you, Mr Donovan.'

'That's *O*'Donovan,' he said. I'm Irish.

'I never would have guessed,' said the spy and sent him on his way.

The IRA men were pleased to hear Michael delivered the message, and doubly pleased when three days later they saw a newspaper article about a large fire in the area where the fuel dump was located. They bought Michael a round in their East End pub, and the new IRA recruit was now officially working for Irish independence.

However, the IRA men would not have been so chuffed had they known the truth. The newspaper article was false, published by order of the government. They'd turned Mrs Grayling nee Ratzinger. The threat of her husband being executed for his pro-fascist views meant she became a double agent, and was now sending useless information to the Abwehr under instructions from the British.

Special Branch added a new name to their list of IRA suspects in Britain, and Michael O'Donovan was put under surveillance. Special Branch declined to arrest him at first, believing him to be the monkey and they wanted the organ-grinder.

Chapter 7

August 1940, Wiltshire England

Louise's palms were sweaty. It was the height of summer but her nervousness came as she was about to meet her mother for the first time in over a year. Her step-father, Sir Anthony Wilding, was a quintessential elderly English gentleman. He married Louise's mother as much out of a sense of duty rather than romantic love believing a woman of her class should never remain a widow.

Sir Anthony wasn't short of a bob and his rambling estate near the village of Great Wishford was "fenced" at the bottom of his garden by the sleepy Wylye River. The house had creature comforts to spare, more wings than a Spitfire, and a glorious garden whipped into shape by Harold the long-serving gardener cum chauffeur.

Louise's mother would spend her autumnal years in style, and as Wiltshire was not on the Luftwaffe radar, only radio and newspaper reports brought the war to Sir Anthony, his wife and spinster sister.

Louise travelled courtesy of the Great Western Railway, took the Salisbury Branch line alighting at Wishford station. Harold stood by the ticket gate, and as Louise was not so much the only young female passenger as the only passenger, he managed to spot her.

'Good day to you, Miss Wellesley,' he said doffing his cap; 'your carriage awaits.'

He took her case, indicated the way, and followed Louise from the station. This was not rush hour and the car owners of Great Wishford could be counted on one hand. Petrol was impossible to obtain for private use and a pony and trap stood still in the shade with the only action in this quiet corner of Wiltshire being a swish of the pony's tail to disturb the odd lazy fly. The gardener offered Louise a hand and she climbed onto the double seat. Harold untied the pony, hopped aboard and gave the beast the universal coded message. 'Giddy up.'

As they travelled, Louise cramped in her stomach. She missed her family and her mother in particular. That alone made her anxious. But so too did a couple of tales she was urged, even required not to tell.

She didn't go to Australia. She did go to France. She wasn't engaged as an actress in a company performing Shakespeare. She was engaged as a sleeper for the Secret Intelligence Service. She didn't play Juliet in Melbourne. She did appear semi-naked at the Folies Bergère. Imagine the reaction if she broke the Official Secrets Act and told her tale. *But what will I invent to explain my absence? And worse, will I be convincing?*

Then another tale caused her grief. Her brother, her mother's second son, sat in a wheelchair with horrible disfiguring wounds from fighting in and escaping from France. He faced major operations to make him even remotely normal. To her mother's question, "How is Edmund?" what will she reply?

All three "upstairs" residents were waiting as the trap came along the drive. Victoria waved a handkerchief and Louise waved a hand. Her heart raced. The trap stopped and Sir Anthony stepped forward offering a hand. Louise stepped down and fell into her mother's arms.

'My darling girl,' she said maintaining her sense of decorum.

'Hello Mummy,' said Louise, struggling with the emotional baggage she'd been carrying for ages.

Sir Anthony and his sister, Clementine provided warm and sincere but less physical greetings and the four settled inside. Tea was served, pleasant discourse ensued, and Louise said nothing remotely controversial or true. Phew.

'Let me show you to your room, my dear,' said Victoria and the women departed.

They sat on the bed, held hands and stared at one another. Louise thought her mother appeared older. Of course she did. Louise knew she too no longer looked 18. Being chased by enraged Resistance fighters and Gestapo officers would age anyone.

Victoria's sons were fighting in a war and her unmarried, beautiful daughter sailed away to the other side of the world. What else could better age a mother?

Victoria thought Louise more mature, more grown-up. Once she would never hesitate to ask her daughter personal questions. Now, she hesitated. They were not so much a mother and daughter as two women of the world catching up on time apart.

'Now you will tell me, my darling,' said Victoria, 'if anything is wrong?'

'Of course, Mummy.'

'If anyone is unwell or having a hard time of it, you will say.'

Louise patted her mother's hands. 'We have always been open and honest with one another, Mummy. That will never change.' She lied.

'Boyfriends, suitable gentlemen?' Victoria asked starting to pry.

Louise did not have to lie. 'Whenever anything serious happens, Mummy, you'll be the first to know.'

They judged one another then hugged. Both knew their relationship was new. Their love for each other was never stronger but the expression "open and honest" no longer applied.

Louise stayed for three days. The only snippet of family news she discovered confirmed what she already knew; brother Henry's wife Georgina was with child and due to make Victoria a grandmother by Christmas.

Louise's acting skills survived their greatest test when she described her visit to the land Down Under and walking across Sydney's Harbour Bridge.

She took the train up to London, and in Edmund's, in *her* new flat, sorted her meagre belongings before heading to the Theatre Royal. She entered via the stage door to be met with the same cacophony in full swing. People eyed her wondering who this striking young woman might be. She saw no-one she knew until Basil Dean came into the wings. He smiled with joy.

'Miss Wellesley; hello, how lovely to see you again.' He turned and called to his friend, Leslie Henson in the auditorium. When told of her arrival, he ran down the aisle.

The men greeted their Shakespearean actress, fussed over her and led her into their office.

'Miss Wellesley,' said Henson, 'we have a problem.' Louise worried but remained calm. 'We have no opening for your marvellous acting skills at the moment but we're hoping to form a company of experienced actors to perform excerpts from the Bard. Does the concept appeal?'

'It does indeed,' said Louise, 'although I am not as experienced as the professionals you may have in mind.'

'Nonsense,' said Dean. 'But we think it's a shame not to be able to offer you something right away. I don't suppose you'd consider anything else while waiting for the Shakespeare troupe to form?'

'Of course,' replied Louise a tad worried she might finish up as a fairy in Cardiff.

'Would you be interested in a fun family show such as a popular pantomime?'

Louise smiled inside and out. 'Oh I love pantomimes. I once played the principal boy in *Jack and the Beanstalk*.'

She thought the ENSA creators were going to dance. They beamed, took hold of Louise's hand and shook it together.

As it happened, their panto production needed a principal boy to play Cinderella. 'We open in Lowestoft on Saturday week, Miss Wellesley. What are you like at learning a script in 10 days?'

Louise smiled. 'Gentlemen, there's only one way to find out.'

She was excited, the ENSA producers were more excited, and the people within earshot clapped.

They whisked Louise back to the costume ladies with orders for the scruffiest rags and finest ball gown for their new Cinderella.

Several women fussed over Louise, measuring and discussing material and designs. The arguments became hectic.

'We can't have that ball gown if she needs to dance.'

'What does the script say?'

'If the show tours, there are sure to be different stage sizes.'

'With her hair colour, she can't wear blue.'

Louise didn't know what to think. One woman undid the buttons on her dress. 'Come on, Miss, we need you to try on these outfits.'

And so down to her underwear, Louise tried on various garments. It reminded her of her former Parisian landlady, Madame Baudin who kept stunning outfits from her days at the Folies Bergère. When Louise asked about work, the landlady as calm and as matter-of-fact as you like said, 'Please Mademoiselle, show me your breasts.'

Pantomime rehearsals began in an old church hall in Battersea and Louise met her fellow performers. She was the youngest by far. Any male of fighting age was needed to give Herr Hitler a black eye. These folk were troupers, Music Hall entertainers who knew their way around a stage blindfolded. They were fun, most of them, and gave her tips like using facial expressions to get a laugh, how timing was everything, and how not to upstage a fellow performer.

With the script in her bag, she hurried home from the Tube station at Maida Vale. Boiling an egg, making tea and learning lines became her life for the foreseeable future.

Cast members were exhausted, especially Louise. Tomorrow the performers, set and costumes would start their tour. Everyone spread out in the stalls of the Theatre Royal and listened to Leslie Henson give his final pep talk. Even the carpenters and costume ladies were there.

'I'm proud of every one of you. You've pulled this show together in a fortnight.'

'*Less* than a fortnight,' called the elderly Harry Bent who played the Fairy Godmother.

'We'll be giving the troops on leave and their families a taste of what life was like before this blasted war began. The pantomime season is a traditional British institution. It's been going for ages and no German bully is going to interrupt our beloved way of life.'

He sounded a bit like the Prime Minister delivering one of his stirring speeches.

'Now there's a small possibility we may perform in a special venue at a special time in a few weeks.' A buzz began. 'I can't say any more right now but I know you'll be thrilled if it all comes off.'

'We're going to sing for the King,' cried a cast member, having a wild guess and trying to make mischief.

The company murmured; it grew and Henson looked horrified. 'It's true,' shouted someone else pointing at the producer who'd been sworn to secrecy, and the response became electric.

Basil Dean stepped from the wings and stood on the stage behind his colleague Leslie Henson. A voice from the stalls bellowed.

'He's behind you!' That prompted an almighty laugh.

An actor in the theatre seats yelled, 'Oh no he's not!

Naturally this was followed by everyone in the company—apart from the two founders—calling as one. 'Oh yes he is!'

Much laughter followed, more to release steam after a hectic rehearsal schedule as much to enjoy the well-known panto routine. Basil Dean held up his hands and a semblance of order was restored.

'Righto ladies and gentlemen, that's all for today. Make sure you see the paymaster to sort out your massive salaries.' A solid jeer erupted. 'We'll see you all tomorrow—on time!'

People headed home. Louise checked with the finance department and was heading for the exit when she overheard the ladies in the costume room.

'I heard them bosses talkin' about it,' said Daisy in her broad Cockney accent. 'We're going to perform at Windsor Castle for the Royal family at Christmas.'

Louise smiled. If true, such a performance would be grand and make a different audience to the one in the church hall for the St Peter's Players in Cambridge. Louise could dine out on such a tale for years.

Clara Rackett was in the group of costume ladies. She said nothing but the news made her think. She appeared miserable, only because she was, and now faced the ongoing and horrendous task of going home to an abusive and drunken husband.

Chapter 8

September 1940, Lowestoft Suffolk

Cinderella was a hit, both the show and the actress in the eponymous role. It was only performed during the day because of the renewed German bombing in many parts of Britain at night. Louise starred. She looked gorgeous and her transformation for the ball scene drew gasps from every audience. The men in uniform skipped the gasp reaction and settled for whistling and calling.

One of the Ugly Sisters, a big, beefy bloke with the softest nature, always escorted Louise from the theatre to her digs meaning randy soldiers, sailors and airmen who gathered at the stage door were cheeky but never brave enough to risk a smack from Lennie the large.

'C'mon, Cinders, let's go for a drink, darlin'?' was heard most afternoons, and Louise would smile and keep walking with her big Ugly Sister now looking like the former Liverpool docker he once was.

There were six cast members in the boarding house where Louise was staying. With no evening shows, the performers would play cards, knit, read and listen to the radio. The comedy *It's That Man Again* and music shows with Sandy MacPherson's *At Your Request* helped pass the time in-between news of the war.

The radio announced what was happening overseas, and Louise paid attention to anything taking place in France. In autumn of 1940, the card playing stopped when the news began.

The Luftwaffe, having failed to cripple Britain's air force in the Battle of Britain, switched tactics and targeted the cities. Daylight bombing made it easier for Britain to attack the bombers and so most German attacks switched to night raids with London the main target.

Night after night tons of bombs rained down on the capital. Massive damage occurred. Incendiary bombs started fires and life for firefighters, air-raid wardens and ambulance drivers was exhausting and bloody dangerous. Poplar, in the East End, saw thousands of houses damaged or destroyed.

Londoners headed for cellars, basements and tube stations. A few reckoned being under the kitchen table or the stairs was a good spot, and a quarter of Londoners hid in their homemade Anderson shelter in the back garden. Lowestoft was much safer than Maida Vale.

This was Blitzkrieg, German for lightning war but in the Blitz, lightning certainly struck the same place twice. Make that four or five times in the same place. For more than 50 nights London copped it.

Clara would go home to her rented terrace in Poplar after her day at the Theatre Royal. Her charming and loving husband would arrive drunk as a Lord demanding his supper. He needed to eat sharpish once the air-raid siren sounded. Forget your grub and find shelter.

Clara chose the local Underground station. It was cold, crowded, and uncomfortable and smelt of stale pee, but was safe. Victor rarely joined her. He didn't have a death wish; he simply didn't fancy walking so far. So long as his food was on the table and he could abuse his wife, he was happy being miserable; he being the world's worst husband.

Victor spent most of his meagre wage in a pub, left fag ends on his dinner plate, and regularly slapped his wife. She easily grew to hate him and often pondered how to escape her prison. *Where will I go? How will I survive?* After ten years, Clara was ready to break free but she would never have guessed who or what helped create a plan.

On night 15 of the Blitz, Victor gobbled his sausages and mash and the always-on-time sirens sounded. Clara grabbed her coat.

'I'm off,' she said heading for the door. She looked back as he slumped on the table. He didn't care about bombs and she didn't care about him. She wished a bomb would land on their terrace and send Victor to hell in a hurry. Then an idea exploded. If Victor dies in the Blitz, I'll be free. She moved to him and shouted. 'Victor, wake up!'

He lifted his head, swore and slumped back on the table. He snored. You never shoot a dog if it's looking at you. She moved to the kitchen and grabbed the large frying pan. Finally, here was the opportunity to end their marriage, her living hell. With pan in hand she returned to the table, swallowed her principles, and did the business. Whack!

As Victor reached the top of a snore crescendo, she swung the pan and smashed his skull. Yes it was against one of the Ten Commandments and English Common Law but if anyone deserved it, the vile Victor Rackett most certainly did.

Emotion swamped Clara. Not having murdered anyone before, she went off her rocker. Revulsion, shame and euphoria collided. A psychiatrist would brand her "unhinged". She took a lantern into the blackened street and waved it to the invisible German pilots above. 'Over here, boys,' she cried trying to attract their attention. 'Flatten this house and bury my old man! Over here!'

Drunk on emotional shock, she didn't hear the air raid warden thundering towards her in the blackout. 'Oi!' he bellowed and Clara panicked. 'What the hell do you think you're doing, woman?'

She came back to Earth and pretended. 'It's my husband. I was calling to him. He's lost in the blackout.' He was lost all right.

'I don't care if he's the ruddy King of England, put out that damn light.' Clara did so post haste. 'So where is your old man?'

She pointed. 'He comes up from the docks.'

'I'll take a look. You go back inside—and stay there.' He set off.

Clara's reply was lost as a German bomb missed its target of the London docks and whistled on its way a hundred yards from Clara's terrace. The explosion burst eardrums as Clara flattened herself on the road. Debris landed nearby and kept landing. Screams and shouting erupted. Then silence. She waited. No sign or sound of the warden and definitely nothing from Victor.

The stray bomb proved a blessing. Clara raced inside, struggled to retrieve her bloodied, drunken and no-longer-snoring husband, and dragged him into the street. Talk about back-breaking work.

It was a labour of love as Victor was lugged towards the end of the road. Houses were obliterated with debris everywhere. Desperate voices called. Clara dropped to her knees. Victor refused to help or complain. The voices faded and the body disposal unit carried on.

But dragging hubby soon proved impossible as a collapsed terrace blocked her path. Victor reached the end of his journey. Clara switched to Plan B, left her "better" half on the road and began picking up bricks. She tossed them onto his lifeless body. They crash-landed on his legs, chest, arms and face. His domestic head wound copped a second serve, this time from the front. Clara's hands were cut as she grabbed building material in the dark.

Finally the burial was over. Or was it? Clara suffered mental and physical abuse from the late Victor Rackett for years. She wanted one last chance to get her own back. In the pitch black she studied the corpse with its smattering of bricks. She saw a part of his body without rubble. She picked up one final brick, stood above her abusive husband and, like a bombardier in the Heinkel He 111 above; took aim at hubby's crotch. Pity he was dead because her action would have brought a tear to his eyes. When found in daylight, Victor was just another Blitz casualty. Would Clara get away with murder?

She scrambled over the debris and headed for the Tube. Down the steps she went and a wave of sound came from below; talking, singing, and babies crying. The platform was covered with people. The smell hit her. Finding a place to sit was tricky. She walked towards the end of the platform. The lighting was dim and she stepped over and between people to squeeze into a spot against the tiles on the wall.

She took an old towel from her bag, put it on the platform and sat pulling her knees up under her chin.

In the darkness, a voice spoke. 'We meet again.'

She turned but couldn't make out the man's face. She thought she recognized him and did thanks to his accent. Michael O'Donovan was taking shelter on the same platform.

'Oh hello,' she said.

'Do you come here often?' he chirruped.

She smiled although you couldn't tell. She pointed to the roof. 'Have you checked for any flying chamber pots?'

He too smiled. 'No but the aroma's the same.'

'When was that? 1937?'

'1936,' he said, 'and the man we went to see is now in jail.'

They chatted away talking about the Battle of Cable Street, Oswald Mosley, the Blitz and the war. Clara made no mention of the holy terror husband. The raid ended, the siren sounded, and they joined the masses making their way back to the streets of London.

'I'd offer to walk you home,' he said, 'only I don't fancy your old man finding me outside your place.'

'You're okay,' she replied, 'he's dead.'

Michael stopped. 'Oh, well, I'm sorry for your loss.'

'Don't be. I'm not, in fact I'm glad.'

They walked. 'When did it happen; if you don't mind me asking?'

'I don't mind, and he died about three hours ago.'

Michael's fascination grew larger. 'Tonight? You mean just before you went to the Underground.' She nodded.

They took a different route as air raid wardens and police directed people from blocked streets. Ambulances and fire engines clanged their bells trying to get through. Screams would erupt when anyone discovered their loved one dead. Cats scurried about no longer having a home. War statistics never mention canine and feline casualties.

Michael was curious about Clara's old man's death, and she was reluctant to say any more. Finally they reached her street and stopped outside her house.

'You never told me how your husband died.'

She stared at him, compelled to speak. 'I killed him.'

His jaw dropped. 'You killed him?' She nodded. 'How?'

She shrugged. 'Does it matter? He's dead.'

He pointed. 'Is he in the house?'

'No, we stepped over him about a hundred yards down the road.'

Michael struggled to speak. 'You killed him in the blackout?'

'No, in the house then I dragged him down there and covered him with debris from the bombed terrace.'

A sickening feeling grabbed her as she realised she'd confessed to a stranger, well as good as, and could now find herself in court and then on the gallows. But he wasn't about to turn her over to anyone. On the contrary he was anxious to help her get away with murder.

'Have you tidied up inside?'

Her face dropped. *Why would I tidy up?* She shook her head.

'He'll be found in the morning. Someone will know him and the police will come and interview you. If they find his blood in the house, he'll go from victim of the Blitz to victim of a domestic, and you'll be charged with murder. That means the rope.'

Clara unlocked her door and they went inside. With the curtains in place, she turned on a light. The kitchen chairs were tipped over, a rug was scrunched up and there was blood on the table and the floor.

'Hot water and soap,' said Michael, and Clara scrubbed. He put the furniture and rug to rights and together they removed the blood of the murder victim, the man nobody mourned.

Clara made tea and they sat in the front room, united in their plan to have the death of Victor Rackett officially listed as an accident.

'You're not the only one who has a secret,' said Michael. She was puzzled. 'In case you're worried I may tell the police about your secret; don't. And to help you stop worrying, here's the secret you could use against me.' He paused. 'I work for the Abwehr.'

Her blank face spoke volumes. 'I don't know what you mean.'

'It's the German Secret Service. If you think I'll tell the police about your husband, you can tell them about me helping German spies.'

She understood. 'Are you in the IRA?'

He nodded. 'Are you in the BUF?'

'No.' She explained how years ago she lived in the same house as Oswald Mosley when they were children, and how she supported his anti-war views.

He explained how he wanted Germany to win the war so Ireland might be united. Their discussion went on into the night.

'I've changed my name, unofficially, I'm now Michael Donovan and I've learnt to speak like an Englishman.' He surprised her by slipping into a London accent. 'Good evening, madam. Do you know the way to Buckingham Palace?'

She laughed for the first time in ages. 'Oh, very good, Mr Donovan.'

'And I'm a part-time air raid warden when I'm not on the docks.'

'And is that your IRA cover as you help Germany win the war?'

He put a finger to his lips. 'Shhh. Loose lips sink ships.'

Clara explained her job and Michael learnt about ENSA and the many acts Clara helped costume. She mentioned one of her latest projects, a pantomime. 'It's on tour in Suffolk but there's a rumour it might be staged for the Royal Family in Windsor Castle at Christmas.'

Michael absorbed the information but said nothing. It was late and he stood to leave.

'Will you have a drink with me one night?'

'I'd like that,' she said and meant it.

He went to the door. 'I'll see you at the Underground.'

'Sure.'

'And you should practice being shocked for when the coppers knock on your door.'

She almost smiled. 'Thanks, Michael and goodnight.'

'Goodnight to you, widow Rackett,' he said disappearing in the blackout.

Chapter 9

October 1940, London England

Huntley, Steadfast and Browne were not from a firm of solicitors in the Aldgate High Street but three Special Branch officers tasked with preventing the IRA harming Britain during its war with Germany.

Special Branch, originally the Special Irish Branch, began in the 19th century with the IRA their number one target. During the Blitz, Special Branch officers spied on IRA members, and even felt their collars.

'So what about this Michael O'Donovan?' asked Browne. 'I see he's changed his name to Donovan.'

'He's not the worry, it's the German woman in Kent we need to watch,' replied Steadfast.'

'What do you mean?'

'She agreed too easily to be a double agent. The information she gave us about the fuel depot was next to useless; fifty gallons is nothing.'

'Donovan was testing her.'

'Or the IRA was testing him.'

'He's never been involved in bombings, here or in Ireland. His bosses on the docks reckon he's a reliable and good worker.'

'And he works as an air-raid warden two or three nights a week guiding people into shelters, helping rescue dead and wounded victims of the Blitz.'

'But is it a cover?' asked Browne.

'I say we put him on the Watch List but with a low priority.'

'I agree,' said Steadfast.

And so IRA member Michael Donovan, formerly O'Donovan, worked on the docks by day, as an air raid warden by night, and went to IRA Meetings in secret.

Was Special Branch doing its job?

The London cell of the IRA met in secret in a pub in Limehouse. Members never came or went via the front door. Even eagle-eyed Special Branch officers never knew where they met.

The IRA Leader was Liam Flattery who thought about killing more Brits than he had whiskers, and his bushy beard made Ned Kelly and W. G. Grace bum fluff beginners.

Liam joined the IRA as a teen and chatted with the Germans. In 1936 he met an Abwehr agent in Belfast. Liam went to Berlin for further talks.

A German invasion of Ireland was a lower priority than menus for concentration camps. The IRA wanted weapons. 'Give us guns, Fritz and we can give the bloody Brits more than a feckin' black eye.'

But the Nazis were reluctant. The IRA did not impress with their boast being bigger than their brawn. In fact, both groups were in the same boat called *Shambles*. The Abwehr were disorganized and the IRA up themselves.

With the Luftwaffe pounding London night after night, the London IRA lads were doubly frustrated. Under cover of the Blitz, they could wreak havoc everywhere; power stations, railways, factories, hospitals. "Just give us the feckin' explosives".

At these IRA meetings in Limehouse, Michael spoke little but when he did this night, he stopped the conversation dead.

'What about the Royal Family?' he asked.

The silence was loud.

'What about 'em?' asked Liam with a mix of hatred for the Royals and fascination with any possibility to damage them.

'I met a woman who is sympathetic to the cause.'

'To us?'

'No, to the Mosley fella.'

The room buzzed with anger. 'That feckin' fascist,' snarled Liam.

Michael waited for quiet. 'She wants the war to end and doesn't care who wins. She knows if the Krauts win, our chance of a united Ireland improves no end, and she supports that.'

He spoke the truth and the others, even Liam, believed him.

He tackled Michael. 'So what's this about the Royal Family?'

'This woman works for a group of entertainers who visit troops all over the country. She reckons a group will perform for the Royals at Windsor Castle this Christmas.'

Daniel from Derry scoffed. 'So are we expecting an invitation?'

Liam saw the possibilities. 'Can we use this woman? Can she smuggle a bomb into the castle?'

Michael lost it. 'Oh for Christ's sake, Liam, use your feckin' brains for once.'

Wow. Stop the meeting. Pistols at ten paces. Liam stood ready to exchange blows. Michael kept at him.

'If we kill a Royal, we'll have the police, army, spy-catchers and the whole feckin' country after our blood.'

They knew he spoke the truth. 'Okay, so what's your plan?

Chapter 10

December 1940, London England

This would be a Christmas like no other. Thousands of Londoners killed, many more injured and bomb damage as far as the eye could see. And in this season of goodwill, Michael and Clara struck up a friendship. Both were alone, both hated the war, and, for vastly different reasons, both wanted Germany to win.

They met regularly in the Underground, taking shelter as the Luftwaffe pounded London. Michael walked Clara home and soon the routine involved him stepping in for a cup of char and a chat.

There was no sexual tension. Their connection was the frailty of life, and the fact that both held a secret; she murdered her husband and he belonged to the IRA. If their secrets became known, both would be in jail and likely executed.

Victor Rackett was officially described as a victim of the Blitz and Clara was free to marry again. Michael stayed clear of part-time IRA work but picked up a third job when Clara took him along to ENSA to meet Messrs. Dean and Henson.

'He's a part-time volunteer Air Raid Warden so why not a part-time volunteer carpenter and driver for ENSA?' she pitched to the producers. They were delighted to have Michael on board.

'I don't suppose you sing as well, Mr Donovan?' asked Dean, and Michael shook his head and laughed, speaking in his London accent. 'I'm afraid not, sir, strictly behind the scenes.'

So to his dock work by day and air raid warden work by night, he added weekend labours as he volunteered for ENSA at the Theatre Royal, Drury Lane.

He liked the place, helping with set-building and van driving.

That night, Clara cooked a meal for Michael before his Air Raid Warden shift. 'This is kind of you Clara,' he said. 'You must let me give you a bob or two.'

'Don't be silly. Two can eat as cheap as one and besides, it makes a difference cooking for a man who appreciates what I do.'

He studied her. 'I don't suppose you'd let me become your lodger?' She hesitated. 'I'd pay you of course and you'd have a man here to keep you safe.'

It made sense. 'Okay,' she said. 'I'll make up the back room. But you'll have to wash out in the yard by the privvy.'

He grinned. 'What else is new?' Both were glad. He got stuck into a piece of the poorest quality cut of meat you could imagine but stopped chewing when Clara spoke.

'The pantomime I told you about is going to be performed for the Royals at Windsor Castle next week and you're driving the van.'

He stared at her. His chewing, which was damn hard work, stopped in mid bite. Both their minds were racing. He dared not ask even one of his many questions. She dared not ask if he was ready and willing.

'I see.'

She paused. 'If you don't want the job, I'll find someone else.'

'No, no,' he spoke in a rush. 'I want the job, I'll take it.'

There was another pause. 'Good,' she said then put a piece of apple pie in front of him. 'Sorry, there's no cream not for love or money.'

At night he put on his Warden's helmet and set off on patrol. As the sirens sounded, the searchlights probed the night sky, and the anti-aircraft guns boomed, Michael stood outside his designated shelter and marked off the names of the locals as they arrived.

'Good evening,' most said not knowing their volunteer was an IRA man and a recent ENSA volunteer. With all accounted for and the bombs beginning to fall, he joined the residents and took cover.

He was the first out when the all clear sounded, and in the darkness saw his supervisor approaching.

'Good evening, Michael,' said the senior man, an octogenarian.

'Good evening, sir,' replied Michael having impeccable manners. He was the most polite and respectful member of the IRA here and abroad.

'Can you cover a spot in the West End on the weekend?'

'I'm sorry, Mr Burke, but I'm volunteering for ENSA.'

'ENSA? You mean the theatre crowd mob?'

'Yes sir. They entertain the troops on leave.'

'So you're a singer as well?'

Michael laughed at the same assumption he heard from the men in the Theatre Royal. He made it clear he was devoid of artistic talent, and remained free to drive the van for ENSA this coming weekend.

Windsor Castle, Berkshire England

Marion Crawford, known as Crawfie to members of the Royal Family, was the governess caring for Princess Elizabeth and Princess Margaret. There was great respect and fondness between the young girls and their young helpmate.

As she supervised their retirement, she gave the girls the news.

'I have a surprise, you two,' she said. The Princesses sat up in bed, eyes wide open eagerly awaiting details.

'Are we going back to London?' asked Elizabeth. 'Mummy and Daddy went today.'

'No, we're staying here, and their Majesties returned late this afternoon.'

'Are we getting less presents this Christmas because of the war?' asked the younger Princess.

'You say "fewer presents", Margaret, and I don't know about your presents except the ones I have for both of you.' The girls trembled with excitement. They adored Christmas even if Elizabeth was 14 and Margaret nearly 10.

'No,' said Crawfie, 'the news is we're going to have visitors with a pantomime in the Waterloo Chamber in two days' time.'

The girls clapped; their happiness on show.

'Which pantomime?' asked Margaret begging.

'I believe it's *Cinderella*.'

'Oh it's one of my favourites,' said Margaret.

'Mine too,' said her sister.

'And can we meet the actors after the performance?' Margaret was desperate to be able to talk to the players especially if they were still wearing their costumes and make-up.

'I shall ask, no promises mind,' said Crawfie. 'Now it's lights out and off to sleep, young ladies.' She walked to the door. 'Goodnight.'

The sisters chorused, 'Goodnight.'

'And no talking.' She left and the excited whispering began.

Michael was not on duty. He and Clara walked to the Underground like so many others, regular as clockwork. He wanted to talk about their trip to Windsor and Clara's plan. He couldn't believe she would want him to plant a bomb or attempt to harm a member of the Royal Family. So what was her plan?

'Clara, can we talk about the trip to Windsor?'

'It's simple. The van is loaded with the costumes and props. You drive with me sitting next to you. At the Castle, you help me unload and store the costumes and props in the dressing rooms.'

'Okay,' said Michael, 'but you know that's not what I meant.'

He stared at her. She wouldn't look at him.

'We play it by ear,' she said.

He stopped. She stopped and turned back. 'That's it?' he asked.

She beckoned and he joined her. 'Sir Oswald Mosley wants a peaceful end to the war. *I* want a peaceful end to the war. So do you.' He nodded. 'So once we're inside the castle, we take any opportunity to help bring about a peaceful end to the war. Are you okay with that?'

He took a while to reply. 'Yes,' he said, 'I'm definitely okay with that,' and they entered the Underground station.

Chapter 11

Theatre Royal, Drury Lane

The day of the pantomime at Windsor was bright and sunny. Clara and Michael headed for the Theatre Royal They never admitted to nerves but both sported sweaty palms, rapid heartbeats and butterflies. Neither knew what would happen. Clara's plan was to take action if the opportunity arose. As they approached Drury Lane, she grabbed Michael's arm.

'Let's not arrive together. You go first to show you're keen. I'll walk around a bit and arrive later. Let's not be seen together.'

'What, not at all?'

'No, of course we'll say hello and work together but let's pretend we're acquaintances rather than lodger and landlady.' He nodded. 'Good luck,' she said and walked away.

Neither she nor Michael saw the Special Branch officer who followed them, making notes. He knew Michael had recently moved house to live with a woman, a widow, Clara Rackett.

The agent followed Michael to Drury Lane, watched him enter via the stage door, and took up a position to continue his observation. He would wait for Michael to finish his stint in the theatre, and walk out again into the London sunshine, or just as likely the London drizzle.

The man from Special Branch didn't know what Michael planned once inside the Theatre Royal. More fool him.

Michael opened the stage door. 'Good morning,' he greeted the head carpenter.

'Good morning, Michael. The van's out the back. You can start loading all these boxes. And you're on the list as the driver. Okay?'

Michael maintained his polite, subservient nature. 'Yes sir,' he replied and carried pantomime material to the van. It was a typical vehicle of the day used to shift furniture for folk on the move. Now it was an ENSA vehicle taking everything from pins to pianos to venues up and down the country.

From deep inside the van, as he shoved boxes into a corner, he heard a voice. 'Good morning.' He turned and saw Clara.

'Oh good morning, Missus Rackett.'

'Are you all set for the big day?'

'I am,' he said as he walked to the back of the van and dropped down to stand beside her.

'There are special costumes, including the ball gown for Cinders, which need to be hung on a special rack. Come and I'll show you.' He followed her into the theatre and to the room where the costumes were made and stored. Backstage people were busy. She pointed. 'That's the rack, Michael.'

He carried it out to the van and she followed with large costumes. He stood inside the van waiting for instructions.

'Put the rack up the front beside the boxes and make sure it's secure,' she said. He did so using ropes which were tied to the wood runners along the sides of the van. He walked to the front and collected the costumes.

'When they're hung on the rack, Michael, please come back for more,' said Clara who disappeared.

Back in the costume area, he was told to collect another rack. Clara followed him with more costumes.

'Put the rack there, Michael,' she said indicating the back of the van close to the back flap.

'Here?' he asked wondering why it was so far from the other costumes. 'Is it too close when the back flap is raised?'

'It's fine,' she confirmed. Then, when he'd secured the rack, she handed him the latest bunch of costumes. Basil Dean appeared.

'Good morning, Clara. Good morning, Michael,' he said. 'Are we ready for the off?'

'Good morning, Mister Dean,' said Clara.

'Almost sir,' said Michael.

'Good, well here's the paperwork. You'll need these passes to enter the Castle.' He handed them each a pass and gave Clara an envelope with other relevant documents. 'Don't lose anything, don't nick anything and for God's sake don't drive on the lawn. Are we clear?'

The driver and costumier understood.

'Well,' said Dean, his chest expanding with happiness. 'ENSA performing for royalty gives one a sense of pride, does it not?' The lackeys agreed, again.

'When will the performers arrive, Mister Dean?' asked Clara.

He checked his watch. 'The coach is due soon and not everyone is here yet. No matter, you head off and have everything ready for when we arrive. Straighten your tie, Michael and please drive carefully.'

Dean left and Clara and Michael glanced at one another. Their nerves became nervous. This was a mission to stop the war. They were the IRA man with links to an Abwehr spy, and the murderess milliner from ENSA who admired the imprisoned fascist, Sir Oswald Mosley. The ENSA duo were pacifists of a sort with the "of a sort" bit a worry.

'Can you fetch the flat with the ballroom chandelier?' asked Clara.

'I thought there was to be no scenery.'

'There isn't but if they think the stage is undressed, we can fix the problem in two shakes of a lamb's tail.'

Michael left. The head carpenter queried his move.

'There's no scenery going.'

Michael thought on his feet. 'Ah, Mr Dean said we needed to have a back-up just in case.' The head carpenter grunted and Michael staggered away with the flat.

At the van, Clara gave instructions. 'Put it against those boxes in front of the wicker basket. He did and the van was ready to go.

Clara climbed in the passenger side, Michael sat behind the wheel, started the engine and off they drove to Berkshire for a Royal panto.

Marion Crawford helped her young charges dress. 'I want to wear my fairy costume,' said Margaret, determined to appear as one of the players.

'But we're in the audience, Margaret, not on stage,' said Crawfie.

'I don't care,' said Princess Determined.

'Crawfie's right, Margaret. We wear normal clothes. That's what people in audiences in theatres wear.'

Margaret stamped her foot. She hated not getting her way.

Crawfie tried to pacify the girl. 'Next year, if we have our own pantomime, you can dress up as one of the characters.'

The girls were impressed, especially Margaret. 'Do you mean our very own pantomime, here at Windsor?'

'Or it might be a play but whatever we have, it will be you and Lillibet performing on stage in your favourite costumes.'

Both the princesses were excited but like most children wanted the event to happen now. Only when they were older, much older would they wish for time to slow down. They dressed in "normal" clothes for the ENSA show in the Berkshire castle.

In the van, Clara and Michael said little. When they were about a mile from Windsor, Clara told him to pull over.

'There,' she pointed, 'by the woodland.' He stopped the van. 'I'll hop in with the costumes. When we're stopped at the gate, tell them the lady in charge with all the paperwork, is in the back.'

He studied her. 'If you have a plan, Clara, I've no idea what it is.'

'I'm making it up as I go along. I suggest if we get the chance to do something for peace and end the war, we support one another.'

He nodded. 'Okay.'

They climbed down and on the quiet road he opened the rear of the van and helped Clara up and inside. He closed the flap, raised the tailboard, patted the side of the van and walked back to the cab.

They drove into Windsor and to the castle.

Chapter 12

Windsor Castle, Berkshire England

As a POW, in 1916 Michael moved from Dublin to North Wales. It was a forced emigration. When released by the British, he landed in London. Since arriving in the capital, in the last 20 odd years he had never once visited a tourist landmark, and certainly none outside the capital. Windsor Castle was a new adventure for him.

The Castle became home to the Royal Family during WW2. At first the government tried to spirit the Royals away to Canada but the King refused point blank. Some argued the young Princesses should be removed for safety reasons; after all, London's youngsters went to the countryside. But the Queen was blunt. 'If the King stays, we stay.'

It was announced the King and Queen were living at Buckingham Palace and in part this was true but actually propaganda because the royal couple returned to Windsor at night. There were too many German bombs landing in London.

A special section of the army was assigned to Windsor Castle with the sole task of guarding the royals. The Castle, a massive edifice was begun in the 11th century. There are hundreds of rooms and a spacious estate with surrounding farm and parkland. Many soldiers were required to cover the entire Windsor precinct.

The two guards on duty at the main entrance were expecting "those thespians, them fairies" with the number plate details of both the coach and van on their clipboards. Michael drove with extreme caution. He was certain his beating heart would attract interest from the Brits. He stopped and leant out his window.

'Pass,' said the sergeant, his uniform so clean and stiff he couldn't help but walk in a military manner. Michael handed him his pass. It was approved. 'Engine off and step out of the vehicle.'

No *please* or *sir*. On the form, Michael was listed as a dock-worker, ENSA volunteer and part-time Air Raid Warden, not a toff, politician or person of rank. He switched off the engine and stepped out.

The private on duty shouldered his rifle and issued an order. 'Arms out.' Michael imitated a scarecrow and was patted down to see if anything not allowed was on his person. The private looked at his sergeant and shook his head.

'Right,' said the Sergeant, 'papers.'

'They're with the costume lady in the back of the van.'

'Open it,' snapped Mr Army.

All three headed to the rear. Michael glanced at these British soldiers, in their uniform, armed, smug in their roles as defenders of the realm. *Are either of these bastards related to the Brits who shot my family and butchered my friends?* If so, he would love to have secreted a pistol about his person.

At the rear, the sergeant ordered the van opened. Michael dropped the tail board and went to pull the canvas curtains. He was beaten to the task as Clara threw them apart.

'Good morning, gentlemen,' she declared and held out her pass and the envelope containing the other official documents required for visitors to the Castle.

The sergeant examined the contents and was satisfied. But was this woman concealing anything illegal?

'You'll need to step down, madam.'

'Officer,' protested Clara in the most subservient of tones, 'I am the former housekeeper of the 4th Baronet of Ancoats. His Lordship will gladly vouch for my honesty and steadfast loyalty to their Majesties and their heirs and successors, according to law.' She neglected to add Sir Oswald Senior kicked the bucket in 1915 and, due to subsidence caused by mining in which her father was killed, Apedale Hall started to sink and was demolished years ago.

Clara was of average build. Any object under her apron or dress would be easily seen. She didn't look like an anarchist or German fifth columnist. The sergeant sniffed and handed the documents to Michael.

'On your way,' he said, and as he strode away, called, 'and if you drive on the lawn, you'll be in the Tower.'

Clara hopped down and Michael raised the tailboard. She joined Michael in the cab, and they drove slowly into the massive Windsor Castle. At another entrance, another army official playing the role of traffic policeman waved them through an impressive opening. Another official beckoned them forward with Michael driving with due care.

When the official raised a hand to stop, Michael did so in a professional way.

A female official stepped forward and spoke to the driver. 'ENSA pantomime people?'

Michael nodded. 'Yes,' said Clara out and walking around the van.

The official set off. 'This way,' and the London duo followed.

Into the castle they went and Michael and Clara were impressed, mightily so. They walked through the vast and beautifully decorated rooms with furniture, paintings, carpets and sky-high ceilings. They struggled to walk without bumping into one another as their eyes were drawn to the stunning interiors. They stopped.

'This is the Waterloo Chamber. You will perform here and the changing facilities are through there.' More walking. 'The lavatories are down that corridor and nobody, repeat nobody from your group is to go anywhere else in the Castle other than the performing space and this area. Do you understand?'

There was only one answer.

Clara added a question of her own. 'Is there another way to bring the costumes through to this area?'

The official glared at Clara as if she'd spilt paint on the centuries old furniture. 'This way,' she said and headed off down another corridor. She opened a door to the outside with the van about 50 yards away. 'Make sure you close this door when finished.'

'Thank you,' said Clara.

'Thank you,' said Michael and wondered whether he should nod or bow. The official disappeared and the duo set off for the van. Michael dropped the tailboard and hopped up.

''Bring those costumes from the front of the van please, Michael,' said Clara. He fetched them and she filled her arms with outfits. 'And please bring the rack and then the boxes marked Panto Props.'

She set off to the short cut entrance and he followed with the rack. The rooms set aside for the performers as dressing rooms were not typical of any theatre but had atmosphere and character aplenty.

Clara put the costumes on the rack. Michael returned with the first of the boxes. He went back for the others and when he arrived, he found Clara setting up the rooms with costumes, props, wigs and footwear spread out ready for use. The performers were treated as professionals.

'I'll finish sorting these boxes,' she said. 'I suggest you go and turn the van around. It will be easy to re-load when we're finished.'

That made sense and Michael did as he was told.

He returned and the duo went into the Waterloo Chamber admiring the magnificent ceiling when a young woman came in from one of the six entrances.

'Hello,' she said. 'Are you the people from the pantomime?'

'Yes, madam,' said Clara.

The young woman extended her hand and both Clara and Michael shook it. 'My name's Marion Crawford. I'm the governess for Princess Elizabeth and Princess Margaret. I have to tell you the Princesses are both terribly excited to see your performance.'

Clara and Michael smiled. 'We're backstage workers,' said Clara but the pantomime has been jolly successful in other places so we hope it will prove popular for their Majesties.'

'I'm sure it will, and there is a small favour I wish to ask. Do you think Princess Elizabeth and Princess Margaret might be able to meet the performers afterwards; just to say hello?'

'I'm sure the performers would be honoured.'

'Oh how wonderful. I won't say anything to the girls beforehand but if you could have a word to the cast, I'll be most grateful, and I know the Princesses will be thrilled. Well, I'll let you get on.' She hesitated. 'Am I allowed to say good luck?'

Clara replied. 'I think the Royal Family and their staff are allowed to say whatever they like.'

All three laughed and the governess waved and left.

Michael studied Clara. He wanted to ask questions but thought better of it. He remembered her previous comment. 'Let's just see what happens.'

The plot thickened.

Chapter 13

Windsor Castle, Berkshire England

The coach arrived with the cast, producer and ENSA creators. Basil and Leslie were never going to miss the chance to be introduced to a certain family. Everyone found the stop and search routine to be great fun. They piled back on the coach and pulled up near the van. They were led through rooms in the wing known as the State Apartments and couldn't stop gasping and bumping into one another.

In the Waterloo Chamber they were awestruck. This was a dream venue with the most important audience; an occasion the performers could only dream about.

The official gave the same speech she gave to Clara and Michael who stood to one side and watched the buzz of excitement generated by the company. When the official left, Clara approached Basil Dean and told him the costumes and props were ready in the dressing rooms. He called for attention and repeated Clara's news which prompted a round of applause. The company would applaud anything right now such was their eager anticipation. They departed to prepare.

The Waterloo Chamber is dominated by massive portraits which cover the walls. They are everywhere; monarchs, politicians, military leaders and even a pope. Not a lot of ladies, mind. A chap by the name of Arthur Wellesley is prominent. A distant relative of his had just arrived. She could have spent an age wandering admiring the art.

A temporary stage was constructed with no wings or walls. Because the stunning ceiling had a raised section allowing daylight in, the matinee was au natural. The players could see the theatre-goers as much as they could see the performers. To some actors this can be disconcerting, and when the viewers include the King and Queen and their daughters, then every performer is super self-conscious.

The venue was not full. This was only partly a public performance. The Royal Family sat in the front row—naturally. It wouldn't do to have the Queen moving from side to side because a large person with an even larger hat obstructed her view.

The plush single chairs took up about a third of the magnificent room. Apart from the Royals, many of the Castle employees were invited as were the children from the Royal School located in the Castle grounds. Being young and little, they couldn't see the whole stage through the backs and heads of the adults in front of them. But, it was a treat, they were close to the King and Queen, and they skipped Arithmetic and Religious Instruction. Hooray!

Backstage, the cast were aquiver. They knew their lines and moves but a Royal Variety Performance was a first for all of them. Their wigs, props, costumes and footwear were fine. Stage make-up without the glare of theatre lights was a bit strange but then consider the venue and audience. They whispered due to their proximity to the stage.

Old Fred Worthing, Ugly Sister number 1, in his awful dress and monstrous wig sidled up to Louise in her tatty dress and messy hair. 'All set, Love?' he asked and gave her his usual wink.

'I'm a tad nervous, Mr Worthing, and can't think why.'

He smiled. 'Is your curtsey ready for the King and Queen?'

Louise thought her upset tummy was about to revolt. She gave Fred a strangled grin. She'd performed on many stages playing many roles but this was a first. She could handle stage door Johnnies and lecherous men in uniform but the King and Queen of England; they were in another universe.

The stage manager appeared and spoke in a soft voice. 'Thank you ladies and gentlemen.' A hush fell in the corridor outside the Waterloo Chamber in the Upper Ward by the State Apartments of Windsor Castle.

The producer stuck to the same opening as used for all previous performances. Cinders would enter sweeping, pause, face front and begin her monologue. She stood in the large doorway, heart racing and ready to start the show.

Basil Dean stole her thunder. He stepped forward and addressed the audience. By the time he finished listing the distinguished guests, most of his allotted speech time had elapsed. His final words were, 'And so on with the show,' as he strode into the audience and took his seat in the second row. The audience applauded, the pianist struck up the musical introduction and the stage manager tapped Louise on the shoulder.

'You're on, Darling,' he said and Louise entered the famous Waterloo Chamber dressed as a skivvy and swished her broom.

The Princesses in the front row were hooked. Princess Margaret's mouth was open as she clasped her hands in delight and wonder.

There were steps at either end of the temporary stage. Louise ascended them with ease and once centre stage, stopped and spoke. The audience loved her.

Clara and Michael sat in the back row by themselves. As the show progressed and as the audience became hooked, Clara made her move. With the audience yelling their responses, she withdrew an envelope and nudged him. He glanced at her, saw the envelope and took it.

'Put it away,' she whispered. 'Read it when you're on your own.'

He shoved the envelope in his dustcoat pocket. He'd been nervous just thinking about what might happen today. Now his nerves edged towards terror. Imagine what the authorities both within the Castle and in Whitehall would think if they knew the true situation.

Here was a member of the IRA sitting a few yards from the entire royal family and nobody knew; nobody except a Mrs Clara Rackett, murderess, and devoted supporter of Sir Oswald Mosley, he who currently resided as a guest of His Majesty in Holloway Prison.

The current situation in the Waterloo Chamber was a "powder keg". Guido Fawkes would be right at home.

The pantomime struck the perfect chord; it began well, got better and finished in triumph. The audience loved the show, their calling out responses to the good and evil made the event a towering success. The King and Queen enjoyed themselves but seeing the joy expressed by their daughters gave their Majesties' royal hearts a boost. Despite the ravages of war, people were still able to enjoy the simple pleasures.

As the company took their bows, Clara whispered to Michael. 'Go and wait by the van. Have it ready to leave in an instant. When we depart, drive steadily, stop when required and above all, stay calm.'

He studied her eyes. They displayed a certain fire, a passion and he didn't think, he *knew* something big was about to happen. He left.

The children from the Royal School were ushered out of the Chamber away from the Royals. The cast remained on stage. The

Castle employees filed out, heading back to work. The ENSA founders hovered around awaiting a Royal introduction.

An official representing the King brought the producer to meet the Royals. He in turn introduced Dean and Henson and then the players which lead to lots of bobbing and bowing, and smiles and congratulations. It was a moment every ENSA employee would remember for the rest of their lives.

I performed for the King and the Queen!

The Royals and the players and officials broke into smaller groups. The Princesses begged Crawfie to let them meet Cinderella. The governess caught Louise's eye then beckoned with a finger. Louise, in her most fancy costume, headed to one side of the Waterloo Chamber. Two excited young sisters were thrilled to meet the star of the show. She was beautiful and her costume stunning.

Crawfie introduced the Princesses to Louise.

'How do you do?' said Louise finding it hard to bob and shake hands with each Princess.

'Congratulations,' said Elizabeth. 'We absolutely loved the play.'

'Thank you,' said Louise not sure what to call the young girls.

'I thought you were super,' said Margaret, 'and I love your dress.' She reached out to touch the material.

Louise saw Clara standing nearby. 'Well there's the lady who made my dress.' The royals turned and saw the dressmaker. Crawfie did her beckoning routine again and Clara joined the group. She was introduced and explained how she made all the dresses in the pantomime.

'Even the Ugly Sisters?' asked Elizabeth. Clara nodded.

Princess Margaret imitated a chatterbox but talking to the dressmaker was not nearly as exciting as talking to the star. She addressed Louise. 'Cinderella, have you seen the other parts of the Castle?'

'No, only these rooms.'

'Oh there's so much more.' She held out her hand. 'Come and I'll show you.'

Louise froze. How do you say no to a Princess?

Crawfie took control. 'I think Cinderella has to change, Margaret.'

The Princess objected. 'Oh please Crawfie, just for five minutes.'

'I would like to meet the Fairy Godmother,' said Elizabeth putting the governess in a bind.

Clara spoke. 'If you like, I could go with Princess Margaret and Cinderella and make sure they're back in five minutes.'

Ten minutes,' said Margaret being determined to win.

'Oh would you?' sighed the relieved governess.

'Come on,' said the younger Princess dragging Louise out of the Waterloo Chamber. Clara followed giving a friendly smile to comfort Crawfie. She and Elizabeth went to find the Fairy Godmother.

The trio entered the fabulous dining hall and Margaret became the tour guide. 'This is where we have those big dinner parties with all the important people. Would you like to come? I could arrange it.'

Louise smiled at Clara. 'Thank you,' said the actress, 'but I'm not sure I'm important.'

'Of course you are,' contradicted the Princess and headed off through another massive door in the massive castle. 'Come this way.'

After a few minutes, Louise worried. 'I think we should go back, Princess Margaret. Don't you agree, Madam Costumier?'

'Well yes,' said Clara but as we're so close to the van, I could give the young Princess a special dress I've made for her.'

Louise worried but the royal celebrated. Her eyes had never been so wide. 'You've made a special dress just for me?'

Clara smiled. ''You could keep it and wear it on special occasions.' For once, the Princess was struck dumb. Clara pretended. 'But I'm lost. I don't know the way out.'

'That's easy,' said the royal and set off. 'I'll show you.'

Louise was seriously worried and hissed. 'Clara, this is not right.'

'Nonsense,' said Clara giving Cinders a shove. 'The King will think you're a huge star for making his daughter so happy.'

They followed the young Princess through the castle until they reached a large door. 'Help me,' she said and the women needed all their strength to open the door just enough for the Princess to scamper through. In the sunshine she pointed. 'Is that your van?'

Chapter 14

Windsor Castle, Berkshire England

Michael sat on the back of the van, his feet kicking the tailboard. He read the note Clara gave him inside the castle. It was a map with a few directions. What it all meant, he didn't know. He didn't have to think much longer because from around a corner of the castle came three females. One was a child who happened to be a member of the Royal Family. Another was an actress dressed in a ball gown as Cinderella. And last was the woman in whose East End terrace he was currently a lodger. Middle-aged she might be but Clara kept up with the other two much younger females.

Stunned, Michael dropped to the ground. *What the hell is happening?*

Clara yelled from a distance. 'Help us into the van. We must find the special dress for the Princess.'

Margaret reached the van first and held out a hand to be helped. She was up for anything. Michael obliged. The Princess was in the van when Louise arrived and was helped aboard. Clara arrived puffing.

She pointed. 'Go the front of the van,' she called to the others and Louise and Margaret disappeared. 'Help me up,' she whispered, and Michael did so. Still puffing, she hissed instructions. 'Lift the tailboard, leave the canvas open, hop in the cab and when I yell, drive. Did you read my note?'

'Yes.'

'Then you know what to do. Destroy the note and go!'

She disappeared into the van and he lifted the tail board and left the canvas blinds open. He moved to the cab, climbed into his seat and checked the ignition key was ready. He could hear voices in the back. The Princess sounded excited. The actress seemed to be urging a speedy exit. Then there was silence.

A different voice called out; one with fear. It screamed No! No!'

Then it too stopped and Clara yelled. 'Go! Go! Go!

Back in the Waterloo Chamber, the glad-handing ended. The players returned to their changing area to remove make-up and costumes.

Marion Crawford was in distress. The younger princess and her two adult friends were nowhere to be seen. She approached an equerry of the King and explained the situation. He immediately spoke to a security person who disappeared to alert others.

The governess, with Princess Elizabeth in hand, approached the Queen. 'My apologies, Your Majesty, I have left Margaret to entertain Cinderella. I'll go and fetch her immediately.'

She departed leaving the Queen worried. Her husband grinned. 'What else would you expect?' he asked and with Princess Elizabeth in tow, they headed back to their apartments.

The van reached the exit gate where the same two military officers stopped the van. 'Pass,' said the sergeant. Michael handed over his ID. It was given scant investigation.

'The costume lady has the other papers in the back.'

'Open the back,' said the sergeant.

Michael thought Clara was mad. The kidnap, if that's what it was, would be discovered, he'd be arrested and, if lucky, spend the rest of his life in jail. Far more likely, with his IRA and POW record, he'd be executed for treason. His hope of a united Ireland died.

He followed the soldiers to the rear, dropped the tailboard but realised the canvas curtains were closed. Not for long as they were opened by a smiling costumier.

'Good afternoon, gentlemen,' she said handing down the papers. Both officers peered into the van. It seemed the same as before. The rack of costumes was in place with a couple hanging on the wall of the cab. The flat with the chandelier was exactly where it stood before. The boxes were there, not all mind but most. Several smaller boxes sat atop the large wicker basket.

'The King and Queen loved the show,' said Clara. 'It's a pity you didn't see it.' She pointed back to the Castle. 'Now I don't want to tell you your job, Sergeant, but you're about to cop a coach load of excited actors, and you know what they can be like.'

The Sergeant paused, glanced inside again then gave an order.

'Right, you can go.'

Michael raised the tail board, Clara closed the curtains and soon the van took off, at a gentle pace mind, leaving the ancient castle, and heading into Windsor and beyond.

It took a while for the truth to dawn. The Princess Margaret, Cinderella and the costume lady were missing. So too was the van in which the costume lady arrived. Panic set in but this was an English panic. No screaming and shouting, at least not anywhere near the Royal Family.

Security was alerted. An officer raced to the exit gate and the Sergeant and Private sprang to attention.

'Has the ENSA van been here recently?'

'Passed through only a few minutes ago, sir,' replied the Sergeant feeling his skin go all prickly.

'Did you check the van?'

'Yes sir.'

'Thoroughly?'

It was the hesitation that sealed the soldier's fate.

The officer moved to the phone in the soldier's hut. He spun the handle. 'Get me Major Johns.' He was connected. 'The van's gone sir and it wasn't searched.' The officer was given instructions and hung up. He glared at the Sergeant now literally shaking. 'You're on a charge, Sergeant,' he said with venom; 'both of you. And if you breathe a word of this, I'll have your guts for garters.'

Number 10 Downing Street

If good news spreads like wildfire, bad news travels faster. The PM's assistant private secretary, Jock Colville, knocked and entered. Mr Churchill, cigar in hand, ploughed through a raft of war documents.

'Excuse me, Prime Minister.'

He looked up knowing his assistant private secretary only interrupted with important news. 'Tell me,' he said.

'There appears to be an issue with the Royal Family.' Churchill dropped everything. He stared at Colville.

'What man? Spit it out.'

'Princess Margaret appears to be missing.'

'Missing? What do you mean, missing?'

'She may have been kidnapped, Prime Minister.'

It was easy to see when Churchill was upset. He chewed as opposed to smoking his cigars, his eyes bore right through you, and he found it impossible to take a backward step.

'For God's sake, man, tell it to me straight.'

'There was an ENSA concert at Windsor Castle. After the performance, Princess Margaret took one of the actresses and the costumier on a tour of the Castle.'

'What? Alone?'

'It would appear so.'

'My God!'

'The van with the costumier was allowed through security and no-one has seen the actress, costumier or the Princess since.'

'Get Canning. No-one else; only Canning.' Colville picked up the phone on Churchill's desk.

'Get me Special Branch. It's urgent.'

Churchill fumed but was good at keeping control. 'Canning handled the Royals on their trip to Canada. And if we have the police and MI5 involved, they'll all want to run the show.'

'Superintendent, it's Jock Colville speaking. The Prime Minister would like to see you in his office immediately.' Canning instinctively understood. Colville replaced the phone. 'He's on his way, Prime Minster.'

'You'd better check and see if the others know. Tell them to be here in thirty minutes.' By others he meant the Army, Metropolitan Police, MI5, the Secret Intelligence Service, and even the War Office.

Churchill puffed his cigar and his assistant secretary began puffing air as he hurried from the room.

Special Branch, London

Ten minutes before Mr Churchill heard the news, the head of Special Branch, Albert Canning, received a call. He was told the officer waiting outside the Theatre Royal had not seen the person of interest, the Irishman Michael O'Donovan, now calling himself Michael Donovan, for hours. The officer made discreet enquiries and discovered O'Donovan left the theatre by another route and drove an ENSA van to Windsor.

Canning couldn't believe the officer made such a schoolboy error.

'Apparently he's always exited through the same door and gone home via Drury Lane, sir,' said an underling.

''Find O'Donovan,' snapped Canning.

Then the phone rang again and the officer in charge of the army detail at Windsor Castle advised Special Branch of the situation. Before Canning could take action, the PM's assistant private secretary requested an immediate audience with Mr Churchill. The balloon was well and truly up. At that stage, the missing van driver and the missing Princess were dots which remained to be connected. The head of Special Branch set off for Downing Street.

The PM's plans and speeches in response to anything Herr Hitler threw at him did not cover a kidnapped Royal. Finding the missing princess was a whole new kettle of fish. *Could she be found? Will she be harmed? Killed? What will I say to her parents?*

Canning arrived and he and Churchill remained calm but only just.

'Prime Minister, she most likely was kidnapped by the driver of the ENSA van, Michael O'Donovan, an Irish national and member of the IRA.'

Churchill's eyes widened. Canning knew it best to keep talking.

'As soon as the Princess was found to be missing, the army group guarding Windsor Castle sent out vehicles to find the van. They informed the Chief Constable of Berkshire without disclosing the reason for the search and so police vehicles are also involved.'

'What have the King and Queen been told?'

'We believe they were told Princess Margaret wanted to show an actress the sights of the castle and the Princess may have taken the actress and the woman in charge of costumes for a lengthy tour.'

'Not that a kidnap was involved?'

'I believe they're keeping it as low key as possible, Prime Minister.'

'They have to be told what's happened.'

'Of course,' said a worried Special Branch boss. He felt wretched as his agent had made a terrible mistake allowing the kidnap to occur.

'What about the actress and costumier? Are they involved?'

'Possibly, sir. O'Donovan has recently moved into the house occupied by the costumier.'

'My godfather, it gets worse. And the actress?'

'We know nothing about her, sir, other than she's young and recently returned from a tour of Australia with a Shakespearean touring company.'

'Find them. See if she's part of the team.'

'Sir.'

'Anything else?'

Canning was bilious. He knew Special Branch could have prevented this possible tragedy by not following O'Donovan. They blew it. But Canning knew lying or not telling the whole truth was madness. 'The Irishman has dealt with the Abwehr here in England.'

Churchill's face could have stopped not one clock but every ticking timepiece in Whitehall.

'I want reports every 30 minutes, Canning and if you need anything, failure to demand such help will see you in the Tower. I am at your service. Just find her alive, man, and soon.'

'Prime Minister,' said Canning as he hurried from the room.

'Find her, please,' said Churchill to an empty room. 'Find her.'

Chapter 15

Somewhere in Berkshire England

The brain behind the kidnapping was the murderess formerly of Apedale Hall, Shropshire. When Clara heard about the ENSA trip to Windsor Castle, her mind caught fire. Having Tom, as she referred to Sir Oswald Mosley, released from prison was the key to ending the war. He knew Herr Hitler personally. The German leader was a guest at Tom's wedding. Tom could make a deal with Adolf. This horrible war could be ended in next to no time. All this bombing, death and destruction must stop and will stop with the right person in charge.

Michael followed the instructions on the note inside the envelope handed to him by Clara in the Waterloo Chamber. It was a map with instructions. A week ago, Clara had taken the train to Windsor and a bus to Lower Hatch. She walked around and found a hiding place.

Michael took the route they took in arriving at Windsor Castle. Once they reached the crossroads with the pub, *The Fox and Hounds*, he turned left instead of right and drove for about a mile until they approached the village of Lower Hatch.

Turn left before the bridge. A hundred yards down this dirt road is an old abandoned barn. Turn in and park behind the barn.

Michael wanted a united Ireland. He didn't want bloodshed other than that of British soldiers. Harming, God forbid killing, innocent people was not in his armory. Having a member of the Royal Family involved sent his nervous system into meltdown. But he knew, liked and trusted Clara. Her wretched late husband deserved to be late.

He parked the van, hopped out, ran around to the back and dropped the tailboard. Clara appeared and he helped her down 'What have you done?' he gasped.

'Don't panic. They're both okay.'

'Where are they?' He stared into the van not seeing anyone.

'They're bound and gagged, with silk ribbons suitable for a Princess and leading lady, and resting in the wicker basket.'

'How did you do it?'

Clara was a tad sheepish. 'I got the Princess to try on a dress. As it was over her head, I asked Cinderella to help. When the actress was pre-occupied I gave her a tap on the head.'

'No!' cried Michael.

'But she's okay. Apart from Cinders having a headache, they're fine. I asked the Princess to put her hands behind her back and tied them then put a silk ribbon over her mouth. I did the same to the actress and put them both in the wicker basket.' He shook his head. 'Now it's your turn, Michael; you and your IRA pals. There's a phone box in the village, the one just over the bridge. I've a change of clothes for you as disguise.' She reached in and grabbed a bag. 'Change, then go and contact your follow freedom fighters.'

He changed his clothes. 'What do I say?'

'Say nothing about our special guest. Tell them they have a chance to help Germany win the war and thus speed a united Ireland.'

'But what do you want them to do?'

'Oh for Christ's sake man, you said you fought in the Easter Rising. Use your brain. We need transport and a safe house. Once there, we'll send our demands for Mosley to be released. Now move yourself, man.'

He finished dressing. She handed him a cap and a false beard.

'And I tell them to come here?'

'No, tell them you'll meet them before the bridge on the road into Lower Hatch. Have you coins for the telephone?'

He felt in his pockets. 'Yes.'

'Then go and tell them to be quick about it.' She checked his attire and especially his beard. It was an excellent prop from the ENSA collection. He headed down the dirt track and towards the village and she called, although not loudly. 'And don't draw attention to yourself.'

Special Branch, London

Albert Canning was a bright fellow. In 1936 he was involved in a spot of wire-tapping. Two brothers spoke on the telephone. One brother was Edward and the other George. Special Branch had an officer crouch in bushes in a park opposite the house in which the then King of England resided. This was old-fashioned cloak and dagger stuff. Edward and George chatted away unaware Special Branch listened as

Edward the V111 told his bother his love for Wallis Simpson was so great it was time to abdicate. And so Canning knew of the historic event before the PM, the government, the media and the world.

But that was five years ago. Now Canning faced a serious problem, some would say a national calamity. Where is the King's younger daughter, and how can she be returned safe and well to the bosom of her family?

He joined officers from Special Branch, the Army, MI5, MI6 and high-ranking officers from the Metropolitan Police.

'Gentlemen, the Prime Minister is not interested in apportioning blame—yet. Like all of us, he wants the Princess found alive and well with a minimum of fuss. Naturally there is a press embargo in place.'

He told them what he knew about Michael O'Donovan, IRA member and friend of the Abwehr. The sullen mood in the room switched to despair or fury.

'Of course the rescue of any kidnapped person is a matter of urgency but in this case, we are risking the nation's safety in this world war. If the IRA can escape with the capture of a member of the Royal Family, the morale of the British people will suffer enormous damage. Throughout this so-called Blitz, the men and women of this country have been magnificent, remaining stoic and steadfast. Let us not make them suffer an extra and terrible burden. So, what do we know?'

An officer from Special Branch spoke. 'There is an on-going search for the van within 30 miles of Windsor Castle. All known IRA members in London are being watched. As yet, no demands have been made.'

The police sat on their opinions which included caustic comments about Special Branch and the Army.

Then the police stirred the pot. 'Surely this IRA fellow couldn't be working alone. What do we know of the other two women?'

'O'Donovan lived with the costumier so it would appear she's in on the kidnap.'

The police persisted. 'What do we know of her?'

'Not much,' replied a Special Branch officer. 'She's a widow and has lived at the same East End address for many years.'

'How did her husband die?'

The officer studied the file. 'He was killed in a bombing raid'

'Killed or murdered?' asked the nosy Superintendent.

Silence.

Canning continued. 'And we know nothing of the young actress and assume she was kidnapped as well. Information from inside the Royal Family suggests the Princess was enamored with the young actress and was most keen to meet her.'

'She's a part of it,' said the policeman. 'All three are in on the kidnap with the actress being the bait.'

Another burst of silence.

'It's not true,' said a voice, and everyone turned to Major Ralph Bunting of the Secret Intelligence Service. Few knew who he was and understandably so as he now resided in a broom cupboard and was being pushed aside by more ambitious M16 operatives and the recently created Special Operations Executive—Winston's baby.

'And you are?' asked Canning.

'Major Bunting from SIS in Baker Street, sir. I can assure you the actress, Miss Louise Wellesley is definitely not involved in this kidnap other than as a victim. She has not recently returned from a tour of Australia as a Shakespearean actress but has spent the last year in Paris where she did splendid work for the Secret Intelligence Service including uncovering the notorious double agent Godfrey Silsbury.' His words rocked the men in the room. 'If you want an insider on this kidnapping, you could not wish for a better person than Miss Louise Wellesley and, if he could do so, I believe her Great Uncle six times removed, the Duke of Wellington would attest.'

The mood in the room copped one almighty whack. The police were stunned, and Special Branch didn't know what to say. Canning glowed knowing his news would please Winston.

'Thank you, Major,' said Canning, 'for such excellent news. And you think this actress could leave a trail or send us a message?'

'On previous form, sir, she could do that and more.'

'Excellent. Well, our plan is to continue searching for the van, watching every known IRA man in London and researching this woman, Clara Rackett. What else, gentlemen?'

The Metropolitan Police Superintendent wanted back in the game. 'We will pressure every known kidnapper and IRA sympathizer and send you any information the moment it comes to hand.'

The M15 man wanted to be involved. 'So we assume it's a kidnapping and if so, what for? Money? Hardly. Surely if the IRA is involved, it'll mean politics. What are the German implications?'

Canning explained. 'We know O'Donovan has long been involved with Irish independence. He was a POW after the Easter Rising. He moved to London some 20 years ago and works on the docks. He's a part-time Air Raid Warden and now, apparently an ENSA driver, and surely it can't be a coincidence. He recently made contact with an Abwehr agent but she's been turned which is how we know he contacted her. So yes, we are convinced this has nothing to do with money, so if and when we hear from the kidnappers, their demands will be all about a united Ireland. The IRA believes their best chance of achieving same is to have Germany win the war. I think we have to admit holding a member of the Royal Family, and the youngest and most vulnerable one, is a brilliant tactic. To lose the young Princess will be a bitter blow to British morale and a serious boost to Lord Haw Haw.'

Canning's words hit hard. The miffed chief cop made a grab for the moral high ground.

'I would say the King and Queen's feelings might be the most important item here,' he said, his anger simmering at having been left out of the chase. 'The police would never have allowed this dog's breakfast to have happened in the first place.'

The Army representative, a Major Hitchcock, fumed.

'Thank you Commissioner,' replied Canning, annoyed at the one-upmanship taking place. 'Our main goal, gentlemen, is to save the Princess. Now, is there anything else?'

Nobody spoke and the meeting broke up. 'Oh Major Bunting, may I have a word please.'

The man who knew Louise Beatrice Wellesley, a.k.a. Juliette Beauchamp, a.k.a. Plum, a.k.a. Cinderella, better than anyone, gave Special Branch chapter and verse on his favourite sleeper.

Chapter 16

Lower Hatch, Berkshire England

Michael, dressed in his new disguise, walked to the nearby village. He worked on his patter should he be stopped, crossed the bridge, which once assisted Cromwell's men, and passed the local pub. It was nearly closing time and a bunch of gents enjoyed a pint in the afternoon sun.

'Good day to you, sir,' called one drinker.

Michael switched to his Londoner accent. 'Good day. Am I in the village of Lower Hatch?'

'Aye. Can we be of help, sir?'

'Michael stopped and moved closer. 'How kind. My horse pulled up lame about a mile back and I need to telephone my master. His Lordship is most particular about his animals. Is there a public telephone in the village?'

The locals pointed out what he already knew. He thanked them and set off. If the police or army asked about strangers in the area, a Londoner with a beard and driving a trap for Lord So-and-So might not raise much, if any, suspicion. At least such was the plan.

Michael reached the phone box and placed a call. It was to an IRA member not known to Special Branch. The cell employed one member who never attended meetings and remained under the Special Branch radar.

'Finchley and Sons, Undertaker,' said the voice.

'Hello Mr Finchley. There's been a sudden death in my family.'

'Oh, I'm sorry to hear that, sir?'

Michael spoke in code meaning a body—or in this case two bodies—needed to be collected.

'The address is 2 The Mews, Lower Hatch in Berkshire. How soon can you be here?'

That too was a code meaning the matter was urgent. Was it ever?

'As soon as we can, sir. What name is it?'

The question was a code and the correct answer confirmed the caller was genuine.

'Ramsbottom,' said Michael, and the undertaker clicked into gear.

Passing the locals a second time, Michael simply waved to the drinkers who were being told it was time, gentlemen please.

He arrived back at the van making sure he wasn't followed. Walking around the back he panicked when Clara was nowhere to be seen. He peered in the van and whispered. 'Hello.'

Clara stood inside beside the open wicker basket. She spoke to those inside said basket. 'Won't be long, ladies. You'll soon be on your way back home.' She closed the lid, tied the clip, and headed to Michael. 'Everything okay?'

'Are they all right?'

Clara was annoyed. 'They're fine. I said there'll be no bloodshed. Once Sir Oswald is free, they'll be released unharmed.'

'What about Cinderella?'

'She's has a headache.'

'What about food and water?'

Clara glared at him. 'Listen, Michael, you sort out the transport and I'll run the catering.'

'And the ransom note?'

She hissed. 'Oh for the love God, it's all under control. Now are your friends coming?' He nodded. She softened. 'Here's a sandwich. When I come back, you'll need to wait for your mates. I won't be long.'

She headed off. 'Where are you going?'

'If you must know, I need the Ladies which I've decided is behind those bushes.'

It was almost dark when Michael saw the vehicle approaching. He stepped out and knelt to tie his shoelace; the signal. The hearse stopped beside the IRA man who climbed aboard. There were two undertakers in the front and a coffin in the rear. Michael gave directions and they soon pulled in behind the van.

Clara stepped out of the van cab and greeted them. Both undertakers were dressed in proper garb.

'My God,' she said, 'the IRA does things in style.'

'What's happening?' asked the boss, the driver of the hearse.

Clara explained. When she mentioned the name of the special guest, both "undertakers" swallowed. Their eyes widened and they slipped into their Dubliner accents.

'Holy Mother of God,' said the assistant.

'The feckin' royal family,' said the boss. 'This is unbelievable. Well done, Michael. I always knew you was the real deal.'

Clara spoke. 'So where do you hide them and don't tell me in the coffin?'

The boss, like Clara, didn't take kindly to being questioned and treated like an idiot. 'You make the sandwiches, Mary, and we'll drive the Brits out of Ireland.'

Michael stepped in to keep the peace. 'We'll get the passengers and pass them down to you boys.' He guided Clara to the rear and helped her up. He followed. They reached the wicker basket and Clara opened the lid. This was Michael's first viewing of the prisoners since they ran towards him at Windsor Castle.

They were lying close together on a mattress of soft linen, their hands tied with silk ribbons with more ties over their eyes and mouths. Louise had lost the bottom half of her ball gown leaving her lower body dressed in long bloomers.

'Now ladies,' said Clara, 'remember you'll be released as soon as the Prime Minster signs a piece of paper. Until then, you'll be driven to a special place where you'll be well cared for and those horrible straps over your eyes and mouth will be removed. Cinders, we'll take you first. Both of you; please remain still.'

She glanced at Michael. They leant in and each took one of Louise's arms lifting her to her feet. Then Michael put an arm around her waist and another under her bottom lifting her free of the basket. He carried the actress to the rear of the van and to the waiting undertakers.

Michael returned and the kidnappers did the same with the Princess. Louise was light and Margaret even lighter. She was passed down and Michael and Clara followed to the hearse.

Clara was confused. The coffin was on the ground, the back of the hearse open and inside was a large grave shaped space. Peering in, Clara could see Cinders lying in the well-lined space.

Margaret was picked up and gently placed alongside her favourite actress. The boss spoke to the victims.

'It will be dark but there are air vents. You will be able to breathe but not see. If you make a sound, the air vents will be closed and you don't want that to happen.' To Louise, with her head still thumping from being coshed by Clara, the man with the Irish accent sounded sincere; matter-of-fact but real. The Princess felt numb.

Clara worried, never wanting any violence, and having to strike Louise from behind still played on her mind. Clara knew violence from an abusive husband and here, she worked with desperate men.

A lid was placed over the space in the floor of the hearse and then the coffin lifted and placed in position. It was screwed down and the wreath attached to its lid.

The boss examined the ENSA vehicle. 'If we set fire to it, it'll only draw attention. Take what you need and we'll drain the petrol.'

Michael went through the cab and Clara the back of the van. They came out with very little. With the van's petrol in the hearse, all four kidnappers squeezed in the front of the vehicle and away they went.

They travelled on back roads until they approached civilization. The hearse stopped. 'Walk through these woods,' said the boss pointing. When you reach the lane, turn left and we're the double-storey farmhouse with a five-bar gate and the name Gillespie on the letter-box. Don't be seen.'

Clara and Michael hopped out, watched the hearse head to the main road then walked into the woods. The hearse turned at the next intersection. It was dark with the moon excellent for German bombers lining up parts of London, Liverpool, Southampton, Coventry and more cities.

Full headlights were banned even in this less populated part of England. As the hearse approached the road leading to their safe house, an army patrol appeared in the gloom. A man in uniform held up a hand. The hearse stopped and the driver wound down his window. He spoke with a flat English accent.

'Good evening, officer,' said the boss. 'Is there a problem?'

'You're a bit late for a funeral,' said the army man.

'Funeral is tomorrow and we have brought the dear lady a long way. You can't be late for your own funeral, officer.'

'Open the back.'

The IRA men froze 'But officer, you can see through the windows.'

The army chaps were under pressure. It was some of their own who caused this catastrophe and the pressure to find the missing person was immense.

'Out and open the back,' snapped the officer; his words oozing venom.

The IRA men muttered and opened the back of the hearse. 'You cannot dishonor the dead.'

The officer shone a torch inside the hearse. All one could see was the coffin. 'Open it,' ordered the officer.

Now the IRA men became more angry than shocked. 'That I will not,' said the boss lapsing towards his Irish accent. He bit his tongue.

'You either open the coffin or you'll be arrested and spend the night or longer in prison. Now, open the damn coffin!'

Shaking their heads, the undertakers climbed into the back of the hearse and began work. The wreath was removed and placed carefully to one side. The boss muttered using the word *sacrilege* more than once. The screws were undone and the lid was now ready to be lifted.

'I strongly protest at this gross act of indecency and I shall report this to your commanding officer.'

The army man feared his superior officer more than anyone else in the world and so followed through on his command.

'Open it.'

Slowly the lid was lifted and the IRA men held their breath. The officer leant in and raised his torch. He gagged as the face of a dead elderly woman, sans teeth stared back at him. He sucked in fresh country air and spat his response.

'Get her out of here.'

Inside the space beneath the freshly opened coffin, Louise and the Princess heard muffled voices. They couldn't see or speak. It was pitch black anyway and the silk scarves over their eyes were unnecessary. At times in the wicker basket and now in the hearse, Louise hummed. She kept it quiet but performing tunes from the pantomime she hoped would comfort her companion. They did.

When the hearse was stopped by the army, Louise thought about kicking the sides of their cell. The walls were padded. Would the kicking sounds be heard? She remembered the words of the kidnapper who told them about closing the air vents if they tried to make a noise.

Obviously Louise didn't want to die but most certainly she wanted her travelling companion to be rescued and returned to the King and Queen. Louise remained still although the soft humming continued.

The hearse moved, drove for ten minutes then turned into a driveway then a garage which sat beside a large two-storey weatherboard house with trees all around. The garage doors closed, the two men got out of the hearse and were joined by a third IRA man with a nose pointing sideways. Big Kev spent years as a professional boxer although had been in the paddock in recent years and was going to seed.

'All okay?' he asked.

'Yes,' said the boss opening the back of the hearse. 'Help us.'

All three men unlocked the coffin, and placed it on the garage floor. The driver and boss undid the top of the hidden compartment. They were about to lift the lid when Kev whispered with alarm.

'Wait. I heard something.' All three men froze then moved silently towards the doors. One opened out and stopped after a couple of feet. Someone stepped into the darkened garage. In an instant, Kev grabbed the intruder in a strangle hold. The victim yelled.

'Stop,' hissed the boss. A torch shone on Michael's face, turning red by the second. 'He's one of ours.'

Michael was saved and Clara dragged into the garage. The boss and assistant returned to the hearse and removed the cover of the false bottom. In the dim light, the two victims lay snuggled into one another, their hearts racing, and their breathing tricky.

One by one they were lifted out. Kev took the heavier one and the dainty Princess was carried by Michael. Out of the garage and into the old farmhouse kitchen they went where lighting was still dim.

'Upstairs,' said a woman.

She led the way and the victims were carried upstairs, a door was unlocked and the blindfolded females were placed gently on a double bed which had been made by a one-armed paper hanger. The pillow slips needed a good wash. The IRA team left and locked the door.

Downstairs Kevin and the woman were told the identity of their new house guests. The reaction was loud. Having a member of the Royal Family under their control gave great delight. Louise tried whispering to the princess. Her gag was too tight.

The woman climbed the stairs and entered the room. She bent and spoke quietly with a rich Irish accent.

'There are sandwiches and hard-boiled eggs on the table. Plenty of water. There are two chamber pots so you won't have to share. The ties and blindfolds will be removed. The door is locked and the window boarded up. You are miles from anywhere. The sooner you settle down, the sooner we can arrange for you to go home. Nod if you understand.' Louise nodded. 'Now lie on your stomachs.'

Louise and Margaret struggled but did so. The woman undid the ties on the hands of the Princess and left the room. The door closed and the lock clicked.

The Princess removed the silk ties over her eyes and mouth. 'I'm free,' she said and Louise grunted. Margaret struggled but untied the ribbon binding Louise's hands. Louise removed her other ties, blinked, and in the darkness, saw a teary but strong Princess Margaret. Louise opened her arms and the two hugged with feeling.

'You have been extraordinarily brave, Your Royal Highness,' whispered the actress.

'Oh do please call me Margaret and I shall call you Cinders, if you don't mind,' whispered the royal princess.

Louise smiled; a rare event of late. 'Thank you, Margaret, I'd like that. Now let's explore but be careful.'

The room was large with a double bed, a small table, a wardrobe, and a chest against the end of the bed. The light bulb had been removed, and with the window boarded up, only a chink of light crept in from under the door.

Louise found the food on the table. 'Ah, food. Are you hungry?'

Margaret moved towards Louise. 'I am but I need to pee.'

'Me too,' said Louise who went exploring again. She felt under the bed and found two enamel chamber pots. 'Can you see these chamber pots?' She tapped them together and Margaret followed the sound. 'One each, Your Royal Highness but to use it you'll need to become Your Royal Lowness.'

Margaret giggled. 'Oh, Cinders, you are so funny.'

'I'll go over here,' said Louise and the two ladies adjourned to their respective corners.

Chapter 17

The Theatre Royal, London

The players, the backstage staff and ENSA founders chatted nineteen to the dozen as the coach headed back to London. Those who met the Royal Family basked in the glow of their once-in-a-lifetime moment. Others talked about the success of the show, the awe-inspiring Waterloo Chamber, and the people they would tell about the event.

Everything was going swimmingly until someone piped up.

'Hey, where's Cinders?'

Many conversations began.

'I saw her going off with Princess Margaret and the costume lady,' called one performer.

'Lucky so-and-so,' said another.

'I reckon the Royal Family has hired her as a scullery maid.'

That prompted the biggest laugh and Louise was forgotten.

Dean and Henson worried. 'What do you think?' asked Leslie.

Basil shrugged. 'Did Miss Wellesley choose to travel with the costumes?' Neither liked the idea of a missing actress.

The coach reached Drury Lane and the exhausted travellers piled out making their way home in the blackout.

10 Downing Street

Churchill required constant reports on the missing Princess Margaret even if the news was bad or non-existent. Canning rang Number 10. 'Much searching, Mr Colville,' said Canning. More searching of the area surrounding the Castle and we're going hard on IRA hideouts. And there is one bit of good news. Please inform the PM the actress taken with the princess is more than an actress; she's a former operative with the Secret Intelligence Service and has just returned from 12 months serving as an undercover agent in Paris.'

Hearing the news, the secretary silently cheered, and it led his report to the Prime Minister. 'What!' he cried. 'That's brilliant.' But his joy faded instantly when he discovered no sightings or other good news was to hand. His cigar suffered from friendly fire.

IRA Safe house, somewhere in Berkshire

The five IRA members plus Clara sat in the kitchen. 'So tell me the plan, and make it foolproof,' said the boss.

Clara showed no nerves. Her plan, risky and relying on so many parts falling into place, had so far worked a treat. But her follow up scheme now needed help from the IRA. Having their prized asset upstairs under lock and key was one thing. Being able to use her as leverage was something else. Clara produced an envelope.

'As soon as possible, this needs to be posted in London.'

The others, except Michael, launched their objections.

'London?'

'That's hours away.'

'Every cop in the country is searching for us.'

Michael shouted. 'Shut up.' He was so loud, the others fell silent. 'This woman has pulled off the biggest kidnapping the IRA has ever seen. Now we have a chance to shorten, even end the war, leave Britain weak, and gain a united Ireland.' He paused berating them. 'At least let her explain.'

Clara studied the quiet group. 'Thank you, Michael,' she said then gave details. 'This is our demand letter addressed to the Prime Minister. He will be desperate to hear from us and terrified when he does. If we post it locally, it will take much longer to reach him and betray our location. So, how can we post this in London?'

'The hearse is too risky and there's little petrol,' said the boss.

'There's a motorbike in the back yard but why would it be out at night?' asked Big Kev.

The woman spoke. 'Go by train. There are troop trains going up to London all the time. There are military uniforms in the basement. Another soldier on a crowded train will get away with it.'

'I'll go,' said Michael. 'All I have to do is stick it in a postbox. If I'm caught, they'll take the letter and the job is done.'

'If you're caught, you'll be dead,' said the undertaker's assistant.

Clara was thrilled but showed no emotion. Her plan to have little Tom (Sir Oswald) released was within grasp.

'Well done, Michael,' she said. 'Go and find yourself a uniform.' He and the woman left. As a costumier, Clara knew about props. She called. 'And he'll need a kitbag as well.'

The two undertakers and Kev stared at Clara. They knew she wasn't IRA. She was English with no incentive to see the Brits out of Ireland. Was she some sort of stalking horse?

'So what's in the envelope?' asked Kev.

Clara hesitated. *Do I tell them?* 'What do you think? Our demands.'

'Which are?' asked the boss.

The atmosphere grew colder. She didn't like being questioned and the IRA men trusted nobody who wasn't one of them.

'I think the fewer who know, the better our chance of success.'

Infuriated, Kev stood to intimidate the much smaller female. 'Give it me,' he said with malice aforethought.

Clara hated bullies; she killed one, and held the envelope away from Kev allowing the boss to reach forward and snatch it.

'Hey!' she yelled and tried to lunge. One of his Kev's massive hands attached to one of his massive arms stopped her dead.

The three men moved to one side leaving Clara helpless and alone. The boss grabbed a kitchen knife and slit the envelope.

'You bloody fools,' Clara groaned. 'They'll think it's a plant now the envelope's been tampered with.'

The paper inside was withdrawn and the men studied it. A waste of time as the assistant scored an A+ for illiteracy and Kev failed going to school.

'Oswald Mosley,' sneered the boss. 'He's an English toff and a lunatic. What could he do to help unite Ireland?'

'You ignorant oaf,' snapped Clara. 'He supports a free Ireland, knows Hitler and while we have the King's daughter, the government will be forced to appoint Sir Oswald as the acting Prime Minister which will lead directly to you getting your united Ireland!' She screamed the last few words and her passion and logic put the IRA chaps on the back foot. 'Now give me the letter you bloody Eejits!'

Normally, such a remark would see the speaker smacked, and if uttered by a woman, several smacks. Such was about to happen when heavy footsteps were heard, and Michael entered dressed as a British Tommy complete with boots and packed kitbag on his shoulder.

'Well?' he asked, and the fight over the envelope faded.

The woman found a new envelope and Clara addressed it, pinching the stamp from the first envelope and re-attaching it.

The only way of getting to Slough, apart from walking, was by bicycle. It was a good 12 miles and nobody knew anything about troop or train timetables. It was dark and a bicycle could be hidden if patrols blocked the roads. Clara walked Michael off the property.

'If you're caught, Michael, your best bet is to hand over the envelope.' This confused him. 'If you toss it away or hide it, we'll never succeed. If a patrol grabs it, I reckon they'll deliver it.'

'So why not just give it to the first patrol?'

'Because you'll be arrested and, as an IRA man, executed.'

He studied her and wished he knew her better. 'Take it easy in there,' he said. 'Those IRA men are hard nuts. They hate everything English, including their women.'

'I've noticed,' she said.

'I'm not sure I'll see you again, Clara.' They stopped speaking and stared at one another. He spoke the truth. 'I think you're a brilliant woman and I hope to God your plan works.'

'It might if you post that envelope in London.'

In the darkness, he reckoned her eyes seemed to sparkle.

He spoke in Gaelic. 'Adh mor ort,' (Good luck to you) he said, kissed her cheek, mounted the bicycle and wobbled into the night as the only Irish postman delivering long distance to London.

Chapter 18

The country lanes of England

Michael took a while to master bicycle riding after so long out of the saddle but when he did, he made good progress. The travel instructions from the IRA woman were sound. They needed to be because in anticipation of Germany winning the Battle of Britain and thus invading this green and pleasant land, road signs were either missing or deliberately pointing the wrong way.

With no light, Michael cycled, watching and listening for the enemy—the British police or army. He stuck to lanes searching for signs he was on the right track. A hay shed on your right, take the left fork after the mill by the river, and keep going beside the high wall of the manor house and more. All was going well until panic set in when he turned a bend and a bloke, having just splashed his boots, stepped out of the woods. Michael yelled in fright, the bloke responded in kind, and the cyclist took a tumble. He silently cursed.

'Are you all right, mate?' asked a male voice.

Michael struggled to collect his kit bag and right his trusty steed.

'I think so,' he said using his London accent.

'We're so sorry,' said a woman who was with the bloke.

Michael recovered.

'We was taking a short cut through the woods,' said the man. The woman giggled. 'We never expected the army to come flying along this country lane.'

'Well I'm about to be shot for going AWOL unless I can reach Slough and catch my train. How far is it?'

'About five miles,' said the man.'

'More like six,' said the woman, born and raised in Berkshire.

'But there's a short cut,' said the man. 'At the end of this road, take a right then first on the left. It's a bit rough in parts but you'll shave a good mile off the trip.'

'He's right,' said the woman.

'Thanks a lot,' said Michael and mounted.

'My brother's in the Army. Who are you with?'

Michael stared at the young man. It was hard to see in the dark. 'Now, now,' said Michael. 'Careless talk costs lives.' The couple understood and the boyfriend apologised. 'Thanks for your help. Bye.'

They muttered their goodbyes, waved then stood in the middle of the road and resumed their previous activity involving osculation.

10 Downing Street, London

Canning was let straight in to see the PM. 'Some better news, Prime Minister. No sign of the missing Princess but we've found the ENSA van which carried her away from Windsor.'

'Where?'

'It's been abandoned about 4 miles from the Castle near the village of Lower Hatch.'

'And we're sure the actress is a former SIS operative?'

'Indeed and she could be the difference between the Princess being found dead or alive.'

Churchill baulked. 'Dead? For God's sake, man, I don't want you even thinking like that.'

'Sir.'

'What else?'

'We've reduced the search area to within 10 miles of the van. We are making progress, Prime Minister. More men on foot, horseback and in vehicles and daylight will give us a much greater chance. And a side benefit means all the forces—police, army, MI5, Special Branch—are working together.'

Churchill puffed. 'Thank you, Canning. Bloody Adolf is a major problem but I fear a kidnapped Princess going missing may be far worse. Come and see me at any time. Good night.'

Slough Railway Station

The lovers were correct. The short cut saved time but added a sore bum. The road was liberally sprinkled with pot holes, wheel ruts and the odd fallen branch. Michael ran out of oaths and used all the swear words he learnt in both London and Dublin.

Finally the outskirts of Slough appeared and Michael travelled on proper roads. He headed for what he hoped would be the centre of town and the railway station. His major asset at present was hope.

It was late. Not a light anywhere. Dogs barked and a cat flew across in front of him scaring both of them. Of course finding the station was his aim but an empty platform was of no use. Having a train stop there en route to London was essential.

Then it happened. On a still, chilly Berkshire night with plenty of cloud cover, a locomotive whistle called to the sleeping world. It was but a short toot probably to remind the station staff to wake up and have the gates open. Not that there was much traffic about unless you counted the masses of searchers hunting for an unnamed VIP.

Michael was exhausted but pedalled through the pain to reach the damn station. His thighs screamed. Still he pounded the pedals. He could hear the loco and, like Michael, it too was puffing.

He flew around a corner and almost collided with a Bobby doing his rounds. The policeman overbalanced and fell back. Michael veered across the road, hit a fence which stopped his mode of transport but not him, and he settled in the largest rhododendron bush in Slough.

Constable Plod's older bones meant he took a while to arrive at the accident scene. 'Are you okay, officer,' he said not seeing Michael's stripes in the dark indicating he was Corporal O'Donovan.

'I think so,' said Michael disentangling himself and doing his best to sound like an Oxbridge type chap.

The Bobby helped him stand, found his kit bag, and the duo staggered back to the street to view the unroadworthy bicycle.

'I'm afraid your bike's a goner, sir.'

'Forget the damn bike. I must catch that train.'

'No problems,' said the policeman putting Michael's arm over his shoulder and half carrying the IRA man and his kitbag the hundred yards or so to the station.

Imagine what Albert Canning or the PM would say if they knew of this situation. Every copper in the county had been told to keep a look-out for the van, its driver, the costumier and the actress and arrest any or all of them on the spot. Now one of the main culprits in the kidnap was being assisted by the law thus helping the criminals to put their dastardly kidnap ransom demand into operation.

The Up platform was crowded. On the outskirts of London, the line was bombed the night before forcing this troop train to be delayed. Hundreds of Tommys stretched their legs. Some kind-hearted ladies set up an urn with mugs of tea for all. The Bobby grabbed one for his wounded friend then helped Michael into a carriage and to a seat.

'God bless you, mate. You're a credit to King and country.'

Not quite true as the soldier was a fake and up to his neck in kidnapping the King's younger daughter.

The Bobby slipped away and as soon as he was gone, Michael scoffed his tea, dumped the mug, and moved into the corridor and the darkest corner he could find. He wanted as little conversation as possible with anyone, and especially not with soldiers.

The train moved and the envelope set off on the next part of its journey to a London post box and eventually to the Prime Minister.

Chapter 19

IRA Safe house, somewhere in England

Alone in the upstairs locked room, Louise and the Princess sat on the bed and spoke quietly.

'I'm so sorry this has happened to you, Margaret. Your family must be worried sick.'

'I was worried when they first tied and blindfolded us but once you started humming, I didn't worry nearly as much. I kept thinking how Cinders escaped from her Ugly Sisters, and soon she will escape from these horrible people and take me with her.'

Louise smiled in the dark and squeezed a royal hand as she pondered the situation.

A positive attitude is wonderful but has the young girl suspended disbelief? Does she think I'm the character who won the heart of the dashing prince and lived happily ever after?

'I'm sure the police will rescue us as soon as they can,' said Louise.

'But how?' asked Margaret. 'They don't know where we are.'

Out of the mouths of babes and young princesses, thought Louise.

'We must be patient,' she said.

'Why don't we escape ourselves? We could run to the nearest house and ask the people to telephone the Castle. They might if I tell them my parents are the King and Queen of England.'

Louise whispered. 'What a splendid idea, Your Royal Highness.'

'Margaret, please, I want you to call me Margaret, Cinders.'

In the darkness Louise nodded with no idea how they could make their escape. The boarded-up window, the locked door and the isolated farmhouse gave little opportunity.

Footsteps sounded. 'Someone's coming,' said Louise. 'Stay still and don't do anything to upset these people.' Margaret didn't readily agree.

Footsteps stopped. The key turned in the door. It opened and the woman stood there with a small lantern. 'Stay on the bed,' she said.

The prisoners obeyed. The woman put the lantern on the floor and entered with a tray of food. She looked at the table.

'You haven't all the other food.'

'We're not hungry,' said Louise, 'but we might be later.'

The woman grunted, moved towards the table and as she put the tray thereon, Margaret slipped off the bed, reached in and grabbed a chamber pot before Louise could say or do anything. The woman saw movement in the corner of her eye, turned and copped the contents of the pot in her face and all down her front.

Revulsion and anger turned to rage. Louise joined the party, sprang from the bed, grabbed the woman's arm and tripped her. The tray, now minus the flying food, became a weapon and the woman, struggling to rise, screamed as would anyone soaked in urine, then copped an almighty whack from the tray and stayed down.

Louise turned to grab the hand of the Princess to drag her from the room but froze. The screaming brought Kev, the only other resident, upstairs and his hulking body filled the door frame. He growled.

Louise pushed Margaret towards the bed. Kev decided the royal could wait. First up was the woman in the fancy costume.

'Come here, English bitch,' he snarled, and moved in for the kill with kill being used in a literal sense. One round-arm punch connecting with the head of Cinderella would send her through the wall and into the yard and eternity.

He spat. He needed physical violence as a fix. Margaret huddled on the bed in terror. Kev moved forward. His feet were huge. He was the giant from *Jack and the Beanstalk* in the wrong fairytale.

His brawn overpowered his brain. One short jab would fracture Louise's nose or cheekbone or both. But no, Mr Muscle went for the one-punch, the haymaker knock-out, swinging so hard he overbalanced. Louise ducked and Kev stumbled. Her glass slipper would have come in handy right now. She kicked him with her shin smashing between his legs and the shock was worse than the pain. As he gasped, Louise snatched the empty chamber pot and cracked it against Kev's right temple. He dropped and slept.

'Come on,' cried Louise and Margaret didn't hesitate.

'Oh Cinders, you really are a star.'

Louise closed the door, locked it, kept the key and led the Princess down the stairs. They dreaded the other IRA men being there. They weren't. They'd used the hearse to deliver Clara to a spot where she could walk into Slough. Louise led the way. They crept outside and down the driveway towards the road. Cinders chucked the key.

Pitch black, no cars, cattle or crims. Silence.

'We need to find a friendly family,' said Louise. 'Let's go this way and if I tell you to hide, Margaret, be ready to run off the road.'

They walked and Louise trembled with excitement, or was it fear? She remembered the night she hid in the Tuileries Gardens in Paris when a Gestapo madman and a British traitor both wanted her dead. The men shot at her, several times. Her escape was deadly. So far, this was a doddle.

Kings Cross Railway Station, London

The train arrived in London. At the end of his carriage, Michael kept to the darkest part of the corridor. One soldier asked him for a light but he spoke to no-one. He wondered about the gate at the end of the platform. With no ID, he could well be a deserter if his unit, according to the marking on his uniform, was overseas, and he believed he might have his face plastered on display boards in every police station and army barracks. And that's not even counting Special Branch.

He moved with the flow. A packed and dimly lit platform was his best method of escape. All he needed to do was exit the station, find a postbox, post the ransom demand, and then find cover for the night and for the rest of his life.

It was hard to see ahead. Men with kits, hats and rifles blocked his view. The pace slowed then stopped. A loud voice issued an order.

'Have your papers ready for inspection.'

Michael swore softly. He'd cycled through miles of countryside in darkness, crashed twice, tricked a Bobby, enjoyed the luck of the Irish, boarded a troop train and was within yards of being free only to be caught at the gate, a hundred yards from victory.

His mind raced. He decided. *I'll do what Clara suggested. I'll get arrested then hand over the envelope. It might be delivered quicker than by post anyway. Only one problem; being arrested, like so many of my fellow Irishmen before me, I'll be shot.*

The troops formed single lines. Again the booming voice sounded the order. Only then did Michael twig. This whole procedure was for his benefit. The only reason to put a check on passengers was to try and catch the IRA man who drove the getaway van. If he tries to reach London, we'll catch him.

And so the trap was set.

The line shuffled. Now only two blokes were ahead of him. He held the envelope, the only papers he possessed. Then he was about to be next in line. A siren sounded and the world became discombobulated.

'Keep moving,' shouted the booming voice. The soldier in front of Michael was waved through. An officer held out his hand for Michael's papers. Then the whining sounded louder. Men panicked. Some ran. Officers shouted and were ignored. Officers panicked. A bomb exploded in the street. 'Take cover!' screamed an officer.

The noise was deafening. Fragments of glass, brick and metal rained down. Forget the inspection. Save yourself!

Michael raced through the gates. Nobody tried to stop him. Others were doing the same. Another bomb exploded and Michael flattened himself on the platform. Terror reigned and debris rained.

He ran for the streets of London. The bombs were dropped by a pilot with a couple of spares and who didn't fancy taking them back home to Germany.

In the streets people crouched in shop doorways. Ambulances and fire engines clanged and hooted. An air-raid warden appeared calling to people to take shelter. Michael knew the man so turned and hurried into the darkness.

I must find a postbox. But where?

A taxi crept along. 'Oi,' cried Michael and ran to the driver.

'Where to, mate?' asked the cabbie.

'Ten Downing Street,' he said and hopped in.

'Blimey, you must be important.'

Through the Blitz, the taxi found its way but stopped in Whitehall.

'Sorry mate, I can't go no further. You'll 'ave to walk.'

Michael thrust coins in the cabbie's hand and ran. He reached Downing Street and No. 10. A Bobby stood outside the famous door.

'Oi, where do you fink you're going, soldier?'

'Special delivery for the PM from High Command,' puffed Michael giving even more credence to his name-dropping.

The Bobby was impressed. He perused the envelope. It wasn't a gun or a bomb. He read the writing and studied the serious soldier.

'Righto.'

'I need to tell my CO it was delivered in person. What's your name officer?'

Michael's acting was first rate. He would have been right at home on stage in the Waterloo Chamber.

'PC Donald Hopkins, sir.'

A Corporal didn't warrant a sir nor did a Constable but Michael gave the copper the sharpest of salutes. '*Now*, PC Hopkins,' he said and watched as the front door was knocked, opened and the envelope passed to a lackey inside. When the Bobby turned, Michael was already striding down the street and heading into the blacked out city he adopted. He wanted to telephone Clara and give her the news but to do so would have Special Branch in the IRA safe house in no time. Mind you, he had no idea where she was or her phone number.

10 Downing Street, London

Jock Colville knocked but didn't wait for the Prime Minister to bid him enter. Churchill was instantly concerned.

'This just arrived by army courier, Prime Minister.'

Colville had opened and read the letter, replaced it and literally ran to deliver same. Churchill read the letter. 'Where's the courier?'

The assistant secretary panicked. He forgot the delivery boy.

Churchill roared. 'Find the courier!'

Colville's body language yelled panic as he bolted from the office. Churchill barked into his phone. 'Get Canning here now!'

It's fair to say, life became busy in various places. Canning knew something massive had exploded. Security in Number 10 found the Bobby who gave a description of the courier and men went flying towards Whitehall searching for the Tommy turned postman. In the blackout, the chasers had no chance.

Churchill re-read the letter and pined for a very large Scotch. He craved any breakthrough in this potential disaster but when it came, he now wished for no news.

Colville returned to announce security were hunting for the courier. Churchill raged. Canning arrived thinking the news was the worst possible, and was handed the ransom note.

Steam seeped from the PM's pate. 'I despise Oswald "that traitor" Mosley, and all he stands for, but I will unhappily release him if it means the safe return of Her Royal Highness.' He puffed his cigar. 'But making peace with the Berlin psychopath is never going to happen.'

'Agreed, Prime Minister, but how can we negotiate? They give no address or telephone number.'

'Can't you track them from the letter, the envelope? What about fingerprints?'

'Perhaps in time, Prime Minister, but interviewing the courier would help. I assume you detained him.'

Churchill glared at the head of Special Branch. Just as in politics, the PM knew there was intense rivalry between government colleagues, in this case between various law enforcement departments, each wanting to outdo the others. Each wanted the ear of the PM and the funding his patronage might produce. Many in the police, armed forces and cloak and dagger groups despised the PM's baby, the Special Operations Executive.

Canning chose not to cast blame. 'We'll keep looking, sir.'

Churchill fumed some more. 'So what do you recommend, man?'

'We need time to locate him, Prime Minister. As a sign of good faith, and to delay any harm to the Princess, we could release Mosley and allow him to make a public statement.'

Churchill snarled. 'Release, yes; publicity, never. We're fighting tooth and nail to maintain morale, man. If Mosley pushes his surrender nonsense, God knows what will happen?'

'But unless we can contact the kidnappers, we need them to know Mosley is free. We need to show good faith which means some form of publicity.'

Churchill, a man unafraid to make bold decisions, struggled for an answer. A member of the Royal Family being kidnapped by the IRA was a nightmare come true. Giving oxygen to the creator of the British Union of Fascists and Adolf's chum, was equally as bad. Talk about the lesser of two evils. For now, little Tom would stay put.

Chapter 20

Somewhere in Vichy France

As Churchill lost sleep over the missing princess, an RAF pilot tried desperately to land his plane. Having delivered supplies to a well-established Resistance cell in German occupied France, he flew south hoping to avoid the enemy guns which damaged his kite. He knew he should jump but while he could still fly, finding a field or any half-decent space was his goal. His engine misfired then came alive but still he preferred to put down rather than bail out and crash. Was he brave or stupid?

St Nicholas Church, Lyon France

Father Felix Flory gave up shaving as a teen. For years he trimmed his beard and took pride in doing so but not now. The German invasion of France, the evil of war crimes he witnessed every day, the recent arrival of a new bishop at the cathedral in Lyon, and the poor health of his elderly parents in Paris dragged his spirits to a new low. He said Mass without conviction. He heard confession with robotic responses. Even the nuns at the nearby Carmelite monastery noticed.

'Do you think Father Flory is ill?' asked one sister of another.

Not that the sisters were a garrulous lot but even they whispered about their parish priest.

His involvement with the Résistance Français happened by accident. One of his parishioners, the young, fanatical Jean Alpen, confided in his parish priest how he'd joined the Free France Resistance cell recently formed in the forest near Lyon.

'We're only new, Father, but we're gaining members and you could help us, Father.'

'I have enough trouble tending to souls, my son, without dabbling in politics.'

'This isn't politics, Father, this is survival.'

It was a different form of survival for the priest; survival of his sanity and conscience. His sister, who lived with their elderly parents in Paris, wrote to inform her brother their mother had cancer, was in terrible pain and needed to see her son before she died. Their father's problem with alcohol continued. She begged him, 'Come home Father Flory, come home brother Felix.'

Then the new bishop in Lyon was well named; Bishop Vaine. His vanity shone, he dominated every conversation, and he dictated and prosecuted his strong belief in punishment and revenge against his fellow religious. Father Flory failed his calling. There was no cheek turning from Felix who hated his bishop.

So with more than enough on his plate already, getting involved in the Résistance Français did not appeal to Father Flory.

All that changed one night when someone knocked on his door. He was used to being called out to give the last rites when one of his parishioners, usually elderly, decided to accept St Peter's invitation. 'Yes, I'm coming,' muttered the priest who opened the door in his night dress. The man standing there collapsed forcing the priest to catch him.

This was no family member asking for the priest's services. This was no Catholic Frenchman but rather a blood-covered Methodist from Todmorden in West Yorkshire. He was RAF pilot, Brian Wilkinson, who crash landed two miles away. His plane was hit by German fire in the occupied zone and only the skill of the pilot landed the plane in a field near Lyon. The Gestapo raced to the crash site only to miss the escaping pilot by minutes.

Once the plane crash-landed, the pilot set it alight then scarpered leaving a solid sprinkling of his blood behind. He limped into the woods, found a road and came to the outskirts of Lyon. Not being spoilt for choice, a church seemed a likely place for sanctuary and, still losing blood, the Methodist turned to the Catholics for help. Brian made it to the nearby village and the parish church of St Nicholas.

Father Flory helped him into the kitchen and became a medical orderly. There was broken or schoolboy French and English being spoken with grammar the big loser. The priest managed to stem the flow of blood and tipped some brandy into the Englishman. No sooner had the patient regained a glimmer of normality then someone else knocked on the door. This was not soft knocking as in "please help me". This was door bashing as in "open up now", and spoken with a voice decidedly Germanic.

'Gestapo,' whispered Flory and helped the pilot into the church and to the confessional. 'Head down and stay silent,' he muttered in broken English then hurried back to the front door.

Without warning the Gestapo officers were behind him as they entered via the unlocked kitchen door.

Flory attacked. 'How dare you break into the House of God.'

The Gestapo had no intelligence on the politics of this priest and were only interested in a missing RAF pilot.

'We want the man you are hiding, Father. Where is he?'

'What man? I am alone. Now I demand you leave at once.'

The Gestapo leader waggled his pistol and two colleagues moved to search the premises. Flory knew what the Germans did to enemies of the Reich. This was his first face to face experience. He panicked. If they found the pilot, both he and the airman would be shot.

Time moved slowly. He waited for the scream and the gunfire. *Did the pilot have a gun?* Silence. The searching officers returned. Flory held his breath. The searchers shook their heads. The Gestapo boss glared at Flory then stormed out, his fellow thugs following. The church door remained open. Only then did the priest see the blood on his hands and nightdress.

Relief was palpable. Flory waited. When he was sure the Germans had left, he went to the church. There were no lights only some feeble moonlight. He peered in the confessional. It was empty.

Flory looked around. The shadows made the interior spooky. He was puzzled. *Where is the pilot?* The Gestapo used torches. They would have easily found the man in the confessional, under a pew, in the pulpit, behind the organ, in the robing room. *Where is he?*

Someone coughed. At least that's what it sounded like. Flory moved to the altar. A coffin sat on its stand ready for a funeral tomorrow. The priest froze. The lid of the coffin was leaning on the altar. He moved to the coffin and struck a match. The deceased was at repose, hands clasped on chest ready to meet his Maker.

Another cough sounded and this time much closer. Flory peered into the coffin. The flame burnt his finger. He swore then lit another match and heard another cough.

If you believed in miracles your faith would have been rewarded because the deceased moved; not much but enough. Flory realized the corpse was much higher in the coffin than normal and, with great care, lifted and turned the body on its side, and then lifted the cloth beneath it. There lay the RAF pilot in his perfect hiding place.

And that was the beginning of Father Flory's entrée into the world of helping the Allied cause. He hid the pilot in the woodshed. When youthful parishioner Jean arrived for Mass later that day, he was taken aside and told his Resistance cell faced a new challenge—get this RAF pilot out of my house, out of Lyon and France, and back to wherever he came from.

'He says he's English but talks with a weird accent,' said the priest.

Jean was afraid. 'Is it a German accent, Father?'

'Not unless Yorkshire is in Deutschland.'

Jean and his Free France cell did well. The RAF pilot was spirited away, eventually to the Freedom Trail, the chemin de la Liberté.

Walking out of mountainous France into mountainous Spain was not for the faint-hearted. And with German patrols and those of the equally hated La Milice, the Vichy paramilitary force, searching the route, as well as traitorous Frenchmen ready to betray anyone for money, the journey was risky, often deadly.

But Brian made it and back in Blighty, sang the praises of the parish priest, Felix Flory from Lyon. The priest's name reached the ears of Maurice Buckmaster, recently recruited to the F (for France) Section of the SOE. Next thing the good padre was being tapped up to help two new SOE agents ready to be dropped just outside Lyon. The priest's new calling was off and running. Mind you he took on the role under sufferance.

In France, only the Free French Resistance cell in the forest outside Lyon knew of his involvement, while the bishop in the Lyon Cathedral, the nuns at the nearby Monastery, and the Communist Resistance cell in another part of the Lyon forest knew nothing about the local padre now helping fight the Germans. But for how long would his commitment remain a secret?

Chapter 21

An English country lane

An owl and a fox watched the two humans. One was a brilliant actress, the other a right royal princess. The fox, always curious, wondered if a feed was in the offing. Did royal flesh taste better than working-class or middle-class flesh? The owl, who fancied a field-mouse supper, simply hooted to announce its whereabouts.

'Keep going, Margaret, you're doing a brilliant job.'

She was but struggling. The Princess was tired, almost exhausted but refused to admit same. At home, she could twist Crawfie around her little finger but this actress, Cinderella, was no pushover.

'There!' cried Louise, 'a light.'

Margaret's spirits soared then fell. 'Where?' she asked.

It was gone and Louise cursed herself. She'd given hope then snatched it away. Was she wrong? It flashed again and was gone.

'This way,' said Louise, 'we're getting close.'

The woods were on one side and farmland on the other. Staying on the road was vital but potentially dangerous. Walking in the woods or fields was slow and risky.

Louise too was dog tired after such an unusual day. Performing the eponymous role in a panto at Windsor Castle for the Royal Family was a first. But that was followed by being kidnapped with a member of said Royal Family and driven around Berkshire, first in a wicker basket and then in the hollow hidden bottom of a hearse. That's definitely unusual. But then so too was attacking two members of the IRA with a kitchen tray, a chamber pot and a bout of unarmed combat before escaping in the countryside in the dead of night. Again, that's decidedly unusual. Not knowing where they were or going didn't happen every day. Louise's nerves copped a kick in the pants. Yes, unusual just about covers it.

Louise took Margaret's arm. The poor girl was about to collapse. 'There, Margaret, look.' The Princess saw a sliver of light. It came from a farmer's cottage hiding behind a copse of trees.

The joy for the females brought tears to their eyes.

'Come on,' urged Louise and helped her companion along a dirt drive. They were about ten yards from the front door when they heard the sound. They froze. It grew louder, much louder.

A motorcycle raced along the same road the females had traversed and to their horror, it swung into the cottage.

Louise grabbed Margaret and pulled her into the trees. 'Down,' whispered Louise and dragged the Princess with her. The motorbike roared past them. With only a pencil thin headlight on the bike, the escapees remained hidden.

The rider stopped the engine. As he dismounted, a worried man and woman opened the door.

'Hello,' said the rider and Louise and Margaret recognized the voice of the IRA man from the hearse. 'I'm sorry to trouble you,' he said sounding normal and pleasant. 'My sister and her cousin have been sent from London to stay with us in the countryside and they've gone for a walk and are lost. You haven't seen them by any chance?'

'No we haven't,' said the concerned farmer.

'Oh that's terrible,' said his wife. 'How can we help?'

'Well if you see them, it's important you keep them safe indoors. Don't let them out under any circumstances. They'll be terribly scared.'

'Of course,' said the wife.

'If we find them, how can we contact you?' asked the farmer.

'Oh my family will be out searching all night and we'll check in with you later, if that's all right.'

'Of course,' said the wife, 'and I hope you find them soon.'

'Thank you,' said the IRA man and kicked his motorcycle into gear. 'Goodnight,' he called turning and riding away.

The couple went indoors. 'That sounded like the man from the house,' said the Princess. 'What shall we do?'

'Knock on the door and ask for something nice to eat. Come on.'

The door knock was a surprise. The elderly couple glanced at one another confused the motorbike didn't return. They opened their door and gasped as the two missing females stood there looking somewhat bedraggled. One looked like a princess and the other a transvestite.

'Good evening,' said Louise, 'we're the lost sister and cousin. May we come in?'

To say Arthur Dunn and his wife Gertrude were shocked would be accurate. They stepped back and welcomed the visitors. Louise used her brilliant acting skills and combined them with her inventive mind. She needed a good imagination to explain their situation and doubly so as she didn't want to reveal the identity of her VIP companion. The actress became a playwright.

What a yarn. The Dunns accepted everything Louise said. She simply repeated what her IRA captor told the locals. The dim light in the kitchen with just the one lantern, and the fire in the stove meant Margaret's face was never well lit.

After the tall tale with added comments about how they escaped the Blitz in London, Louise popped the question. 'Would you happen to have a telephone, Mr Dunn?'

'Oh I'm afraid not, Miss. A horse and cart, a cow and a butter churn is about all we can stretch too 'ere. The nearest telephone would be up at the manor.'

'But that's more than two miles to the gate, Arthur,' said his wife.

'Not if you go through the scrumper's 'ole.' He turned to the visitors. 'There's a spot in the wall where the kids squeeze through when they goes scrumpin'.

'That sounds fine,' said Louise. 'And may I ask who lives at the manor house.'

'Oh that would be his Lordship.'

'His Lordship?' asked Margaret, full of beans. 'I may know him.'

Her comment set off a small explosion. Louise flashed a warning with her eyes and Margaret changed expressions.

'It's Lord Goodlad of Foxhill Park,' said Gertie.

Louise stared at Margaret and frowned. The Princess shook her head and spoke in a quiet voice. 'No, I don't know him.' She lied.

Louise stood. 'Well, if you could show us the way, Mr Dunn, we'll trouble you no more.'

He worried. 'Oh, but what about your brother?'

'We'll telephone him from the manor house. That will stop his worrying about us ever again,' smiled Louise even now thinking she'd said too much. She took hold of Margaret's hand. 'Come along little one, you must be away to your bed.'

Louise led Margaret, and the Dunns hurried to open the door. Arthur grabbed his flat cap and led them down the drive. The visitors waved to Mrs Dunn who, for the rest of her life, never knew she once entertained a wee slip of a lass, the younger daughter of the King and Queen of England.

The scrumping hole in the manor house wall was ideal for children. Margaret made it but Louise struggled; having breasts didn't help. She squeezed through, and then hurried past the apple orchard and followed the sweeping drive. The manor house was more a stately home. It stood in regal splendor in the silent night.

Margaret stopped. 'I've been here before,' she said. 'My parents know Lord Goodlad. He's an awfully nice gentleman.'

An enormous weight floated from Louise's aching shoulders. But she needed a new script. They stepped onto the tiled flooring which ran around the house below the balcony of the floor above. It was early with the first streaks of dawn peeping above the trees. The house was in darkness. Louise rang the bell.

It sounded loud outside so must have woken those inside. Two dogs barked. A light came on and a man, tying a dressing gown cord, approached the door. He peered through the glass.

'Yes?' was all he said.

Louise began her spiel. 'We're terribly sorry, sir, to be calling so early, but my friend and I urgently need to telephone the police.'

'Who are you?' came from within.

'My name is Louise Wellesley and we've been the victims of a kidnapping.'

The man hesitated. 'Do you know His Lordship?'

Louise struggled. 'No, sir, but I can explain.'

'I do,' piped up Margaret, tired and tired of the refusal. 'Tell him Little Meg is here,' she boasted.

Louise stared at her companion. The man hesitated and asked for confirmation. 'Did you say "Little Meg"?'

'Yes, sometimes known as HRH the Princess Margaret and please ask Henry and Flo to stop barking. They know me.'

The door was hastily opened and the butler gestured. 'Your Royal Highness,' he bowed as the visitors entered. Louise had seen a few large rooms in the last 24 hours and this was yet another; and they were only in the hall.

Two Labradors came bounding in from somewhere in the bowels of the home, and the Princess greeted them like old friends.

'Who is it, Smythe?' called a voice from the top of the stairs.

'It's Her Royal Highness, Princess Margaret, my Lord.'

'Little Meg? What the dickens is she doing here at this hour?'

'Escaping with Cinderella,' called Margaret and that stopped the conversation dead.

'Put them in the kitchen and give them a hot breakfast. I'll be down in a minute.'

His Lordship disappeared and the butler led the visitors and the dogs to the massive kitchen. Sitting was a blessing. The cook appeared wearing her night dress, dressing gown, a hair net and a face of disbelief. She recognized the Princess and curtsied.

Pretty soon the best breakfast in England was being consumed. His Lordship arrived. He bowed to Margaret, shook hands with Louise and heard a potted history of the last 18 or so hours leaving out certain violent and unsavory incidents.

'Good heavens,' said His Lordship.

'She's a star on stage and off, my Lord,' said Margaret indicating Louise who now desperately wanted to contact the outside world.

'May I make a telephone call, my Lord?' she asked. 'And I might need your help with a certain number.'

'Of course, do come this way.' He gave orders to the cook. 'Make sure the Princess has a second helping of everything,' he called and led Louise to his office. He closed the door.

'My Lord, I know an officer in the security service and think he should be the first person I contact.'

'Of course but will not their Majesties need to know their daughter is safe?'

'They will be the first to be told, my Lord, but what I didn't tell you in front of the others is that the IRA are behind this kidnapping and we have the chance to capture them. There is no time to lose.'

'Good heavens, of course, please do whatever is necessary.'

'May I ask your address, sir, and the name of the road running beside the wall behind your apple orchard?' He gave her the details.

'Thank you.'

Lord Goodlad picked up the telephone receiver on his desk, tapped it, heard a dial tone and passed it to Louise.

She wondered if she should ask the homeowner to leave the room but then decided the call was too important to wait.

'This is an emergency; Cricklewood 1318 please.' She waited and smiled at the astonished Lord. Someone answered. 'Oh good morning, Major; it's Plum speaking.'

Bunting almost dropped the phone. 'Miss Wellesley? Are you safe? Are you with the VIP? Where are you?'

'We're both safe, sir. We're with Lord Goodlad in his home, Foxhill Park near the village of Lower Hatch in Berkshire. Have you got that?'

'Yes,' said Bunting repeating the details.

'The IRA safe house is in Gatling Road, a mile or so south of this estate. You want a large double-story farmhouse, set behind trees with the name Gillespie on the white letterbox.'

His Lordship stood stunned. This woman spoke as if she was an experienced officer in the police or security service. Louise continued.

'Can I ask you, sir, to contact the Royal Family, the Prime Minister, and Special Branch?'

'Consider it done, Miss Wellesley and many congratulations.'

'Thank you, sir. I assume you recommend we stay put and await further development?'

'Indeed and you sound as if you've been well trained in your work.'

Louise smiled. 'Only by the best, sir.'

'I look forward to congratulating you in person. Goodbye, Plum.'

She hung up and Lord Goodlad smiled. 'I'm guessing we have something in common, young lady. We've both signed the Official Secrets Act.'

Louise smiled in return. 'I don't suppose, my Lord, you'd have such a thing as a hot bath?'

Chapter 22

10 Downing Street

The ongoing tension with the Blitz, the war developing on new fronts, and the possibility of Germany invading Britain were only some of the threats Winston Leonard Spencer Churchill currently dealt with.

The man drank a little water topped up with a decent slosh of single malt, smoked cigars incessantly, and bathed often. His drinking and smoking continued during bath time. Sleep was a luxury.

His current and most pressing dilemma was the kidnapping by the IRA of the youngest member of the Royal Family, the lively, many would say beautiful girl, much loved by her family and the nation.

To have her kidnapped was appalling. To have her harmed or, God forbid, killed because Churchill was unable to meet the demands of the kidnappers, would not only leave an enormous and immoveable blot on his copybook, it would haunt the man to and even whilst *in* his grave.

Progress dragged. The police found the getaway van. They reckoned this reduced the search area. Daylight drew near. The ransom demand was delivered presumably by one of the kidnappers who was allowed to escape. Winston did an excellent line in fury and various senior police officers copped the full force of the PM's rich vocabulary.

At 0700 hours he called a meeting of officers from the Metropolitan Police, Army, MI5, MI6 and Special Branch. War Office aides were outside wondering why they weren't invited to whatever was happening next door. Despair lingered in Winston's office. He chewed on cigars and chewed off high-ranking officers.

His phone rang. He snatched it. 'What?'

His secretary spoke. 'Major Bunting from the Special Intelligence Service is on the line, Prime Minister.'

'Put him through.' Everyone watched the PM. He was told the news. His face lit up. 'And you're sure they're safe?'

He raised his hands and shouted, 'Hallelujah!' as high-ranking officers shook hands and slapped one another on the back. All that bonhomie was a sham and about to vanish.

The PM's secretary briefed the officials providing Louise's details. There were several major tasks to perform. The first, informing the King and Queen their daughter was safe and well and would soon be returned to Windsor, was handled by the chap with the huge cigar.

But other tasks remained. Apprehending the kidnappers, collecting and returning the Princess, and investigating everything about this whole wretched business were top of the agenda.

Every agency wanted to be in charge. What better way in which to bask in royal glory, avoid criticism, and shift the blame to other agencies than by running the enquiry?

Churchill gave no orders as to who would be in charge leaving them to fight among themselves. Was the PM canny or sloppy? Churchill left the top officials to come up with a plan, which was when the fun began.

The Army stationed a unit at Windsor Castle. Its only job being to guard the Royal family and the unit failed spectacularly. But still they claimed the right to retrieve and return the Princess.

Special Branch dealt with the kidnapper who was working with the Abwehr. Special Branch lost the IRA man who went on to kidnap the Princess. They desperately wanted to redeem their reputation.

The police helped the kidnapper escape twice—admittedly unknown at that stage—but with stations within striking distance of the stately home, they reckoned they were in the box seat to reach the Princess and escort her home to Windsor.

But hang on; MI5 were in charge of the security of the realm. Who better to run the enquiry?

Churchill entered the room and wanted to know their plans. When he discovered they were squabbling over who should do what, he exploded. The high-ranking law-enforcement officials fled. It was every department for itself.

IRA safe house

When the two missing IRA undertakers returned from dropping Clara close to Slough, they heard banging upstairs and quickly discovered the situation. Louise threw the key away so the men needed an axe to release the woman and Big Kev. Both endured sore heads, and in Kev's case sore privates plus shame. There was only one choice—scarper. They did, abandoning what was no longer an IRA safe house.

It took a while but police officers were the first to arrive at the now abandoned property. Finding no-one, they cursed and beat a retreat. Alas their exit was blocked as a truck loaded with soldiers swung into the driveway. These soldiers were good at firing rockets but lousy at copping them. After their giant cock-up at Windsor, they copped a rocket and were hell bent on redemption.

A copper ran to the truck driver's window. 'You're too late, you lazy bastards. They've gone,' yelled the constable to the private. 'Now out of the way and we'll clean up your mess!'

The army boys were having none of that. Item 2 on their agenda was to attend Lord Goodlad's estate and rescue the Princess. The cops were following the same orders. The constable ran back to the car ready to do just that. The army truck reversed but blocked their way. Horns blared. Mine's louder than yours.

The truck reversed carefully onto the road not allowing the revving police car to sneak ahead. Off they went with the army truck leading and the faster police car tooting and trying to overtake on one side of the narrow country road. The truck driver watched in his side mirrors and drifted from side to side forcing the police car to pull out of each manoeuvre. It was madness with shouting the preferred language.

Special Branch sent officers to every known IRA house in London hunting a certain Michael O'Donovan. He wasn't that silly. He went down to the Thames and broke into a houseboat he knew was unoccupied. Clara headed across country and finished back in her home town in Staffordshire. Her East End rented home gave no clues as to her new/old hideaway.

Having made a schoolboy error in shadowing Michael O'Donovan in London, Special Branch dispatched a car to Berkshire and the stately home of Lord Goodlad of Foxhill Park. Better late than never.

MI5 accepted Churchill's request to investigate the whole event and sent a car to the stately home to interview His Lordship. If it meant they could rescue the Princess, so much the better.

All roads led to Foxhill Park and to the Princess Margaret.

After breakfast and a glorious bath, Louise dressed in her odd assortment of theatrical and street clothes and joined His Lordship, his goddaughter Phoebe, and Princess Margaret in the smallest of the drawing rooms. It was huge.

Smythe knocked and entered. 'Another phone call, my Lord, advising another group of officers is coming to collect your visitors.'

'Not another one; that makes four!' complained his Lordship and immediately apologised. 'Oh I do beg your pardon, ladies. But just the thought of a mob of puffed-up officers trampling over my lawn wanting to be the one to return Little Meg to Windsor absolutely appalls me.'

'Why don't *you* take Princess Margaret?' asked his goddaughter.

He shook his head. 'The Rolls hasn't been anywhere of late, not much petrol, and it would take an age to drive to Windsor.'

'Not in the car, in the Fox.'

His Lordship's face lit up. 'I say, what a splendid idea. What do you say Little Meg? Fancy a flying taxi back home to the Castle?'

Margaret's face emulated his Lordship's. Louise needed worry beads.

'Smythe!' yelled His Lordship. The butler appeared. 'Tell Hopkins we need the Skipper ready for takeoff in five minutes.'

'My Lord?' asked a confused servant.

'Move, man!' yelled His Lordship and the butler disappeared.

'My Lord,' began Louise.

'And especially you, Miss Cinders; this'll be the perfect way to visit the scene of your triumph.'

'Do you have an aeroplane, My Lord?'

'Oh it's much than that, young lady.'

'But where will you land, My Lord?'

'Why outside the front door of the castle. We'll taxi up the driveway of Great Windsor Park.'

Margaret was up and clapping. 'Hooray!' she cried. 'And Cinders can tell Mummy and Daddy all about our adventure.'

Louise's heart filled out a complaint form; in triplicate.

One of the highlights of Louise's visit to Windsor Castle and its aftermath was to climb into His Lordship's de Havilland Fox Moth, and soar above his magnificent estate. They took off into the wind and as they turned and headed towards Windsor, not one, not two, but three convoys of law-enforcement officers drove dangerously into the Foxhill Park estate. One had just arrived. Sorry chaps, you've missed the boat.

His Lordship laughed, the Princess waved, and even Louise found it easy to smile.

Windsor Castle, Berkshire

The pilot, Lord Goodlad, was as good as his name. He radioed ahead so as not to frighten the horses, meaning a full complement of soldiers was on hand as the plane taxied to a stop. It's not often any aeroplane puts down in Great Windsor Park.

A government car pulled up and out stepped two important persons; King George VI and his good lady wife, Queen Elizabeth.

Margaret was the first out of the plane and ran to embrace her delighted parents. Louise, not used to suffering from stage fright, couldn't move. An equerry poked his head into the small passenger compartment.

'Are you ready, Miss? Their Majesties are rather keen to meet you.'

Bloody hell, thought Louise examining her outfit. Mummy would die if she knew I looked like this at any time, let alone chatting with you know who.

Chapter 23

Windsor Castle, Berkshire

Princess Margaret was a chatterbox at the best of times so having just been through the most hair-raising experience, her description of the last 24 hours, she held her family, Crawfie, Lord Goodlad and royal aides spellbound. Seated in the midst of this gathering was a young woman, known to some as Plum, dressed in half a stage costume and other sundry garments, while being praised to the heavens.

If ever a glowing reference was provided for anyone anywhere, Little Meg's thank-you speech to Louise was it. Her words sat easily in the chapter entitled *Glorious*.

The Princess finished by moving to Louise who stood as the two young females embraced. Those in the room stood and applauded. Louise had given some convincing, even moving stage performances over the years, but never received such a wholehearted standing ovation.

The aides ushered all but the Royal Family and the actress from the room. Princess Elizabeth moved to congratulate Louise whose curtsy flowed with ease and grace. If Louise knew the older Princess better, she would have sensed Elizabeth's regret that she was not the one kidnapped and taken on so thrilling an adventure.

The King and Queen were genuinely overcome by Louise's bravery.

'We cannot thank you enough, Miss Wellesley,' said Her Majesty. 'You will always be welcome to visit our family. If ever we can be of assistance, do not hesitate to ask. My only regret is that your wonderful heroics may never be made public. God bless you.'

'We have a car for you, Miss Wellesley,' said His Majesty nodding to an invisible lady-in-waiting who stepped forward to escort Louise back to another world, the other world.

She curtsied to the Royals, and walked to the lady-in-waiting. At the door, she stopped because Princess Margaret called. 'Cinders,' she cried and ran in a most un-Royal like way and gave her heroine a full-strength hug. Louise's emotions toppled her nerves. She kissed the Princess, smiled at the Royals and left.

The woman led Louise to a small ante-chamber. 'We have found your make-up case and street clothes, Miss Wellesley. We couldn't find the rest of your ball gown I'm afraid. Is there anything else missing?'

It was all too much for Louise. She checked her belongings. 'No, thank you, I think that's everything.' An equerry entered.

'Good, well if you'll follow this gentleman, there's a car waiting to drive you back to London. I assume you'll want to go home and change because I believe you have an appointment with the Prime Minister at 3 o'clock this afternoon.'

It was not often Plum was lost for words—*the Prime Minister?*

Plum's flat, Maida Vale, London

Flop! Louise collapsed on her bed and groaned, not so much from pain as relief. What a day—what a night. Sleep kept calling. She dozed but wanted news about her brothers, the one about to become a father and the other, horribly disfigured escaping from Dunkirk. Her mother would know about the baby but probably not her son's war wounds.

She walked to the kitchen and saw an envelope pushed under the front door. She found a note inside.

Dear Miss Wellesley
We are most concerned about your sudden disappearance after the Windsor Castle pantomime.
ENSA requires all its performers to behave with the utmost decorum and especially when appearing before such dignitaries as the Royal Family.
Please provide us with an explanation of your departure from Windsor as soon as possible. This is your first and final request on the matter.
Yours faithfully
Basil Dean and Leslie Henson

Louise chuckled and spoke aloud. 'I'm sorry, gentlemen. My lips are sealed. And even if I could tell you, you wouldn't believe me.'

She walked downstairs, into the street, reached a telephone box and made a call to Wiltshire. Her mother was overjoyed.

'My darling girl, how are you? Are you still performing for ENSA?'

'Yes Mummy, still performing. How are you and Sir Anthony?'

'We're both well and I suppose I should now call you Aunt Louise.'

The ENSA actress was delighted to hear that her sister-in-law and brand new niece were well but was not surprised the new mother—it could not possibly have been brother Henry's doing—chose to call her daughter Hester Ottoline Wellesley. The baby's initials were HOW and Louise could only wonder WHY? Victoria asked about Edmund and it was obvious the damaged son continued to remain silent about his battered body.

'He told me he was wounded in France but nothing serious. How did he seem to you?'

'He's the same old, Edmund, Mummy; never say die.'

'Well my darling, with Henry busy on some mission for the War Office, you're the only one to keep an eye on your brother. Please tell me you'll do that.'

'I will, Mummy, of course I will. I'll ring him now.'

She did as promised and made a call to Farnham in Surrey. Mrs Crossley answered.

'Oh hello Miss Louise.'

'Hello Mrs Crossley. Are you well?' She was. 'May I speak with my brother please?'

'Oh haven't you heard? Mr Alexander was to send you a message.'

Louise panicked. 'What's happened?'

'Your brother's gone to that special hospital for an operation.'

'Which hospital? When? What's the address?' Louise sounded rude. She worried about her brother, her mother not knowing anything about the extent of his wounds, and not being told of developments.

'Please hold the line, Miss Louise.' She searched for the details. Louise found her pulse getting busy. 'Are you there?'

'Yes, go ahead.'

'It's the Queen Victoria Hospital in East Grinstead, West Sussex.'

'Do you have the telephone number please?'

Mrs Crossley told Louise everything she knew. The call ended and the hospital receptionist took Louise's next call.

'Hello. I'm enquiring about my brother, Lieutenant Edmund Wellesley. Can you tell me his condition please?'

Louise was transferred to a ward and spoke with a nurse. 'Lieutenant Wellesley arrived yesterday and is due to have his first operation tomorrow.

'Please tell my brother I will be there as soon as I can.'

'Did you say you're his sister?'

'Yes. Please tell him Plum is on her way.'

The nurse went to deliver the message and began by asking Edmund if he knew anyone by the name of Plum. He smiled for the first time in a long time. 'I most certainly do.'

'She asked me to say Plum is on her way.'

Edmund's spirits skyrocketed.

Louise arrived back at her flat to find the ENSA producer from *Cinderella* sitting on the landing outside her door.

'Miss Wellesley,' he said standing. 'I've been sent by Mr Dean and Mr Henson to ask why you left Windsor Castle without permission. Both gentlemen regard this as a most serious matter.'

'I'm terribly sorry but I've just learnt my brother has been badly injured fighting in France and I must see him in hospital before his major operation.' She went to open her door.

The producer didn't expect so serious an answer, expecting her to confess to some jaunt with the royal equivalent of a stage door Johnny. Actually she did go on a sort of jaunt.

'Well, I hope your brother recovers but I still need an explanation for your unacceptable behaviour.'

Before Louise could enter her flat or fire off a retort, another man came up the stairs, stopped and stared at the others. They stared back. His pinstriped suit shouted civil servant.

'Miss Louise Wellesley?'

'Yes,' said Louise as inquisitive as the ENSA producer.

'Carstairs is my name. I'm from the Prime Minister's office, and have come to collect you for your meeting with Mr Churchill.'

That flattened the ENSA chap. Did it ever? He couldn't top that. Louise then flattened the civil servant.

'I'm terribly sorry Mr Carstairs, but I have a family emergency.' She explained Edmund's situation. 'Please tell the Prime Minister my brother takes precedence over any meeting. Good day gentlemen.'

She entered her flat, closed the door and left the visitors open-mouthed, wondering what on Earth they would say to their respective masters.

Five minutes later she emerged dressed for her trip to Sussex. The ENSA producer had exited stage right but the civil servant remained.

'I thought I explained my situation,' said Louise.

'You did, Miss Wellesley, but the Prime Minister insists I offer you every assistance. My car's downstairs. Can I drive you to the hospital?'

That was a pleasant surprise. 'Thank you, no, but you could drop me at the London station for East Grinstead.'

Queen Victoria Hospital, East Grinstead

London Bridge was that station and soon Louise found herself in West Sussex and taking a taxi to the hospital.

With some guidance from staff, she approached the floor where her brother resided. A nurse asked if she needed help.

'I've come to see my brother, Lieutenant Edmund Wellesley.'

'You must be Plum,' said the smiling nurse. 'Come this way.' They set off along a corridor. 'He certainly perked up when he heard you were coming.'

'Oh?' asked Louise, her worry beads working overtime.

They entered a ward and the nurse pointed to the far bed. Edmund was trying to read a newspaper but with only one good eye, the task proved difficult. His damaged face could still manage a smile.

'What are you doing here, you silly girl?'

Both produced tears as she kissed his forehead. She was on his bad side and feared kissing his burnt cheek.

'I don't suppose you've heard the news, *Uncle* Edmund.'

He knew nothing as Mrs Crossley was under strict instructions about what she told anyone. He perked up. 'Marvellous; boy or girl?'

'Girl and the good news is that mother and baby are well, and the bad news is that our niece has the two worst Christian names ever.'

He wanted to know but she waved her hand signaling "don't ask".

She pulled up a chair and prepared for a solid heart to heart conversation. She wanted the truth and went for her brother.

'Mrs Crossley said Alexander was meant to tell me about your operation. At Farnham, he told me he was going to care for you.'

Edmund's damaged face saddened. 'I'm afraid my good looks have faded and so alas, has Alexander. He reckoned caring for a deformed cripple was a bridge too far. So much for true love, hey?'

She squeezed his hand and didn't let go. 'Well here's some good news. When your operation is over and they send you home, I'll be there to take care of you.'

'No Plum, you have your acting.'

Not after the Windsor kidnap I haven't. She changed the subject.

'So tell me about this operation.'

He indicated the other patients who were as bad or worse than him. He dropped his voice. 'I told you, I'm a ring-in. All these chaps are RAF pilots or bomber crew who were burnt when their planes came down. I don't think they know I've sneaked in.'

'But you're as deserving as anyone.'

'Perhaps and this wonderful surgeon, Archibald McIntoe, is a genius in helping chaps with burns. I couldn't believe my luck in joining his list of patients.'

He smiled and she wanted to smile but couldn't. 'Hey,' said Edmund, 'the doc hails from Down Under, New Zealand I think. You could tell him all about your acting trip to that part of the world.'

Louise worried. *No I can't.* Well she could but it would be a pack of lies. She would have to invent yarns about the invented trip. She couldn't tell her brother anything as like him she was in France fighting the Bosch.

'After what's happened, you deserve some good luck, Eddie. But you haven't told me how you came to be here.'

'Oh, and there's another bit of luck; I got a helping hand from the young quack who looked after the old man; you know, Doctor Tom Curzon.'

Chapter 24

10 Downing Street, London

'Louise Wellesley, is brilliant, Buckmaster,' said Churchill. 'What she did in rescuing the Princess was remarkable.'

'It was, Prime Minister.'

'But understandable when you consider her work as a sleeper for the SIS. Do you know in France she made a mess of several Nazis including a leading Gestapo agent and uncovered a British double-agent?

'I heard, Prime Minister.'

'She's perfect for the SOE.'

'Perhaps,' said Buckmaster.

Churchill exploded. 'Perhaps? What do you mean perhaps?'

'She has little training with explosives and firearms, and none as a radio operator. Can she stare into the eyes of a Nazi as she sticks a knife in his heart?' Churchill grumbled. 'Sending agents to Europe can be like sending pilots to Europe.'

'We're at war, man. People get killed.'

'Yes Prime Minister but I like to boost the survival rate. Even in our early days of operation, on average, SOE radio operators are good for all of six weeks.'

Churchill hated those facts. He knew Allied bomber crews had about a 1 in 3 chance of not coming home. For SOE agents to succeed in blowing up bridges, re-arranging railway lines, and harassing the enemy, they needed great skills and terrific luck.

'All I want you to do is train her; all right?'

Buckmaster was relatively new in his post as a leading light with the Special Operations Executive but held firm on some beliefs.

'Prime Minister we believe the best agents are native born. This woman is English and whilst her French might be fluent, she …'

'It is, extraordinarily so, according to Bunting from MI6.'

'But to the French locals, to some Gestapo or Milice, she will have an accent; slight or minor but still an accent.'

'Surely not all Germans in France will be able to tell that.'

'Not all but as you know a more powerful enemy than a German is the Frenchman or woman who is a collaborator.'

Churchill pondered the point. 'Bastards.'

'Even within Resistance groups, we believe there are those who work for the Germans.'

'In the Resistance?' Churchill's eyebrows climbed. 'Does de Gaulle know that?'

'Only a few perhaps but you only need one. And just as the Irish want Germany to win the war to unite Ireland, some French Communists want Germany to win so France becomes Communist.'

Churchill didn't like what he heard. 'But surely this woman has talents we could and should use.'

'I agree, she sounds perfect, almost too perfect.'

'Damn you, man; what does that mean?'

'In our short time of operation, sir, we've found many apply but few are chosen. It's a waste of time and resources, not to mention a life, to send someone abroad who is likely to fail.'

'But with her track record, this young woman is *over*-qualified.'

'Age is relevant, Prime Minister. Her tender years may count against her. I suggest she might wait a year or two before ...'

Churchill's fist banged hard on the desk. 'No! If she fails the bloody training, reject her but for God's sake man, give her a go. Invite her to start training now.'

Buckmaster's caution died. 'Very well, Prime Minster. I'll send her along to Jepson.'

Churchill disliked Selwyn Jepson. 'I don't know why you employ that fellow. He's a novelist who dresses up in some naval costume using a rank he's not entitled to.'

'He's also an expert in selecting ideal candidates for the SOE and especially females.'

East Grinstead Hospital, West Sussex

Louise froze. That name, Dr Tom Curzon, once occupied her thinking on a daily basis, hourly. If someone put the motion that one could fall in love at first sight, Louise would support it. She and Tom Curzon met in Cambridge after Louise appeared in an awful amateur theatre production directed by a kind, selfless and incompetent producer.

Tom thought Louise was adorable. She thought Dr Curzon's voice was but one of his many gorgeous features. It sounded like rich chocolate. His smile dazzled, his flattery oozed sincere charm and Louise melted. Her heart sang.

He didn't live in Cambridge and when he left, Louise thought she would never see him again. She tried to discover his whereabouts but failed. True love wilted and slowly faded away.

Then fast forward to Christmas 1938, when Louise was at home in Farnham with her family when her father collapsed. On Christmas Eve of all times, Charles Wellesley fell seriously ill.

Not even bothering to call an ambulance, his sons drove and then carried their father into the local hospital.

The family was eventually allowed to enter the ward to see their Papa where, the doctor attending to the patient was none other than one Dr Tom Curzon. Amidst the terrible sadness of her father's serious illness, Louise found a joy she struggled to suppress.

After her father's funeral, Tom began to tell Louise his feelings for her only to be interrupted by Louise's mad friend, Matilda Gonzales. Tom stepped away and then he was gone, back to Africa as a medical missionary to fulfill a promise made to his late wife. Louise was heartbroken. The funeral dripped with emotion and sorrow made even worse when Tom tried but failed to tell Louise his true feelings.

So it was back to Cambridge and her studies, the theatre and eventually to the Special Intelligence Service and her role as a sleeper in what became German occupied Paris. Goodbye Dr Curzon.

But now the wheel turned full circle. Dr Curzon treated Charles Wellesley and now apparently his second son Edmund when he arrived back from Dunkirk. Tom knew of the medical genius, Archibald McIntoe, and recommended Lieutenant Wellesley to the surgeon. Out of nowhere, out of nothing, Louise heard the name of the man she once knew she loved. But did he feel the same way about her? And where is he? And how can I find him?

Louise was about to ask Edmund about Tom Curzon but stopped when another doctor arrived. Archibald McIndoe wore spectacles, a white coat and a welcoming smile. 'Well now, Lieutenant Edmund Wellesley and who do we have here?' Louise went to stand. 'Please, don't get up.'

'This is my sister, Louise, Doctor.'

The medico studied the notes about Edmund's accident history. 'Bad luck being shot and then bombed. Greedy are you, Lieutenant?'

'Glutton for punishment, sir,' said Edmund trying but failing to smile.

McIndoe moved in and examined Edmund's face. 'That's a famous name, Wellesley. Prime Minister wasn't he?'

'Twice,' said Edmund, 'and the scourge of Monsieur Bonaparte.'

'I think we can do something with that burnt skin. Might take a few ops so are you a patient man, Lieutenant?'

'I was born patient, sir.'

'Good show.' McIntoe stood back. 'We'll make a start tomorrow.' He smiled at Louise. 'And will your sister be able to help with your recovery?'

'That's why I'm here, Doctor.'

Edmund interrupted. 'I've told her, Doctor, there's no need for nursing and she should go back to being the brilliant actress she is.'

Louise groaned internally.

'An actress?' said McIntoe fishing for details.

Edmund ramped up his praise. 'In fact she's only just back from a tour Down Under having scored another theatrical triumph.'

The doctor was genuinely interested. 'Did you travel as far as New Zealand, Miss Wellesley?'

'Sadly, no sir.'

'I have theatre-lover friends in Sydney. Where did you perform?'

Oh dear. I feared this would happen. It's time to invent, Louise.

'We actually went to military bases and gave impromptu performances wherever troops were gathered.'

Her reply killed the subject but Edmund was not finished. 'Now she's become a regular with ENSA travelling to entertain our troops.'

The doctor was impressed. 'Oh, I say, how marvellous. Could you bring an ENSA party here to East Grinstead? A show in the depths of winter would be just the ticket.'

'Oh yes,' said Edmund. Please Plum, say you will.'

'Plum?' asked the interested medico.

'Family name, sir, but only appreciated by cricket lovers.'

'I'll have you know, as a gangly teenager, I once opened the batting for Otago High School.'

So the origin of the nickname Plum was explained and enjoyed except by Louise. She decided to try and leave.

'Gentlemen, I'm afraid I have a train to catch.'

'But not before I introduce you to Matron,' said McIndoe. 'She's the one to see about your ENSA visit.'

So Edmund scored a kiss from his sis, who met Matron who was even more enthusiastic for ENSA than the surgeon. A taxi took the actress to the station and then a train back to London. She dreaded returning to ENSA. She pondered her missed appointment with the Prime Minister. And one name kept swirling around in her mind—Dr Tom Curzon.

Theatre Royal, Drury Lane London

The founders of ENSA were in a spin. They'd just staged a successful production of their pantomime *Cinderella* for the Royal Family at Windsor Castle. Everything went well except their leading lady, the costumier and the van driver simply vanished along with the empty van. The uncollected costumes and props were piled into the bus with the actors. The leading lady was not available for a chat with the Royals, and the theatricals became both confused and annoyed.

To Dean and Henson, annoying the Royal Family was the ideal way to not get a gong. Damn. They were miffed tending to anger.

The founders sent a hand-delivered note to Louise's flat and heard nothing. An ENSA producer was ordered to the leading lady's abode demanding an explanation. She gave no explanation and then some civil servant arrived telling Miss Wellesley she was wanted by the Prime Minister. Why? What's happened?

Talk about confusing. Sending someone to the costumier's house didn't help—there was no-one home, and the new van driver moved house. The ENSA bosses were a mix of anger, frustration and curiosity.

Then the bombshell arrived in the form of a hand-delivered letter with an impressive return address—Windsor Castle, Berkshire. The founders fought to open the envelope. The letter was one of thanks to ENSA for a wonderful performance. The final paragraph was the killer:

The letter was signed *George VI*.

Dean and Henson stared at one another. 'What on Earth happened after the performance?' asked Henson.

'No idea,' said Dean but we now have two priorities.'

'Which are?'

'Create a new one-woman show for our Miss Louise Wellesley and promote her as an ENSA star.'

'And the second?'

'We must never, ever ask about what happened at Windsor.'

'Never?'

'Never!'

Chapter 25

10 Downing Street, London

It wasn't until the next day that a member of the Prime Minister's office tracked down Louise and made an appointment for her with Mr Churchill. She was chauffeured into Downing Street, shown upstairs and waited until summoned to the inner chamber.

'Miss Louise Wellesley, Prime Minister' said Colville.

Churchill walked towards Louise his hand extended, a cigar stuck between fingers on his left hand.

'My dear young lady, I am delighted to meet you.' His grip was firm and his eyes never left hers.

'How do you do, sir?'

'On behalf of the nation, I wish to thank and congratulate you for your selfless and courageous behavior in saving the life of a member of the Royal Family. My deepest regret is you cannot be honoured in public—at least not for the time being. Now let us have some tea.' He stopped. 'Or would you like something a little stronger.' His eyes twinkled.

'Thank you, Prime Minster, tea will be lovely.'

He didn't even need to look at an aide to set the refreshment order in motion.

'Do, please, sit.'

Tea was served, the conversation buzzed, and Louise enjoyed her moment in the sun. Everything Churchill heard about Louise at Windsor and in Paris drove his admiration for the young woman. Now, having met her in person, he liked her even more.

'Now Miss Wellesley, there is someone I would like you to meet. Maurice Buckmaster works in the F Section of a new organization called the Special Operations Executive. They have agents, not unlike the Special Intelligence Service, although SOE agents tend to use explosives rather than envelopes. Have you heard of the group?'

'I have, Prime Minister.'

'Good, so tell me about your present plans?'

'I'm performing with ENSA when not taking care of my brother who was wounded in France, and then again on a ship coming home from Dunkirk.'

The premier nodded. He heard story after story of the suffering people endured because of this bloody war. 'You and your brother are a credit to your family and country, Miss Wellesley.' He stopped when, after a soft knock, an aide ushered in Maurice Buckmaster. 'Ah, Maurice, come and meet Miss Louise Wellesley.'

Introductions complete, they sat, sipped tea, and Buckmaster spoke. 'I'll come straight to the point, Miss Wellesley. With your track record in dealing with the Nazis and the IRA, I would be interested in talking to you about the possibility of joining the SOE.' He studied her awaiting a response. 'Should I continue?'

'It's most kind of you, sir, but I have no experience in jumping out of aeroplanes, blowing up bridges and firing Sten guns.'

'Those skills can be taught but I'll be blunt with you. Not everyone who applies is accepted. We have weeks of rigorous training and failing any one stage will see you rejected.'

'I understand, sir.'

'What are you doing at present?'

'I'm performing with ENSA.'

'Well you might be interested to know many SOE agents are called upon to play a part where, if the audience isn't convinced by the performance, they don't walk out or boo or yell insults; they kill you.'

Churchill worried Buckmaster was driving away a brilliant future agent. But Maurice played it hard wanting only people with the passion to succeed to apply to join.

'If you wish to be considered, Miss Wellesley, your involvement would come under the Official Secrets Act, and any plans you have for the future, would need to be put on hold. Do you understand?'

'I do, sir.'

'Then I suggest you give the matter some thought over the Christmas New Year break. 'Sadly you can't discuss it with anyone, and we can talk again in January. Will that be satisfactory?'

Both Buckmaster and Churchill stood.

'Thank you, sir,' she said, 'I'll do as you wish.' She nodded to the man with the cigar. 'Prime Minister,' she said, and left with the door magically opening as she approached.

Outside in Downing Street, she took a deep breath. *An agent for the SOE. What happened to my career with ENSA?* She panicked. *Oh God, ENSA!*

She needed to report in person, to explain her sudden disappearance which would have to be invented. She walked to Whitehall, into Trafalgar Square and along the Strand.

What will I say? The Official Secrets Act means I can't tell anyone the truth. But I have to say something polite and believable. If word gets out Louise Wellesley treats producers with contempt, I may never work as an actress again.

She turned into Southampton Street then Tavistock and Catherine Streets and reached the Theatre Royal.

Tell a lie with a grain of truth, girl and keep your fingers crossed.

She entered the stage door. There was the usual activity but not so much at this time. Local ENSA activity took a break over Christmas. Someone spotted Louise.

'It's Cinders!' Others were excited and surrounded her. As she accepted their praise and fielded their questions, the founders came pushing through to reach the star.

'Oh Miss Wellesley,' gushed Henson, how lovely to see you.'

'We were so worried, my dear,' added Dean trying not to fawn. 'Do please, come into our office.'

The men trod on eggshells. Their note to Louise reeked of anger and disapproval. Now the King's letter saw them retreating fast.

'My dear Miss Wellesley,' began Dean. 'We have been thrilled with your performances as Cinders and would like to propose a special new role.'

Louise was surprised, delighted and curious all rolled into one.

'I should explain my sudden exit from Windsor,' she said.

Both men took up histrionics. 'Oh don't mention it,' moaned Dean.

'We've forgotten it already,' added Henson.

'No,' added Dean, 'we want to talk about your *future* with ENSA.

'Your own show,' beamed Henson while praying at the same time.

'In the New Year, you can begin rehearsing for your own one-woman show, and we know the bookings will absolutely flood in.'

'It sounds wonderful, gentlemen, but what …' She was about to ask why she was to receive this special treatment but settled for something else. 'But what form would the show take?'

'Oh anything you wish,' said Dean.

'Anything,' crowed Dean. 'You could recite your favourite Shakespearean speeches, sing some pantomime songs, tell anecdotes of your acting career Down Under, anything your heart desires.'

'Have a think about it and tell us your decision after Christmas.'

What could she say? 'That's most generous of you, gentlemen, and I hope I didn't cause any problems when I left so soon after the performance at Windsor.'

Both men turned on a performance riddled with sentiment. 'Don't mention it ... Not a problem ... You were wonderful ... You have a merry Christmas.'

She caught the Tube home to Maida Vale. There was an envelope under her door. She didn't recognize the handwriting, elegant as it was. It contained a card with an invitation.

> *My Dear Miss Wellesley*
> *If you are stuck for somewhere to spend*
> *Christmas, you are most welcome to come to*
> *Foxhill Park. I'll collect you at the Finchley*
> *Golf Club. Do come.*
> *Kind regards*
> *Lord Goodlad*

'Bloody hell!' said Louise. *Join the SOE and become a spy with a licence to kill. Tour the country with ENSA in my own one-woman show. Spend Christmas with a stinking rich Lord, a pal of the Royal Family. Or best of all, see if I can find a certain Dr Tom Curzon.*

She wrote notes and placed one inside cards she sent to her mother, sister-in-law and brother Henry, brother Edmund, Mrs Crossley, and the Vestys. To Edmund she apologised for a lack of an ENSA visit to the hospital in East Grinstead.

> *So sorry to not be with you this Festive season*
> *but am travelling. Best wishes for a wonderful*
> *and peaceful 1941.*
> *Much love*
> *Louise*

She was early on Christmas Eve and caught a bus in the High Street. It was 7 miles to Finchley. She had a fair walk but found the entrance and walked towards a marvellous Victorian mansion, the clubhouse. There was no sign of any golfers and why would there be in winter during a war? No sign of His Lordship and his roller. She went to what looked like the front door. Before she could knock a man in a suit came around a corner.

'Can I help you, madam?'

'Is this the Finchley Golf Club?'

'It is but for the duration the building is occupied by the Ministry of Defence. What is your business?'

Louise hesitated and worried. *What do I say? Have I been sent on a wild goose chase? Is this really the Ministry of Defence?*

She opted for the truth. 'I'm waiting to be collected by Lord Goodlad of Foxhill Park.'

To the civil servant that sounded highly improbable. 'And what is His Lordship's connection to the Ministry of Defence?'

Louise had thoughts about being banned from the SOE having been caught trespassing on sensitive military property. She guessed.

'I rather think, sir, his connection is to this golf club.'

'The club is closed due to the war. Wait here.'

The official had decided Louise was a suspicious person. As he set off to fetch security, a sound was heard. It stopped the official and made Louise smile.

Hopping over the trees and making a bouncy landing on the first fairway was his Lordship's de Havilland Fox Moth.

'What on Earth is that?' asked the official.

'I believe it's my taxi, sir. Good afternoon.'

She set off down the fairway and as she approached the plane, a door opened and a man with a large briefcase hopped out.

He held the door for Louise. 'One out, one in,' he smiled and Louise entered the plane she last flew in en route to Windsor Castle.

No wonder His Lordship had access to aviation fuel. He played an important ferrying role assisting the Ministry of Defence within the land of his birth.

Chapter 26

St Nicholas Church, Lyon France

Father Felix Flory grumbled. He was hungry, needed to say Mass in ten minutes and news arrived from young Jean Alpen that four Jewish refugees needed help to escape the Nazis. Most of the nuns in the local monastery were elderly, the Mother Superior was poorly, and she and several of her sisters in Christ wanted a visit from their priest. *What else, God?* He thought. *Come on, Lord, give me a break.*

He gobbled some bread and cheese and swigged from a bottle of locally made wine. A soft knocking pushed him towards swearing. He was halfway through dressing for Mass.

He opened the door and met the Zweitel family—middle-aged parents and teenage son and daughter.

'Father Flory?' asked Monsieur Zweitel.

The priest turned and resumed his robing routine.

'Come in and close the door.'

They did and stood watching, their bodies shaking as much from the December cold as the fear of being discovered by French or German authorities. Every Jew in the area knew about the brutality of the Nazis. Do whatever you can to avoid being captured. Inhumanity was alive and well in Lyon.

Once dressed in his robes, the priest explained. 'I can't help you for another hour. You'll have to come to Mass.'

To the family's fear they added horror.

'But Father, we're Jewish,' said Mademoiselle Zweitel.

Flory finished dressing. 'I'm sure Jehovah will understand. You don't have to convert but to survive, you do have to pretend. The pathetic criminals serving the Vichy regime may call here at any time. If they do and find you not in church during Mass, you might as well book your tickets for the concentration camp now.' The family was stunned. He led them outside the room. 'Go down this corridor and enter the church from the front. Once inside the church, face front, bend your knee, put you hand on your face like this,' (He made the sign of the cross) 'and then sit halfway down and to one side. Stay in the pew when the others go forward. Kneel a lot. Afterwards, I will lead you to safety. Now go.'

The refugees didn't hesitate. A Rabbi might question them at some time but he wouldn't be able to if they were dead.

They did survive. After Mass, they waited in the priest's robing room becoming ever more terrified. At midnight Flory appeared and whispered. 'It's time to go. Do not speak, do not make a sound. Watch my hands.' He made hand signs as he explained. '*Stop, get down* and *come on* are the three signs. Understood?' All four refugees agreed in silence. Flory used his hands. The message was *come on.*

Outside in the bitterly cold darkness, in the shadows, across the road, the group was being watched.

Through the suburbs of Lyon they went. The curfew made being caught in the street suicidal. With no moon, the darkness was their friend. Father Flory knew where the enemy would most likely be but not the spy. He took the roundabout way and luck was on their side.

Outside the city, he beckoned. They followed him into some bushes beside the silent river. Now he spoke.

'Follow the river till it takes a turn to the right. Opposite on your left is a path between the trees. Take it. Climb to the top of the hill. You will come to a shepherd's hut. Wait in there for someone to collect you. Understood?' They nodded. 'Good luck,' he said and slipped away in the night.

They wanted to thank the priest but remembered speaking was forbidden. The father hugged his children and wife, and the family set off on the next leg of their journey to freedom.

Foxhill Park, Berkshire

Louise remembered the magnificent estate she encountered a few days ago with Princess Margaret—Little Meg—and seeing it again from the air a second time still took her breath away. His Lordship made a perfect landing and staff members were there to greet him and his guests. Louise was the last passenger collected. On board were Lady Flora Tweedale-Hunt and Sir Percival Groot. Both eyed Louise but for different reasons. Before even reaching their destination, Louise sensed this would be a Christmas she would rather forget.

Lord Goodlad described Louise as an actress—which was bad enough with some still believing *actress* was a synonym for *prostitute*—and someone who recently visited his home with a friend. That was it. No mention of the friend's identity.

Once inside the stately home, Louise met the other guests. Two were neighbours of His Lordship, Colonel and Mrs Faversham. He was an old duffer and she was rightly known as Mrs Old Duffer. The surprise for Louise were two people under the age of thirty, Lord Goodlad's nephew and niece—Randolf and Rebecca.

Randolf was the heir apparent to his uncle's estate and being the eldest son of the Earl of Norfolk, his title was set in stone. Apart from striking good looks, and being an immediate attraction for any red-blooded woman, Randolf had no airs or graces and when introduced to Louise, said, 'Hello, Miss Wellesley, please call me Randolf.'

Louise liked him immediately and enjoyed the fact he quizzed her over mulled wine and hors d'oeuvres wanting to know about her theatrical career.

'My uncle tells me you are an actress, Miss Wellesley.'

'Please, Randolf, you may call me Louise.'

He smiled. 'I can see how your stunning natural beauty would win over any audience, so does this mean talent is not required?'

Louise wondered if his charm was genuine. They chatted about Louise's roles until Randolf was called to explain a family painting. Lady Tweedale-Hunt appeared out of nowhere and whispered.

'Hands off, he's mine.' Flora smiled with a squeeze of venom. She had breeding, wealth and a title but God was rushed off his feet on the day she was born and the cupboard of natural beauty was bare. Flora hated God ever since. According to Flora, Louise with her natural beauty was not just a rival but a bitch as well.

The evening meal was simple fare in preparation for the feast on Christmas Day. Louise sat between Lord Goodlad and Colonel Faversham. She held her own. Being such a small gathering, the ladies did not retire and instead the entire party took coffee together.

Apart from the threat from Flora, the evening passed smoothly and then it was farewell to the locals and bedtime for the guests.

Louise climbed the stairs and headed along the corridor to her room when she heard footsteps, a hand took her arm and she was escorted into a linen press. Sir Percival Groot smiled to assure Louise all was well.

'Just a few questions, Miss Wellesley,' he said closing the door.

'Sir Percival, I must object.'

'The Foreign Office is studying your case with great interest.' Louise froze. 'Who have you told about your work in France?'

'No-one,' said Louise feeling her hackles rise.

'And what about your recent visit to Windsor Castle?'

Louise flushed with anger. 'No-one,' she fired back. 'I am well aware of the Official Secrets Act, Sir Percival.' She glared. 'Are you?'

He paused then grinned. 'Just checking, my dear, and you've passed with flying colours.' He held his hands together. 'Well then, now we have the business out of the way, how about we relax and have a little pre-Christmas fun? He grinned and as Louise didn't reply immediately because of shock, he continued. 'So, is it my room or yours?'

He moved in, held her arms and tried to kiss her. She pushed back, and with limited room to swing her arms, could only shove his chest.

'Let me by,' she said.

He grinned. 'Oh you play hard to get; I like that.' He moved in for a second time only to cop a knuckle in his left eye. It hurt. It was meant to. 'Ow, *ow!* You bitch!'

As he nursed his eye, tomorrow's shiner, she slipped past, hurried to her room and locked the door. Her premonition was right.

Shepherd's Hut, forest in France

The Zweitel family sat on the bunks sans blankets. They shivered. Tired, hungry and scared, they waited for their promised guide. If you call it luck, French Jewry was lucky as many Jewish citizens escaped the Germans. In some cases, Vichy authorities reckoned anyone born in France was French first and Jewish second. The Zweitels prayed that if they were captured, that sentiment would extend to them.

Huddled together, they fell asleep. The son woke when he heard a sound. He whispered to the others. 'Papa, Mama, someone's coming.' The footsteps grew louder. It was at least two people.

In the pitch black, the family stopped breathing. The door opened and a bright beam shone on their faces.

'Ah,' said a snarling voice, 'some more lovely Jews wanting a holiday in Germany. Out!'

Someone betrayed the refugees. What did Father Flory know?

Foxhill Park, Berkshire

Louise trembled. She wasn't cold just outraged. First, one of His Lordship's guests warned her off and then a lecherous mandarin from Whitehall tried to trick her into breaking the Official Secrets Act, and when he failed, decided the damsel was fair game for a bit of how's your father. Talk about an appalling Christmas. She decided to leave.

Assuming she could find it, knocking on His Lordship's door at midnight, seemed a bad idea.

Before dawn, she packed her bag, wrote a note for Lord Goodlad about her wounded brother being at death's door. She simply must go.

With breakfast in the dining room ready to welcome everyone, she left the note on her bedside table and slipped through a rear door used by tradesmen. She knew where to go. Past the apple orchard and straight to the opening in the wall created for those in short pants and with qualifications in scrumping.

She was free. On the road she wondered if any IRA agents were still about. She reached the farmhouse owned by the elderly couple who sheltered her and Princess Margaret. She needed directions so knocked on the door.

It was Christmas morning and when the cottage door opened, Mr Dunn's face was a picture. His wife beamed, welcoming the lovely young lady inside. Suffice to say, Louise was wrong about this being the worst Christmas of her life. It was one of the best.

She kept thinking about returning to London. Going back to Lord Goodlad or heading towards the IRA safe house were not options. But when Mrs Dunn's bachelor brother called to wish his family season's greetings, Louise was fixed. She had a smashing breakfast and then her carriage was ready. Old Bernard's horse was almost as old as the septuagenarian but the biting December air was good for her cheeks and the ride to nearby Langley and the train to London were perfect.

Chapter 27

Maida Vale flat, London

Louise pondered her choices. Go home to Surrey and care for Edmund, and while there, try to track down Dr Tom Curzon. That appealed, especially the last bit. Take up the ENSA offer and travel the country performing her one-woman show. That too appealed, especially if she could choose the show. Or join the SOE, and be sent back to France risking life and limb and love. Having already fought the Nazis in and around Paris and come close to death more than once, this option gave her nightmares. But it dragged her in. Was she addicted to danger?

Wellesley home, Farnham Surrey

With free time between Christmas and New Year, Louise rang Surrey and discovered Edmund was back home between operations with Dr McIndoe. *Surrey, here I come.*

Mrs Crossley and Horatio were the same while Edmund's burnt cheek was covered with a bandage and the skin around his eye seemed less gruesome. His face lit up when his sister appeared.

Their embrace was long and strong despite the difficulty of him being wheelchair bound and still sporting splints and bandages.

'I hope this is a fleeting visit,' he said. 'I'm perfectly capable of caring for myself. A nurse changes the dressing and helps wash me.'

Louise made a sound as if suggesting something cheeky. 'Ooooh, who's a lucky boy?'

'She's 103 and shaves her upper lip.' They laughed. 'So tell me; what has my little sister been doing? Has ENSA come to their senses and offered you a new contract?'

Louise tingled inside. 'As a matter of fact they have.'

Edmund clapped. 'Oh dear, my little sister really *is* a big star.'

'Ha ha,' she scoffed hiding her pride. 'Now tell me what's been happening at East Grinstead? I want to know everything, Eddie.'

He told her. 'There are several ops to go and they've given me a few days off to spend Christmas with my family.' He fondled the Labrador. 'And it's been grand, hasn't it Horatio?'

His tail said yes.

'So no need for you to interrupt your ENSA career, old girl. I'll have the best treatment. But you could stay till New Year if you like.'

She stared at him. 'I would like.'

When the sun came out, they piled blankets on Edmund's knees and Louise pushed the wheelchair around the large garden with an acre of lawn, glorious trees, now most currently leafless, and garden beds with rhododendrons, rambling roses, and privet hedges and more. Come summer the flowers would rejoice in their colour.

On Sunday they talked about going to church. Edmund declined as he thought someone, having seen him, might contact their mother and he couldn't bear to see her suffer. They ate well and dozed in the conservatory after more of Mrs Crossley's fare.

Louise called on friends and one in particular, Beauford "Nightie" Nightingale. Her ENSA performances gave him great delight.

On New Year's Eve the siblings sat in front of a roaring fire, turned out the lights and reminisced. Horatio was the only spoilsport as he broke wind from time to time and fanning became necessary. There were groans but no reprimands from the humans as, being old, the canine was entitled to indulge in his new-found hobby.

So much had happened in the recent past. This time two years ago their father died. Then their mother re-married, a world war began, big brother Henry married and was now a father, Edmund was horribly wounded and Louise, well Louise hadn't done much at all.

She honoured the Official Secrets Act but wondered if telling her brother would be okay. She wanted to ask his advice about the SOE offer and knew he would be like their father and forbid her from even thinking about it. "War is not for women," he would say.

But if she told him about her SIS work and then asked him about the SOE, he might not be so dismissive. In the end, she said nothing.

She was busting to ask about Dr Tom Curzon. *Where did you meet him? Did he ask about me? Did you ever know I was madly in love with the man in the white coat?* She thought about her possible new career as an SOE agent. If that came to pass, she would have no time for romance. She copied Tom Curzon and became faint-hearted.

They saw in the New Year, toasted its peaceful outcome then retired. Edmund pushed himself to his room. 'And get a good sleep ready for your trip to London in the morning and the start of your new ENSA tour. Happy New Year, star.'

'Happy New Year,' she replied thinking of his recovery. She called Horatio. 'Come on, Admiral Nelson, it's time for your evening stroll.'

Theatre Royal, London

She decided on her next career move and opened the stage door. It was fairly quiet. She moved through the wings when a woman came out of the costume room. 'Hey,' she cried. 'We want a word with you.'

'Oh?' said Louise, worrying her secret adventure might be exposed.

'Ladies,' called the woman and two more dressmakers came out and surrounded Louise. 'Where did you go after the panto at Windsor?'

'What do you mean?' asked a seemingly puzzled Louise.

'Clara and the van driver have disappeared.'

'Disappeared?' replied a shocked performer, slipping into her acting mode.

'Someone said you and Clara and the Princess Margaret went off for a tour of the Castle. Is that true?'

'I don't know about a tour; it was just to see where the Princess rehearsed her performing.'

'So what happened to Clara and Michael?'

'Who's Michael?' Louise was acting as well as she could.

'Do you know where Clara is?'

Louise shook her head and for once spoke the truth. 'I'm sorry, ladies, I have no idea.'

'Miss Wellesley,' called Basil Dean striding in from the stage having been told the actress was in the theatre. 'Happy New Year,' he gushed, wanting to see his favourite actress start rehearsals for her new show. 'Please come into my office.'

The costume ladies went back to work chatting about their missing colleague as Leslie Henson came running from the foyer having heard the news of the arrival of the Queen of Sheba.

'Oh Miss Wellesley, are we glad to see you,' he purred squeezing her hand. 'Happy New Year.'

'Thank you, gentlemen and the same to you.'

Dean took over. 'We are dying to discuss your new show. We've been talking about little else over the Christmas break.'

'Indeed, indeed,' bubbled Henson. 'Now what ideas do you have? We want you to have as much input into the show as possible.'

She paused and her face spoke volumes. Two hearts sank.

'I'm terribly sorry, gentlemen, but for the foreseeable future, I won't be able to perform for ENSA.'

Their faces collapsed. Their heartbeats slowed to a crawl. They dried on stage at the Theatre Royal. Their disappointment became pain. Their hopes and plans and ideas collapsed in a heap.

Louise delivered a simple tale about family duty, her seriously wounded brother, caring for her mother who did not know how badly her son was injured, and how the family home was to become a home for children fleeing the Blitz. There were fibs intermingled with the truth and the entrepreneurs wanted to push for a change of heart with their star but saw her mind was made up.

She left, feeling sad at having missed a terrific acting opportunity, and because she broke the hearts of two lovely thespians.

Baker Street, London

It took some thinking to make her next career move, tossing up between ENSA acting or SOE acting. In the end she plumped for the greater challenge. She liked to test herself. She wanted to play against the best players even if it meant possibly getting tortured, bashed, raped and killed. She desperately wanted to join the SOE.

She found their HQ without trouble. She didn't need to be Sherlock Holmes to find 64 Baker Street; she'd been there before. It was a chilly but sunny January morning and there was a spring in her step as she walked through London. Bomb damage dominated most streets but Londoners carried on showing a remarkable spirit and attitude. Their mood received a boost seeing huge signs with such a message as *Carry On London and Keep Your Chin Up!*

She entered the reception area and approached a woman at a desk.

'Yes?' was the extent of her opening line.

Louise wanted a more welcoming greeting but pressed on. 'Good morning. My name is Louise Wellesley. Is it possible to make an appointment to see Mr Buckmaster?'

'Why?' The verbose answers remained hidden.

Louise decided to use her big guns. 'I met Mr Buckmaster and the Prime Minister in Mr Churchill's office before Christmas, and Mr Buckmaster asked me to contact him about possibly working for the Special Operations Executive. Am I in the right building?'

Little Miss Tightlips needed a change of attitude and fast. Before she could speak, a man walked into the area and Louise recognized him as the gent who challenged her when she called to see Major Bunting on her return from France.

'Oh, this gentleman can vouch for me. He tried to have me arrested in the Secret Intelligence Service offices.'

If the best way to get on in the SOE was to belittle people, Louise was in cracking form. The gent had discovered the exploits of Louise Wellesley and the woman in Reception wore a sign, "I'm a goose".

Louise was escorted upstairs and asked to wait in a corridor. The hard seat matched her welcome thus far. The wait of more than 20 minutes didn't help. Finally Maurice Buckmaster came out of his office, smiled and approached Louise.

'Miss Wellesley, I'm so sorry to keep you waiting and it is lovely to see you again.' They shook hands and Louise purred. 'Do come in.'

She sat in his office complete with maps, charts, photographs and files. Papers to the left of me and papers to the right …

'Did you have a good Christmas?' he asked.

'Yes thank you.'

'Good, well I assume you've decided to apply to join the SOE.'

Crash! Louise turned rigid. *Apply to join? I thought the job was mine to decline.*

'Yes, I guess that's correct.'

'You guess, Miss Wellesley? Surely I explained in the PM's office how many apply but few actually join. Our standards are high and if you can't meet them, I regret to say you'll be rejected.'

She breathed more steadily. 'Thank you, yes, I understand.'

'And you should not need reminding, your signing the Official Secrets Act applies to everything you see or hear in the SOE.'

'I understand.' She worried about repeating herself.

'Excellent, now I'd like you to meet a gentleman who will conduct the first stage of your training. His name is Selwyn Jepson and you being an actress may have heard of him. He's an author of many novels. Have you read *I Met Murder* and *Love in Peril?*'

Louise pondered her answer. She'd never heard of the author or his work. If she lied in the hope of impressing Buckmaster, would she bring herself undone?

'I'm afraid not, sir.'

He showed her a card. 'There's the address. He'll expect you within the hour. Ask for a gentleman by the name of Mr Potter, and good luck in your quest to join the SOE.'

Louise stood, shook hands and left. She headed towards the interview to be held in a London hotel. She passed a bookshop, stopped as an idea popped into her head, and entered.

'Yes Miss?' asked the bookseller.

'Good morning. Would you have any books by Selwyn Jepson?'

He muttered and searched. 'Ah, Jepson, Jepson.' He found something. 'Only the one and it's the last copy.'

She perused a copy of *Tiger Dawn*. 'How much is it?'

'One and nine, Miss.'

'I'll take it.'

'Shall I wrap it?'

'No thanks.' She put the coins on the counter and the book in her bag. 'Have you read it, may I ask?'

'No, Miss. My brother's the crime expert. He'll be in tomorrow.'

'Thank you,' smiled Louise and set off. She passed a small park, entered, sat on a bench and read. She worried she was cheating, trying to impress the examining officer. Would he see she was pretending to know about him and his books? If so would that have the opposite effect and see her fail?

She kept checking her watch and having read, or rather skimmed, the first two chapters, the blurb, and the last few pages, she set off for the hotel.

Sent to Room 114, she took a deep breath and knocked. Opening the door was a middle aged man in a naval uniform and half a smile.

'Good morning; Miss Wellesley I presume?'

'Mr Potter?' He ushered her into a blacked-out room with its lights on. *Understandable at night*, she thought, *but why on a sunny day around lunch time?*

Once the interview began, he struck her as being intelligent, someone who knew their job and frankly, far better suited to being in charge than Mr Buckmaster.

'I'm told you've caught the eye of some important people, Miss Wellesley.' She knew who he meant but played it straight.

'I've been lucky with some of my acting roles, sir.'

'Tell me, what's the worst part about getting a bad review?'

She wasn't expecting such a question. 'Oh, feeling disappointed I guess; and more so if you believe the critic is correct.'

'Has anyone ever thrown something at you?' Another question she wasn't expecting. 'No tomatoes, rotten eggs and the like?

She smiled. 'So far, no, I must have been lucky.'

'And have you ever been raped, Miss Wellesley?'

This totally unexpected and crude question shocked her. Before she could answer, he apologised.

'Forgive my crass interview technique, Miss Wellesley, but being dropped behind enemy lines is one of the most dangerous jobs in the war and I want to prepare you. Being a woman makes it even harder.'

Louise decided to show some mettle. 'Are you saying women are not up to being an SOE agent?' Her anger meant she left out "sir".

'We've one thing in common, Miss Wellesley; we've both met the Prime Minister. I went to see him about my belief that females make better agents than males.' Louise hid her surprise. 'He, like many in the SOE, didn't agree. I told him why the fairer sex was better, and then pushed for his support. He paused, agreed and wished me luck.'

Louise hesitated. 'I see.' She'd misjudged "Mr Potter".

'And because I'm so keen on recruiting women to work for the SOE, I want them to fully understand the dangers involved. Of course I don't wish to shock or offend you, but I'd rather do so than have you happily sign up unaware of what might, even probably could happen. My goal is to find the absolute best candidates.' He studied her. She said nothing. 'Do you know anything about cricket, Miss Wellesley?'

She smiled inside. 'As a matter of fact I do, sir.'

'Good then you'll know the expression, "It's just not cricket".' She nodded. 'In war, the enemy fights dirty, and women are tortured and executed without a moment's hesitation. If you're captured as an SOE agent, then being female inspires your captors. And worse still, there are many who will delight in betraying you. Even someone you think is your best ally may turn out a Judas.' He paused and waited for her to speak. She said nothing. 'Not ready to leave, Miss Wellesley?'

'Thank you, sir, I'll advise you if and when such a situation occurs.'

He pressed harder. 'The upshot of being captured is usually horrendous torture and death, meaning you will never see your home, family or friends again. And to rub salt in the wound, your achievements may remain secret to protect others being unmasked.'

She remained silent. He admired her and changed the mood.

'So, do you have any questions, Miss Wellesley; anything at all?'

She cursed not having a question to hand. Without thinking, she took out the book she bought.

'Just the one, sir. Will you please sign my book?'

He was genuinely and pleasantly surprised. Having interviewed dozens of men and a few women, no-one ever produced one of his novels and asked for his signature. He liked her and her prospects as a future agent for the Special Operations Executive.

He'd already passed her as being mentally fit for the next training stage, and didn't think she was trying to join the SOE via flattery. He signed the book, handed it to Louise and stood.

'Thank you for coming to see me, Miss Wellesley. I'll be recommending you proceed to the next stage of your training, and the best of luck.' He gasped. 'Oh dear, I'm not supposed to use such an expression to an actress.'

She smiled, thanked the novelist cum spy trainer and left.

Back in Baker Street, she again waited to see Maurice Buckmaster, and while waiting, took out Selwyn Jepson's novel and read. She was so absorbed in the novel she didn't see the man standing beside her.

'Good book?' he asked.

She looked up. 'Oh yes, it is.'

'May I?' he asked holding out a hand. She gave him the novel which he perused then handed back.

Buckmaster appeared. Louise stood. 'Have you two met?'

'No,' both said and Buckmaster made the introduction.

'Mr Ian Fleming, Miss Louise Wellesley.' They shook hands and Louise was whisked away to deal with the boss. 'I believe congratulations are in order, Miss Wellesley.'

Louise smiled. 'Thank you, sir.'

'You have passed what is by far the easiest stage of your training.' She lost her smile. 'Soon you'll be off to bonny Scotland for weeks of intense physical training. Survive there and you're only half way through the course.' Louise worried. 'You would have done some physical training with the SIS, yes?'

'Yes sir.'

'In Scotland?' She nodded. 'Well to give you fair warning, the SOE training is in a steeper, denser part of the country, and the tasks are more numerous, much longer and harder. This part of SOE training has the highest failure rate.'

She stared at him. 'Are you suggesting I'm not up to it, sir?'

'If you're not desperate to join, then yes I am.'

She paused, building the tension. 'I'm desperate to succeed, sir.'

'Good. Succeed in Scotland and you'll move to Stage Three which is probably the scariest part. Are you afraid of heights?'

'I will never admit my fears, depriving my enemy of an advantage.'

Buckmaster admired her answers but gave away nothing. 'You'll learn how to jump from an aircraft with the aid of a parachute.' She said nothing. 'And if you succeed, you'll be off to yet another venue to learn about unusual warfare such as producing propaganda, how to avoid being captured, following someone undetected, writing with invisible ink, how to send and receive messages using Morse code, and more.' He paused. 'That gentleman you met, Ian Fleming, knows a bit about dirty tricks and, like Selwyn Jepson, does a spot of scribbling.'

She spoke in a calm, cheeky tone. 'Is that all, sir?'

'It is. You see we want our agents to be prepared for anything and everything.' He waited for her response.

'Thank you for the detailed information.'

He handed her some forms. 'Please complete these then hand them to my secretary, Vera Atkins, at the end of the corridor.' Louise smiled. He extended a hand. 'I look forward to welcoming you to the Special Operations Executive, Miss Wellesley.'

His firm handshake and warm smile set her heart rate racing.

Chapter 28

SOE Training Camp, Inverness-shire, Scotland

In 1939, before WW2 kicked off, Louise went on a training course in Scotland with the Secret Intelligence Service. She survived. But when she trained for the SIS, the war was yet to begin, Paris was not an occupied city, and pressure to train spies, agents or sleepers was nothing like today in 1941. Now bombs rained down on British cities. The German invasion was on everyone's lips, and so the need for quality spies and saboteurs was never greater. SOE agents needed superbly fit bodies, intelligent and clever minds, and skills. For Louise, this second training camp was nothing like the first.

Applicants who passed the psychological assessment were sent north for a wee romp in the heather. The romp was more a gruelling slog with bruises, scratches, strains and sprains included free of charge. Broken bones were an optional extra.

About 10% of SOE agents were female and in this course, Louise found herself in a group of one. The training manual was gender free meaning the women did exactly the same activities as the men.

The agents travelled by train heading north to Arisaig, Inverness-shire; a beautiful place to visit but a hell of a place in which to train. The hills were covered in dense vegetation. They were lovely to admire but murder to conquer.

Her group alighted at Lochailort Station and admired the stunning scenery. The trees and bushes waved to welcome the agents all the while chuckling at the suckers they were about to torture. With kitbag in hand, the would-be agents, headed off to their home for the next month or more. It was cold, more like freezing beneath a clear sky. Snow crunched under foot and the right footwear and socks were essential. The walk through the silent forest was peaceful even invigorating. But not for long.

Bang! The explosion was loud. Were the Germans expecting them? Pine needles, leaves, twigs, snow and Scottish soil danced in the chill air. Like everyone, Louise hit the deck.

Silence. The agents were uncertain. *Are we under attack? Is this part of the training?* It was. A loud voice with a Glaswegian accent sounded loud and clear.

'All right, wakey wakey, on your feet, look lively.'

It was a dummy explosion to set the mood. It worked. Louise and the others stood brushing foliage, snow and soil from their coats. Someone mumbled. 'Is the train still there?'

That broke the tension, comedy often does, and the trainees set off to walk a couple of miles to their new home, a magnificent house with walls a foot thick, strong and solid to withstand an army. If Hitler tried to bomb this SOE residence, he'd need half the Luftwaffe.

The food was excellent, the beds comfortable and the open fire welcoming. But dear God, the training; it proved horrendous. Those in charge of the exercises were under strict instructions to weed out anyone not suited for SOE work. They reckoned it was pointless sending an agent to a war zone who wasn't capable of living rough, escaping though forests and over mountains, operating alone behind enemy lines and being fit and capable in hand to hand combat with no holds barred. The bar was set very high; these were tough standards.

The day they arrived, apart from the dummy explosion, was a settling in and time-to-relax day. Tomorrow, hang on to your hats.

Much of this part of Scotland was hilly and thick with vegetation.

The activities involved climbing hills, crawling on your belly through undergrowth, crashing through streams and fording icy rivers, swinging on ropes, marching with heavy packs, and all the while being yelled out, and accused of being soft. Forget words of encouragement.

'I must be soft,' gasped Louise following one exercise as she examined her arms and legs to reveal scratches, cuts and bruises. She wasn't alone. She wondered what she might be doing for ENSA right now. Lapping up the applause from her latest stunning performance?

Technical skills were hammered home. In Paris, Louise dodged bullets from the Gestapo and a double agent. Never did she carry a gun. Now she became an expert on certain firearms.

'Not like that,' barked the instructor explaining a Sten gun. 'Put it on your hip and fire twice.' She became better and then much better.

She could strip and put a weapon back together in seconds—blindfolded. She experienced more training in unarmed combat, and was glad the men showed her no mercy. It gave her great satisfaction to put some of them on their back. Silent killing was an important part of an SOE agent's repertoire. Slashing another agent's throat with a wooden knife became de rigeur.

She gave everyone a fright once by smearing red lipstick on her wooden blade. The instructor saw the red mark and screamed.

'Jesus, you crazy bitch, you've killed him.'

The "victim" knew of the stunt beforehand and so played up his "wound". It caused a great laugh within the agents but the instructor harboured a grudge to "Ditch the bitch". She wondered if all this violent activity would ever be necessary but to ask such a question aloud never entered her head. She'd be shown the door if she did.

She buckled down and learnt about explosives and how to derail a train. The local railway company even provided a locomotive for the agents to place dummy explosives. 'Get the wiring wrong and you're dead,' was the oft-repeated message.

Did she pass? On the last day of training, she came down to breakfast and saw a few empty places. She enjoyed a bigger bowl of porridge and turned to the chap next to her.

'What's with the empty places?'

'They've gone.'

'Gone?'

'They failed.'

She was stuck for words. 'Does that mean ...'

'Yes, everyone still here is off to Manchester to break their necks.' Louise didn't understand. 'We're going parachute jumping.'

RAF Ringway, Manchester

Tens of thousands of paratroopers did their parachute training here and the budding SOE agents joined the queue. Their tutor was a brute of a man, Flight Sergeant Harold "Beefy" Mootlake known to everyone as Beefy Fruitcake. His voice doubled as an air raid siren, and his hatred of anything female was as blatant as his huge gut and voice. His first wife left him for a young merchant seaman with a stinging remark about Beefy's manhood giving rise to his rampant misogyny. His second wife was an alcoholic and would marry anyone who bought her a drink. She cleaned out his modest nest egg and did a bunk. Beefy wasn't up for third time lucky.

So he grabbed with both hands any chance to belittle a woman. Seeing Louise Wellesley in the latest batch of trainees set his blood boiling. Being the only female in this batch of trainees, she copped it.

'Should you be in here, lass?' he asked. 'The canteen's next door and we'd all like a brew. Two sugars, darling.'

She remained calm. 'I'm one of the trainees, Flight Sergeant,' she replied in a flat voice.

He scoffed. 'You're wasting your time, woman. Did you hear me?' he asked with a sting in his voice.

'I did, Sergeant, and your flies are undone.'

The room erupted. A punch in the face or a kick to his privates would have been water off a duck's back to Beefy but to be the butt of a joke which everyone enjoyed at his expense, cut him to the quick, and signed Louise's death warrant. Of course he deserved everything he got and more but like the prehistoric elephant he was, he wouldn't forget. All he thought about was how he could make the little bitch fail.

There were lots of short jumps from a tower aimed mainly at getting your feet in the right position to prevent breaking legs or ankles. Then you would sit on your bum and whiz down a big slide. After days of lectures and warm-up exercises, it was time for the real thing. One jump was from a hot air balloon and the other from a low-flying plane. It needed to be low-flying because over enemy territory, the plane flew under 400 feet, even lower, to avoid German radar. The drop took about 15 seconds, and Isaac Newton was right; gravity exists.

Beefy could not control the jumpers from the plane but could try his evil best from the balloon. Four jumpers plus Beefy plus the pilot floated above a Lancashire field. Even in close quarters the bully didn't know how to speak softly.

He ordered various jumpers to take off. They dropped through a hole in the middle of the basket's floor. He ignored Louise. The others dropped and landed safely. He turned and pretended to be surprised.

'Oh, you're still here. Well come on, get your arse into gear.' She moved. He stepped forward and pushed her to the side of the basket. In happened in the blink of an eye; an assault in the sky. He spun her round, placed one hand on the top of her chute and another between her legs and lifted her up and out of the basket. As she was about to plunge overboard, she threw back a foot. Her boots were made for walking and one solid heel smacked Beefy's nose.

He screamed in pain and Louise fell head first, struggling to right herself and release her chute. The ground rushed towards her. Whoosh. Her chute opened enabling her to land safely—just. Another few seconds and her SOE career would have been over, permanently.

In the balloon, the pilot stared at Beefy struggling to stop the bleeding from his broken nose. 'Head between your knees, sir,' he said. 'My Mam always said it was the best thing for a blood nose.'

Beefy snarled a threat but his mangled moosh diluted his power. Louise thought about reporting him but one viewing of the wounded tyrant and for her it was a case of honour is satisfied.

In the canteen, all the talk was about Louise's lucky escape and the giant bandage on Beefy's hooter. All the agents in Louise's group passed and were preparing to head south for the final phase of their training. A couple of chaps studied maps, noting the distance from Manchester to the New Forest in Hampshire. Train timetables were examined and groans became popular.

The men knew that even with the trains running express and on time to London, which was never going to happen, and with perfect connections and no bus delays, which also were highly unlikely, they'd be travelling for ages. As German bombs played havoc with transport timetables, the trip could take forever.

A woman slipped into the empty seat beside Louise. 'Hello,' she said, 'I'm Trinny.

'Louise,' replied the heroine of the parachute team, and the women shook hands.

'You deserve a medal,' said Trinny. 'One female with all these blokes, and you appear to have survived and thrived.'

'Just,' said Louise. They chatted and Louise bubbled having not just a friendly face but a woman to talk to.

'What's it like being the only team member without a beard?'

Louise laughed. 'It's a real competition to see who has the bushiest. One bloke reckons chicken shit makes it grow faster.'

Trinny laughed. 'I know I'm not allowed to ask, but I overheard your colleagues talking about heading off to Hampshire.'

Louise sensed danger. 'Sorry, my lips are sealed and it wouldn't surprise me to learn you're a stooge sent by that tyrant of a flight instructor to have me thrown off the course.'

Trinny laughed. 'I wish it were so, ah, me being an important spy catcher I mean, but no, I'm only a run of the mill pilot.'

Louise frowned. 'Only? Pilots are not run of the mill.'

'I'm in the ATA, and ferry planes all over the country.'

Louise shook her head. 'I never knew.'

'So do you fancy a free ride to Hampshire?'

'In a plane?'

'Well I'm not offering the rear seat of a tandem bicycle.'

Louise was more than impressed. 'Yes please, I'd love a free ride.'

'You're going to the Beaulieu Estate in the New Forest, right?' Against her better judgement, Louise nodded. 'Well I'm about to deliver a plane to Southampton. Once we land, it's about 15 minutes by bus to the Estate.' She grinned. 'So is it chocks away?'

Louise struggled to speak. 'I can't believe my luck.'

'Your colleagues will be stuck on trains till Whitsun while we fly free to Hampshire. We take off in 20 minutes; hangar Number 3.'

Trinny left and Louise glanced at her colleagues. They continued planning and complaining about their next journey. She smiled to herself, finished her tea and went to collect her kit.

As with the SOE, women were initially denied entry to the Air Transport Auxiliary. Trinny was eventually allowed to join. ATA pilots provided an invaluable service ferrying planes. Britain needed all the pilots they could muster, and to have men taken out of active service to be taxi drivers was a scandalous waste of resources. Up stepped the equally capable female pilots and let's crack on with the war.

Jo thrilled to the scenery, the fabulous flying skills of the female pilot, and at Southampton thanked Trinny for a great experience. The bus ride to the training venue was all of 20 minutes and Louise arrived more than 30 hours before her colleagues with facial hair.

Beaulieu Estate, Hampshire

This magnificent property oozed history. French monks settled at Beaulieu and the ruins of their abbey remain, as do magnificent stately homes, glorious rural scenery and a picturesque river. In WW2, the estate was borrowed by the SOE, and the trainee agents were assigned a house according to their destination. The French agents were situated on a bend of the River Beaulieu and a more beautiful spot you could not find. Lectures were more dignified with no Beefy Fruitcake type persons or explosions on the way to work.

When her colleagues arrived, they asked Louise which carriage she sat in on the train up to London. No-one remembered seeing her. She fell into her actress mode and lied with conviction.

One lecture involved a more peaceful form of warfare—propaganda. Agents might be required to perform all sorts of tasks even creating leaflets or newspapers. The content was all important; being to inspire the locals and confound the enemy. The propaganda lecturer was an Englishman, always in a suit and tie, and with an Oxbridge accent. His name was Kim Philby and looking at him and listening to his erudite lectures, you would never guess he was a fifth columnist of the highest degree although his greatest betrayals were yet to come.

SOE agents became experts in sabotage. It might take bombers, tanks and infantrymen to achieve a victory but one SOE agent could divert a train, destroy a power station or blow up an armaments factory all by themselves. They needed to know their onions.

Louise and her fellow trainees were taught about devices and dirty tricks. It could be a compass in a pen top, lemon juice as invisible ink, a cigarette gun which fired a bullet, a shoe with explosives or a silk map which could only be read when urine was deposited thereon; a sort of twist on finding your way home when pissed.

Then there was communication. Every agent needed to learn Morse code and practised until they could dream in Morse! An agent without a radio was handicapped, possibly useless, but a radio with an operator having no Morse skills was worse than useless.

One of the most terrifying lectures was about being captured. If having a weak stomach meant you weren't up to being tortured, you could always end your life quickly and painlessly. They discussed suicide pills containing cyanide.

As their training drew to a close, pressure built. Each new day and night ramped up the stress. Every agent knew to fail this final stage meant all their previous efforts would count for nothing. To fail now was too painful to contemplate.

Finally their training was over and the results announced. In Louise's group, everyone passed. Let joy be unconfined. Louise scored more kisses in an afternoon than in a year. As the only female in her class, her satisfaction was even greater.

Now it was bugger off to some nominated safe house and await your call up. Once it comes, next stop France.

After their final meal, the new SOE agents went to their rooms to pack. As Louise walked from the dining room, an SOE officer caught her eye, gave her a subtle finger wag and her heart sank.

The bastards are letting me down gently. They didn't want to humiliate me in front of the others. I've failed.

She followed the man into a small room; mind you small in a stately home meant large in anyone else's abode.

'Take a seat, Miss Wellesley,' he said. 'I have some good and bad news. Which would you like first?'

Louise struggled to believe how all her hard work had come to nothing. 'The order doesn't matter, sir. Please just tell me.'

'The good news is, as you've been told, you've passed the training and you are now officially an SOE agent awaiting a posting. The bad news is we think you are suited to a unique job, and if you agree to take it, it will mean additional training.' Louise ground her teeth and clenched her fists.

'I see.' She struggled to keep calm. 'May I have the details?'

'Of course,' he smiled. 'In the Lyon region of France, where you've never been before, we have a problem. Our contact, the man who is the link between the SOE agents and London has an unfortunate record. He has lost two SOE agents.'

'Lost, sir?'

'They're missing and our contact doesn't know where they are.'

'Could they have been killed?'

'Or captured or turned, yes of course. And to make matters worse, of late the contact has been sending low grade intelligence.'

'Has *he* been turned, sir?'

'We don't know but if so, we need to know. If he's working for the Germans, sending a third SOE agent to Lyon is sending him to his death. We need an alternative plan.'

Louise wanted to tell the officer to come up with the punchline.

'Being an actress, we thought we could send you as an agent but in disguise. You will not be announced as an SOE agent. The contact will be told nothing. You will arrive and work undercover making your life even more tricky. Every SOE agent has a contact in their area. You would have no-one to help if you're caught. If you volunteer for this job, you, Miss Wellesley, will be unique, the first SOE guinea pig. Now, have you any questions?'

Her list was long. 'Who is this contact who may have been turned?'

'He's a Catholic priest in a small church on the outskirts of Lyon.'

'And how would I approach him?'

'That's the easy part. You simply knock on his door and he will invite you inside.'

Louise decided enough was enough. 'Why would he do that if I've not been announced as an agent? I wish you'd spell it out, sir. This isn't a play where the denouement comes in the final line.'

He smiled. 'I apologise. The priest will invite you inside because of your disguise. We want you to go to Lyon as a Carmelite nun.'

Shock slapped her hard, and for one of the few times in her life, Louise Beatrice Wellesley was stuck for a reply. He continued.

'As part of his duties, the priest attends the Monastery where the nuns live. He says Mass, hears confession and is a regular visitor to where you would live.'

'So my additional training is to learn how to act like a nun?'

'Bless you, Sister, and may the Lord have mercy on your soul.'

Louise sat there, thoughts buzzing, trying to make sense of the news. She reckoned this would be the hardest role she'd ever played.

'Have I understood the job? I must fool the other nuns and the priest into believing I'm a real nun while investigating the priest to see if he's a double agent?'

'Exactly, and while you're there, it would be a great help if you could discover the status of the two main Resistance groups in the area.'

'Oh,' mocked Louise, 'is that all? Would you like me to obtain the Fuhrer's autograph while I'm there?'

The officer let her response wash over him. 'I take it you're interested, Miss Wellesley? I heard you like a challenge.'

She refused to accept but kept asking questions. 'So why am I arriving in Lyon? What is my back story?'

'You're a nun from Paris, have been caught helping the Resistance so have fled south for your own safety.'

Louise responded with scorn. 'That won't work.'

'Oh, you have a better idea?'

Louise pondered. 'If my cover story is I'm helping the Resistance, and the suspect priest has in fact been turned, will he not turn me over to the Germans before I've been able to investigate him?'

The officer deliberately gave a poor back story knowing Louise's reputation for improvisation was first class. 'He would so can you think of another reason why you would flee Paris?'

'Several.'

'Such as?'

She remembered her experiences in Paris as a sleeper with the SIS. 'It could be I upset the Mother Superior and have been banished to the country to learn humility and obedience.'

He nodded. 'It's possible. I like it.'

Louise decided to accept the challenge but wanted answers. 'So if there's no-one expecting me, and no-one there to help me, how do I send any findings?'

'The usual and quickest way is by radio.'

'So I'm dropped into Lyon with a radio?'

'Obviously a radio would be more than helpful, but carrying a radio into a monastery may arouse suspicion.'

'I think specifics are better than sarcasm,' she said without fear.

'I agree and there will be time for planning long before you depart.' More questions remained and her mind was in such a mess. 'Oh, and one more thing,' said the officer. 'Discovering the truth and sending us the detail is obviously essential but if you discover the priest has been turned, you must kill him.'

She paused. 'I understand.'

'So I take it, Miss Wellesley, you wish to volunteer for this role?'

Her mind raced. *It's not a conventional SOE agent role. It's dangerous. What's the difference between a dead SOE agent and a dead nun? I'm certainly not playing Cinderella.*

She forced a smile at the officer. 'Yes sir, I wish to volunteer.'

'Jolly good,' he said which Louise found disappointing. She would have appreciated an enthusiastic thank you plus congratulations. But no, he ploughed ahead as if persuading a young woman to tackle an enormously difficult task was something he did every day.

'But for your acting skills to work, you will need to know how a nun behaves. Is that what an actress calls her preparation?'

Does this man know anything about theatre? 'It is.'

He perused her file. 'Your religion is listed as Church of England.'

'And I'm afraid, the word *lapsed* applies in my case.'

'Never fear; your additional training should fix that.' He smiled. 'We're sending you to a nunnery.' He paused to gauge her reaction. All SOE training officers looked for chinks in the armour of their students. Louise said nothing. He failed to spot a chink.

'It will be both a learning experience and a test. You will study the way the nuns move, pray, chant, sing and whatever nuns do, and thus be convincing for when you land in France.'

'You mentioned a test, sir.'

'We have an anonymous contact in the nunnery. Her brother is an SOE agent and she's been told about your arrival. This nun is there to help should you land in a spot of trouble.'

Louise wondered what sort of trouble she might find in a nunnery.

'And if I fail the test?' she asked.

He smiled. 'Let's remain positive. No-one in the nunnery has ever heard of you apart from the nun I mentioned. Your test is to survive without the other nuns seeing through your disguise.'

Louise took a deep breath. 'It's a different type of acting. I'll need time to study.'

'All the training reports suggest you like a challenge.'

'I do.'

'Then allow me to say gird up your loins, Sister, and give thanks to him and praise his name.'

She tried to smile at his attempt to lift her spirits.

'Thank you, sir.'

'Mind you, there is a benefit if you fail this test.' He paused and she craved the answer. 'You won't be tortured and shot by the Gestapo.'

Chapter 29

SOE HQ, London

Louise went up to London to Baker Street with her gold star certificate. Actually the agents received nothing as a graduation memento. Louise was welcomed by Maurice Buckmaster and Vera Atkins.

'Congratulations, Miss Wellesley, and I believe you're soon to start a religious life.'

'So I'm told, sir.'

'You'll need to see the costumier for your black and white kit.'

Her confusion vanished in the fitting room when shown the habit. 'Try it on, Sister, and may God bless you,' smiled the SOE staff officer.

She changed, stepped out of the "robing room" and did a sort of twirl as if showing off to her family before attending her coming out ball. Her headpiece and veil waved freely and she grinned.

'Charming,' said the officer, 'but I'd lose the society debutant routine before you leave this office.'

She understood and switched to demure.

'Now I suggest a prop, Sister. Many nuns are young but, at the risk of sounding impolite, not all are pretty or, in your case, as beautiful as you, hence the need to make you as inconspicuous as possible.'

Louise blushed. She wasn't only being flattered but rather prepared to remain safe from the enemy. He handed her two pairs of glasses. 'Try these.' She did and they agreed one pair was better.

'Make sure you scrub your face to remove any trace of make-up, including fingers and toes, then tie your hair so tight it hurts, and keep to the rule of never speak unless spoken to. Understood?'

'Understood,' she replied realizing this was no longer a game.

'With male agents I often recommend they add a moustache but being a female, that may do more harm than good.'

She stroked her chin. 'And I'm not old enough to shave,' she said.

He wasn't up for jokes. 'The secret is to fool everyone including your enemies. Now you'll need a cover story for this first visit and something French seems obvious.' She understood. He handed her an envelope. 'This contains your personal details. Memorise them and destroy the document before you leave the building. Any questions?'

'Should I change for my trip to the monastery? It won't be easy travelling all the way to somewhere in Inverness-shire in this habit.'

'You will leave and return to this building in your habit as Sister Claudine, and heading to Scotland will not be necessary. Where you're going is, I think, about six stops on the Underground.'

Louise gasped. 'Here in London?' She thought he was teasing.

'It's the Carmelite Monastery in St John's Square, Notting Hill.'

She set off with her meagre bag of possessions and wondered if her "costume" would give her away. She took no jewellery, watch or perfume, nothing worldly. What about knickers? Should she be wearing some special religious undergarment? Would she be examined? She knew the SOE obsessed with getting every detail spot on but this wasn't war-torn France. Would it matter if she failed this test?

En route she struggled with comments from people.

'Good morning, Sister.'

'Have a good trip, Sister.'

Many people nodded and said, 'Sister', showing respect to a young woman who had given her life to God. Louise wondered if and how this disguise would help once she landed in France.

On the short trip across town from Baker Street to Paddington to Ladbroke Grove, she planned a cover story. The thought kept returning. *Talk about topics you know, not something you invent.*

Carmelite Monastery, Notting Hill, London

The front gates were huge and the facade intimidating. She took a deep breath and rang the bell.

Remember Louise, someone in this order knows who you are.

An older nun opened a small wooden door to one side. 'Yes?'

Louise decided on being a French nun and so spoke in English with a French accent.

'Hello, I am Sister Claudine from the Carmel de Montmartre in Paris. I have come to find my brother, a French officer brought to England from Dunkirk. May I stay for a day while I look for him?'

The small door was fully opened. 'I am Sister Josephine and you are welcome, Sister in the name of Christ.'

Louise stepped inside and waited. She concentrated. *How does a young nun behave? Do I make eye contact? Do I bow? Do I walk beside or behind another nun? Do older nuns receive more respect?*

'I will tell the Sisters you are here. Sadly our Mother Superior is unwell and we are all praying for her. Come this way.'

Louise, the pretend nun, followed Josephine, the real nun inside. They passed rooms where nuns were busy with craft work. The guiding nun kept a steady pace and pointed at places. 'Chapel,' she said, 'Mass 6am.' She spoke quietly and what impressed Louise was the lack of sound. In this sanctuary of silence the sounds of London were non-existent. No-one spoke.

They stopped outside a door. The nun knocked, a voice spoke quietly, 'Enter,' and they did.

Louise was introduced to Sister Regina, the nun in charge, and the situation was explained. 'You are most welcome, Sister. We are at a loss with Mother Superior unwell. There will be prayers in the chapel in ten minutes. Sister Josephine will show you to our guest room.'

It was like nothing Louise had slept in since joining the SOE. It was basic, plain and spotless, a small crucifix being the only decoration. She looked for anything to give her a clue about a nun's routine. Nothing. With her watch at home in Maida Vale she had to guess when prayers began. Hearing soft footsteps outside her door, she opened it. Several nuns walked past in silence. Louise assumed they were heading to the chapel. No-one looked at her or spoke. Louise stepped out, closed her door and followed.

She wanted to be the last to enter. Once in the chapel, she kept her head low but watched. Once the SOE told her about this additional training, she began to rehearse genuflecting, bowing and making the sign of the cross. Now, she copied those in front with as little movement as possible. In the back row, her lips moved as she mimed the liturgy about which she knew nothing. She mimicked those in front.

The key word appeared to be silence. It was easy to pray silently. Louise wondered if being a nun in France would be as easy. There was no word on the Mother Superior's health.

At the dinner table, her arrival was announced without comment from any of the nuns. She knew about the vows of chastity and poverty but for an actress, a vow of silence seemed impossible.

Come to think of it, she thought, *no money and no sex would be off the menu too.*

She tried to learn by observation. There was no chance she would put on weight should she decide to take up holy orders.

After the "slap up meal" of thin soup, and bread washed down with water, the others stood, placed their wooden bowl, cup and spoon on a space beside the sink and left the dining room. *Am I on washing-up duty?* With no-one speaking, Louise followed. Each nun opened the door to their room and disappeared. Louise did likewise.

Now what? She pondered her situation. She'd been told Mass was at 0600 hours but until then, prayer and contemplation seemed to be the sole or soul activity. The only time she would remove her habit was to sleep. She wanted to relieve herself and carefully opened her door. Nothing. No movement or sound was seen or heard.

She crept along the corridor hoping to find a door marked *Ladies*. She stifled a giggle at the thought of finding a door marked *Gents*.

A door opened and a young nun stared at her. Louise mimed the word *Lavatory*. The nun remained frozen. Louise whispered, 'Toilet'.

The nun shook her head. Louise slipped into actress mode, bent a little and made a face of discomfort. She pointed to her abdomen. The nun's face showed signs of life. In perfect French she said, 'Oh, oui.'

'Yes,' whispered Louise, 'wee.'

The nun set off walking silently beckoning Louise to follow. Along the corridor they went, down a flight of stairs and, in serious darkness, stopped at a door. The nun indicated with her head.

Louise smiled, mouthed her thanks, and entered. *My kingdom for a candle,* she thought finding a cubicle and wondered if alongside their vows of chastity and poverty sat another of bladder control.

She found her way back to the guest room, sat on her bed and the pangs of boredom crept up her spine. *Once it hits my brain, I'm dead.* She forget boredom when a soft tap sounded. Rather than call, or rather whisper, a "come in", she opened the door and found her guiding nun with a face pleading to be let in.

Louise did what felt natural but wondered if this was breaking rule number 27. The nun was young, tender and afraid. In perfect French, she said, 'Pardon Sister, but do you speak French?'

'Oui.'

The young nun's face changed to one of joy. 'Are you from Paris?' Louise nodded. 'Tell me please, has the city been bombed? My family is in the Boulevard de Strasbourg in the 10th arrondissement.'

Confident, Louise replied. 'No, sister, Paris has not been bombed. The Germans occupy the city and while they do so, it is most unlikely the Luftwaffe will do to Paris what they are doing to London.'

The young nun moved in and hugged Louise such was her happiness. The door opened and Sister Regina stood there glaring. 'Out!' she hissed and the young nun, now terrified, fled.

Louise tried to explain but was stopped. 'How dare you entice a novitiate to break her vows. You must leave immediately.'

Before either could say another word, a chilling scream sounded somewhere within the Monastery. Sister Indignant left in a hurry. Louise moved to her open door and observed. Nuns came from their rooms and hurried towards whatever caused the scream.

Louise shrugged and packed her bag. The young nun appeared. 'Mother Superior has died. I must leave and return to France.'

The teenager pleaded. Her voice, her face, her body language all begged. Louise knew it was wrong but agreed. 'Grab your belongings,' she said and the nun disappeared.

As the Monastery suffered overwhelming grief, Louise and the young nun walked out of the building and into the streets of London.

Not sure what to do with her rescued nun, Louise took her on the Tube back into central London. She worried Mr Buckmaster would be displeased with her exit and rescuing a stray waif. Louise would have to explain her new friend to SOE but wondered what to say. There was no need. When they reached Paddington, the young nun stood.

'Merci Sister, I will leave now as I know where the French Embassy is located in London. Merci.'

She squeezed Louise's hand and disappeared into the crowd. Louise was hardly going to restrain her and wondered if she would even mention her fellow traveller when she returned to Baker Street.

Entering the SOE HQ, she caught everyone's attention dressed as a nun and made her way to F Section. Maurice Buckmaster was advised of her arrival and invited her to his office.

'That was a short visit, Miss Wellesley. What did you learn?'

'Not much at all, sir, but the Mother Superior died causing widespread distress and I was compelled to leave in order to rescue a young nun who desperately wanted to escape.'

'Are you sure of your facts?'

Louise wanted to be sick. 'The young nun was certainly distressed.'

'And she did as requested.' Louise froze. 'The novice was working for us and did what she did to test your abilities in a nunnery.'

Louise swore silently in mime and misery.

'Were you told there was a nun in the monastery who knew you?'

Louise wanted to vomit. To pass all those SOE tests and then fail at the death was devastating. She nodded. 'I failed a simple test.'

'Never believe someone is who they claim to be. You are a pretend nun who can handle explosives, kill someone with your bare hands and survive in the wild. The pretend nun you rescued fooled you. There will be more clever, more devious people in France. Trust may sometimes be your best hope but it can easily bring you undone.' She understood. He wanted her on the SOE team and particularly for this task.

'I apologise, sir.'

'Don't, but learn the lesson. Now Miss Wellesley, you need to collect all your magic toys, papers, clothes and what not, and settle in the safe house. Your next stop is a monastery in Lyon in the south of France.'

Her relief was real. 'I'm sorry, sir. Does this mean I've passed?'

'Indeed and you are now an active agent of the SOE, F Section.'

Louise's face came alive. 'When will I leave, sir?'

'That depends on the weather, the war and the waves. It could be tonight, tomorrow or next week but it will be soon.' He stood holding out his hand. 'Good luck, Miss Wellesley.'

'Thank you,' she said and went to collect her many tricks of the trade including the all-important suicide pill. Some agents placed it in a button of their jacket or coat. Nuns and buttons didn't go together, so, rather inventively, her poisonous pill was placed in her rosary beads, the one with a speck of red. Damn clever these SOE boffins.

She set off for her final port of call before a certain parachute jump.

Chapter 30

St John the Baptist Cathedral, Lyon France

'Simply magnificent,' said tourist and worshipper alike when they first set eyes on the Cathédrale Saint-Jean-Baptiste de Lyon. It had to be eye-catching as hundreds of years ago those in charge employed the best builders, sculptors, glassmakers and stonemasons who took centuries to build it right.

At its rear, the cathedral nudges the Saone River. At its front, its three main doors open to a wide cobblestone area surrounded by many buildings. It claims to be the oldest church in France. It has an astrological clock, two organs, a bell tower with six bells and a ceiling where ornate is far too weak a word.

At the time when Louise Wellesley, a.k.a. Plum, a.k.a. Sister Claudine was about to make her first visit to the Cathedral, it was playing host to large crowds with many conservative Catholics supporting Marshal Pétain and his puppet regime.

When the Vichy Government took over the south of France, the heavy lifting at the cathedral was down to a new and enthusiastic bishop, Marc Vaine. In the seminary he was known as Weather as his moods and demands changed on a whim. He even looked like a tyrant. He gave the clergy a hard time insisting on canon law being followed to the letter. He kept busy constantly saying Mass and hearing confessions. Many in the pews loved him. He wasn't afraid of travel and was often out and about visiting outlying churches.

One of his biggest fans was a young man, Jean Alpen, who loved the country of his birth and joined the Free France Resistance cell recently formed in Lyon and based in the surrounding forest. Jean slipped into Lyon from time to time.

'Good morning, Your Excellency,' he called to Bishop Vaine after Sunday morning Mass. He approached the cleric to kiss his ring hand and was shocked to be hustled aside.

'You fool, are you mad? In here.'

The young man thought something terrible must have happened. 'Excellency?' he blurted.

'The Germans are everywhere; the Gestapo, SS and even the Wehrmacht. Just because Marshall Pétain is in charge here in Lyon, doesn't mean you won't be arrested, tortured and even killed.'

Jean recovered but worried. 'But I need to come to Mass and confession, Excellency, and I want it to be with you.'

'Thank you, Jean, but it will be safer in your village. In Lyon you will be seen. There are French men and women who happily betray their own people. Do you understand?' He nodded. 'Are you all right? Have you joined the Resistance like you said?'

'I have, Excellency but I still live with my parents in the village.'

'And do you have everything you need?

Jean settled. 'Thank you, Excellency. We always need more arms and better intelligence but for now we are okay.'

'Go home and if you want any help, ask Father Flory in your village, not here. I know he is a good man helping Jews find refuge, and downed British pilots escape to Spain.'

'He is a good man, Excellency, and thank you.'

'If you think Father Flory needs help, come and tell me but do it in secret. Understand?'

'Yes Excellency.'

'Go and God bless.'

Jean slipped away keeping a keen eye out for enemies in both uniform and civvies.

There were two Resistance cells in this part of France. Jean belonged to the one where men hated the Nazis, wanted a free France and would join any army led by General Charles de Gaulle, currently decamped in London.

The other Resistance cell boasted a membership of Communists. They too hated the Nazis and they too wanted France free but only so it could become Communist. Their leader, Raoul Fin, was twice mad being both angry and insane. His hair and whiskers lived a life of their own. His breath often caught fire, and his brutality towards Germans and traitors spawned tales of terror. He treated dogs badly and women worse.

He hated the fact the other Resistance cell in the forest outside of Lyon seemingly captured the ear of the SOE in London receiving many RAF parcels with goodies.

'We need more guns, ammunition and intelligence, Raoul,' his men would say.

He exploded. 'Don't tell me what I already know.'

'Can we send a message to London?'

'How? With what? Those other bastards have the only radio in these parts and even if we could contact London, they'd still favour their favourites, the de Gaulle arse lickers.'

'Can we ask de Gaulle's men for some of their guns?'

Raoul exploded. 'I never ask,' he screamed, 'I take.'

The men called his bluff. 'Okay, when?'

He stared and glared at them. He hated backing down but knew civil war between Resistance groups would aid the Germans. 'Tonight we will find them and try to reason.'

'They hate us. They will never reason with Communists.'

'If they will not help us and give us access to their radio then we will encourage them to change their mind.'

Smoke seeped from his curly locks. His men worried.

SOE safe house, London

The training never stopped. Those agents waiting for the tap on the shoulder kept reading reports on the Resistance, identifying planes, tanks and insignia while polishing their French. Summer was a comin' in and the French people were in strife. Jews were found and sent to labour or concentration camps. The need for a stronger Resistance in the cities and rural France was never greater.

Louise went over her notes noting her main task. Is the SOE contact, Father Flory, the real thing? If she could investigate the two main Lyon Resistance groups, that would be a bonus. Mind you, if she discovered Father Flory was the real thing, she could reveal herself to him and have him help her investigate the Resistance groups. He might have that information already. But whatever she discovered needed to be relayed to London. Fine, but how? Where are those missing SOE agents and their radio?

She studied photos of nuns and read about Catholic dogma. The days and nights dragged and she longed for action.

The waiting depressed her but more so the lack of contact with her family. Not having spoken to her mother by phone or enquired about her brother Edmund brought on sadness, ramping up her depression. Her life became hectic, relentless, and communication free. Of course having signed the Official Secrets Act, whatever she said must be a lie. She penned a short note to both mother and brother using ENSA touring as her excuse. If only it were true.

She fought to remove the thought she would go to France, be captured, tortured and executed and her family would never know. Or they would be told and the shock and sadness would be devastating. Thinking such thoughts brought on a pain in her chest.

A forest near Lyon, France

Raoul and his communist Resistance fighters moved silently through the darkened forest. They needed to find the Free French Resistance fighters and make some sort of pact. They knew the general area where their fellow Resistance fighters might be and Raoul sent two of his men, Barrack and Nic forward. They found the Free French cell and ran back to Raoul and his men.

'Their camp is just over the next ridge. They're resting and we couldn't see any sentries.'

'Spread out,' said Raoul.

'We're not going to shoot, Raoul,' worried one of his lieutenants. 'You said we were here to talk.'

He raged inside. 'Stop telling me what to do. We'll spread out along the ridge. I'll call to them and if they agree to talk, we'll move in but always have your guns ready.'

Most of his men worried. Raoul the firecracker could explode at the slightest provocation. The Communists crept forward knowing this could go badly wrong. If they were mistaken for Germans, the other cell would open fire on them.

The line of Communists spread out on the top of the ridge. They peered down into the darkness. A hundred metres below was the Resistance camp. A single campfire beneath a large tree cooked a meal.

Raoul checked his men, saw they were in position then stood beside a tree, his position of cover, and prepared to yell.

Before a sound left his lips, the night sky filled with light as shells rained down. The fighters by the campfires panicked as mortars exploded. Terrified Free French fighters ran for their lives, fleeing into the forest. Raoul and his communist mates were stunned. They weren't firing. Who was firing? These had to be German mortars.

It was a German attack. Was it luck? Surely in such a vast forest, finding a small band of local militia would be tricky. Finding both cells meant somebody must have tipped off the Bosch. It couldn't be luck. Discussion and retribution would follow but for now, every Resistance fighter fled.

SOE safe house, London

Louise waited. She watched as, on a regular basis, an SOE official would arrive and collect an agent or two. The ones remaining would offer best wishes, back slaps and hugs. Would the departing agent survive? Was this a final, a permanent goodbye? Some SOE agents disappeared and were never heard from again.

Then it was Louise's turn. She was more surprised than nervous. All the remaining agents were men and each kissed her. A couple of gents, no, more than a couple, once wanted to do more than kiss her but tried nothing during the long nights of training. The fear of being rejected was real but after the parachute training, so too was the memory of Beefy Fruitcake with his broken and bloody nose.

She travelled with two other agents and a car drove her to RAF Newmarket. The weather was good for a Channel crossing. She triple checked her kit. She was travelling in mufti with her stage costume folded and crammed in her bag. The joke was if her habit flew up, a nun's underwear would be exposed and "we simply can't allow that to happen, Sister". The real reason being the habit could indeed fly up, block her face and even entangle her parachute. No, it was jump, land safely, get dressed, and then carry on with the business.

With a handshake from the SOE official, and a helping hand into the plane, she and two fellow agents made themselves comfortable, and she left the land of her birth.

The crew member asked, rather yelled, if the agents were all right. Each gave a thumbs up sign. It was noisy and chatting pointless. They flew low over the Channel and as they approached France, dropped below 400 feet to avoid German radar. The darkness dominated.

Louise didn't think she was nervous because, being terrified, gave little time for nerves. She was the first to depart.

The crewman called. 'Oi, oi!' She struggled to hear him. He pointed. 'Over here.'

She moved to the drop place. Her chute strap was clipped onto a metal rod in the roof of the fuselage. The crewman tapped her on the shoulder and when she looked at him, he pointed. She looked up. He tugged her strap a couple of times to assure her the chute was locked and ready for action. She nodded.

A hole appeared in the floor and the darkness below stared back at her. She sat and waited. A red light shone.

'Stand by!' yelled the crewman and the sound of the plane grew even louder. Louise's legs dangled below the fuselage and were smacked by the wind.

She decided there wasn't time to pray and she was right. The RAF was like a good executioner. Pop the hangman's rope in position, slip the bag over the head, and don't muck about. The red light became green, the crewman shouted and dropped his hand, and Louise disappeared into the French night.

Chapter 31

A field, somewhere in France

Being so dark it was tricky to see the ground. As Louise's jump lasted all of 16 seconds, there was little time for sight-seeing as she plunged out of the black sky. *I think that's the ground.* Thud. *Yes, it's the ground all right. No injuries. Great.*

She followed her training and dragged in her chute, removed the small shovel fastened to her leg and found soft ground. The chute disappeared. She checked her possessions and thought about her instructions.

'We'll put you down near Oullins, south of Lyon. Change into your habit and have your shoes handy but start walking in your boots. You'll land about an hour before dawn. Use the darkness to travel but only enter the village when it's daylight. Head north.'

Getting changed in a field in France was a first. She wore appropriate clothing and it was now on show—albeit to a herd of cows—as she struggled to add her nun's habit. All she wore or carried was essential for her role as a nun doubling as an SOE agent. It was time to move. Break a leg, Plum.

She checked her small compass hidden in a pen, faced north, and set off. Would she be spotted? Local cows clocked her but what about local farmers, Germans, or Resistance fighters? Was being a nun an advantage? Were Gestapo agents alive and well in this part of France?

She reached a fence and searched for a gate. Nothing. Dawn peeped over the horizon. Beyond the fence she thought she could see a road, more a track. Getting over the fence was easy when dressed in trousers. Wearing the flowing robes of a Carmelite nun's habit proved tricky. She tossed her bag over the fence and climbed. She heard a sound and turned. A bull trotted in her direction. Louise cleared the fence with ease but in jumping, her spectacles fell off. She spoke a word definitely not part of a nun's vocabulary then spent minutes patting the grass before eventually finding the specs.

The track was more east and west but it made walking so much easier than trying to negotiate wet fields.

After a mile or so, the sun was putting on its hat. She exchanged her boots for her shoes and lost her boots. Totally and appropriately dressed, she set off. The trees on her left thinned then were no more and in the clearing stood an old farmhouse. Smoke lazily drifted from a chimney. She pondered asking directions. "Pardon, but am I on the right road for Lyon?" seemed the best question. Walking miles in the wrong direction didn't appeal.

A door opened and a woman came out tossing grain as chickens scurried toward her and pecked.

It was now or never. The SOE agent in disguise began her adventure in a foreign country. 'Bonjour, Madam,' called Louise waving and thinking a married state was the better assumption. To say the woman was surprised would be an understatement. She was stunned. There were rarely any humans out walking on this rural road at any time let alone so early and certainly not dressed as a bride of Christ.

What the hell is a nun doing here?

'Bonjour, Sister,' replied the woman. 'Are you lost?'

Louise went for the honesty routine. 'Oui. I am going to the church of St Nicholas in the village of Cachés.'

'You are going in the wrong direction, Sister. My husband is going to market soon. He can take you. Come and have some breakfast.'

Louise, if pressed, would scoff at superstition but endured a tweak of pain wondering if she'd used up all her luck in the first hour since touching down in occupied France.

The breakfast was superb. There's nothing like ham and eggs which have travelled the short distance from farm yard to kitchen table.

Louise saw a chance to test her tale and discover a bit of local knowledge during her meal and trip into Cachés.

'I am joining the order of nuns at Carmel de Lyon,' she said in as rustic a French accent as possible. 'But I have been told to report to Father Flory at St Nicholas first. He is to be my parish priest.'

The farmer and his wife knew of the priest but not in great detail. Their church was in another village.

Her free taxi was ready. The horse kept a steady pace with Louise enjoying the ride. The cart entered the village and locals became onlookers as the nun on a cart moved along the street to the church.

''Merci, Monsieur,' she said climbing down in as dignified a way as possible. She gave a small bow, waved as the farmer moved off then stared at the parish church of St Nicholas. Here lived the priest Father Felix Flory who, according to the SOE in Baker Street, London, is either an ordinary but active SOE contact or a turncoat.

Time to find out, Louise, she thought and walked to the church door with no idea how to discover the truth. How about, *Good morning, Father, are you a double agent?*

A forest near Lyon

The free French Resistance cell members were lucky. In that night attack by the Germans, one man was killed and three injured. Fleeing into their neck of the woods, literally, helped them escape. But how did the Germans know where they were? It's a bloody big forest and it was the middle of the night.

And having the Communist Resistance cell almost caught in the same attack, meant both cells were sprung together in this vast space. What, by chance? Hardly. Someone betrayed both Resistance groups.

Two of the youngest members of the Free French cell, Jean and friend Remi, arrived from their homes in Lyon. They were shocked to see the wounded men and learn of the attack.

'But how could the Germans find you?' asked Jean ever so glad he wasn't there at the time of the attack.

'Is this why you've moved to a new location?' asked Remi.

The older Resistance fighters questioned them, explaining the cost of being a traitor. As both young men were absent during the attack, they were now under suspicion. Jean and Remi looked at one another. They realised their situation, and were angry or scared or both.

St Nicholas Church, near Lyon

'Who is knocking at this hour?' growled Father Flory as he strode to the door. He was only just out of bed after a late night and having drunk too much wine. He threw open the door.

As she waited, Louise repeated a new religious mantra in her head. *Speak rural French. Speak rural French.* 'Bonjour, Father. I'm Sister Claudine. I hope you were expecting me and I'm sorry I'm late.'

If any acting or drama judges were watching, Louise would have scored highly. Basil Dean and Leslie Henson would have applauded. She convinced the priest with both her script and delivery.

He flustered. *Did I forget this sister?* No, he'd never heard of her.

'Oh, Bonjour, Sister.' He stepped back. 'Welcome.' She entered and waited for him to close the door. 'Come this way.'

He headed off to the priest's house and she followed. They reached the kitchen. She kept observing although surreptitiously, asking herself questions.

Is there a radio on the kitchen table? Are there are maps or code books tucked into bibles or newspapers? What does an SOE contact need for his work? And how can I discover if he's contacting Berlin and not Baker Street?

'I am to join the sisters at Carmel de Lyon, Father. I've been sent by the sisters in Venice.'

'Of course, that explains it,' he grunted. 'One of their vows is to never communicate with anyone, ever.'

An old woman dressed entirely in black came into the kitchen. 'Madame Bardin, this is Sister Claudine. She is joining the sisters in Lyon. Some breakfast if you please.'

'Bonjour, Sister,' said the housekeeper busy at the stove.

'Bonjour, Madame.'

Two breakfasts on my first day, thought Louise. *I can't say no.*

'I'll take you into Lyon, Sister. It is my turn to say Mass today.'

'Merci, Father,' said Louise trying to create a character of humility.

'I am your parish priest although not for much longer.' Louise was mystified and Madame Bardin tut-tutted as she cracked eggs in a pan.

'We have a new bishop at the Cathedral and he is a man who likes to be all things to all men, including nuns. He has chosen to say Mass on certain days at your monastery pushing me aside. Now I suggest you eat up, Sister, because once you enter the Lyon monastery, you'll not have a breakfast like this ever again.'

Louise struggled to eat a second big breakfast so soon after a first but managed. She thanked the housekeeper then responded when Father

Flory called. They headed back through the church. He went to open the door but stopped when Louise spoke.

'Father, before I join my new monastery, I need to confess.'

He sighed, despairing. 'Oh do you have to, Sister?'

'I want to join my new Sisters in a state of Grace, Father.'

He grumbled some more and headed into the church. She followed. He indicated the door and they entered the confessional. Her heart was racing. She was a pretend nun trying anything to discover the political status of a current or former SOE person. She was an agent and he a contact but for which side was he working?

She'd learnt her lines and hoped they were right. 'Bless me, Father for I have sinned. It's been a week since my last confession.'

He mumbled asking for her transgressions. He invariably found a confession from a nun to be tedious. Nuns saw faults in their character which no-one else could see let alone consider a sin.

He set her penance and Louise accepted with gratitude. He was up and out of the confessional. She was slow to respond.

'Come on, Sister, it's a good walk to the Monastery and I can't be late for Mass.'

She came into the church and decided to be proactive. 'Before we go, Father, might I ask if there are any dangers I should be aware of here in Lyon?' He studied her, wondering what she meant, and why a nun about to enter an enclosed order would ask such a question. She worried. *Have I blown my cover already?*

'I come from an area where war was far away, Father, and do not wish to say or do anything to upset my fellow sisters or my priest.'

He relaxed. 'For you, the war is still far away. You're lucky being in an enclosed order. Now please, let's go.'

He headed to the front door of the church and she followed. He opened the door and this time groaned. There stood a young man with hand raised ready to knock.

'Bonjour, Father,' said Jean Alpen, the young local lad now a Resistance fighter. 'Have you time to hear my confession?'

The priest found Jean to be a pain in the neck. His enthusiasm for the faith was to be encouraged but too much passion for God is, well, too much. Jean loved to confess. 'I'm sorry, Jean, I'm taking our new Sister Claudine to the Monastery. You will have to wait.'

'Bonjour, Sister,' said the young man. 'Welcome to Lyon. Have you met our wonderful new Bishop Vaine?'

'No,' replied Louise keeping her eye contact to a bare minimum.

'You will love him.' He corrected himself. 'I mean you will love his passion for the work of the Church.'

Louise almost smiled. So far she'd met a cleric and two parishioners and learnt next to nothing related to her SOE tasks.

'I'll be back at 12, Jean. Try not to commit any sins before then.'

Carmelite Monastery, Lyon

Father Flory carried Louise's solitary bag as they walked into the city. From the priest's house it was about half an hour to either the cathedral or the monastery. Both were within easy walking distance of one another. Louise kept her head down and her headpiece covering her face. Almost everyone in the street greeted the priest.

'Bonjour, Father,' was spoken dozens of times.

He would mostly nod or even raise a hand in greeting. Louise kept slightly behind him avoiding eye contact.

They reached the monastery. 'Here we are, Sister.' He rang the bell. You will find you are somewhat of an exception here. I think only one of the sisters is under 50, or it might be one under 70.' An elderly nun opened the grand door.

'Bonjour, Father.'

Flory shunned small talk. 'This is Sister Claudine. She has come from the sisters in Venice. As usual, they sent nothing in writing.'

He handed Louise her bag and headed off to the chapel. The elderly nun smiled. 'Welcome Sister. I am Sister Angelica. Come and meet the Reverend Mother.'

The elderly nun walked slowly into the heart of the building and Louise followed. She worried she'd not said a word but reckoned silence was her best strategy.

I am young, have only recently taken holy orders and am humble and shy to boot. And I only speak when spoken to.

They walked down a long corridor with a polished floor on which you could eat your meal; not that food was of any interest to Louise at the moment. They passed another nun who said nothing. They didn't stop and Louise relaxed in her no-speaking role.

They reached a door. Sister Angelica knocked, paused and entered.

Louise followed the nun into the office of the Mother Superior. She sat behind a desk upon which lay absolutely nothing; not a piece of paper, pen, pencil, book, religious artefact, nothing. Another older nun, they were all ancient, stood behind and to the right of the Mother Superior.

'Bonjour, Mother,' said Sister Angelica. We have a new arrival. This is Sister Claudette.'

Louise went to correct the mistake but stopped, thinking her first words should not be remotely harsh or critical. As it turned out, her incorrect name was of little consequence.

The Mother Superior gave the warmest of smiles giving her many wrinkles a solid workout. 'Bonjour, Sister. How are you today?'

Louise struggled. The question suggested they knew each other and here was an enquiry about the wellbeing of a friend. Louise spoke in as demure a voice as possible. 'Bonjour, Reverend Mother.'

'Have you finished your duties this morning?'

New confusion set in. *What duties? I've just arrived.*

Before she could speak, the older nun behind bent and whispered in the ear of the Mother Superior who again gave a wonderful smile.

'Oh, you're new. Why didn't you say? Welcome Sister ...' She turned to the nun behind her. 'What did she say her name was?' There was another whisper in Mother's ear. She smiled. 'Good morning, Sister Claudette. What did you think of this morning's Mass?'

Louise felt a hand on her arm and Sister Angelica whispered. 'Come this way, Sister Claudette.'

Louise struggled to remember her lines. *I've forgotten my stage directions.* She bobbed to the Mother Superior and walked out with her housemistress Sister. In the corridor, boasting the Best Polished Wooden Floor Award, Sister Angelica explained.

'Mother's not been herself of late. We think the stress of war has made her a little forgetful, and we would like you to pray for her.'

'Of course,' said Louise. 'I will pray for her every day.'

Sister Angelica smiled. 'Thank you, Sister. Please follow me.'

They set off and Louise remembered her brief stay in Notting Hill when she wanted the lavatory. The same request returned.

I'm sure my room's fine but could we first find the Ladies?

Chapter 32

Carmelite Monastery, Lyon

Having been shown to her quarters, Louise placed her bible and rosary beads on her bedside table and explored the room. The search took all of eleven seconds. On the journey to her room, Louise spied the chapel, the dining room and lavatory. As that covered the Mass, meals and motions, she now needed to either remain in her room, meditate and go mad, or go exploring. She chose the Columbus option.

If I'm caught, what is the worst that can happen? I'll just say I'm new and seeking the chapel.

She left her room and found the lavatory. She exited, saw no-one, headed along the corridor and turned left. Reaching a door with no signage, she opened it revealing a spacious rear garden. With confidence growing, she set off exploring. Lawn dominated with shrubs and trees against the high garden walls. Walking across the lawn would expose her to anyone looking out of the many windows. She headed towards flower beds and then into the mini forest. Finding a garden bench in the shade, she sat trying to appear pensive, even in a prayer like state while observing the buildings, the garden and whatever else the monastery provided. Her training taught her how to evaluate a building, remember its entry and exit points, places to hide, etc. Apart from two chatty birds, deep in conversation, not a sound was heard meaning her fright was sharp when she heard a voice.

'Bonjour, Sister.'

Louise turned to see another nun holding a book and sitting on the ground beneath a tree a few metres away. *This must be the only nun under 70*, thought Louise. She approached Louise who stood.

'Oh, bonjour, Sister. I did not see you there.'

'May I sit?'

'Of course,' said Louise and both sat on the garden bench.

'You're new. Did I see you arrive before with Father Flory?'

'Yes.'

'I'm Sister Gabrielle.'

'Sister Claudine,' said Louise finding it difficult to not behave like a young woman on Civvy Street wanting to chat and be social.

'Have you settled in?'

'I have, thank you.' They paused and observed one another. Louise guessed the nun was about 30 with natural beauty and, like her in terms of age, they were the odd ones out. 'Forgive me, Sister, but should we be talking like this?'

She laughed. 'I am welcoming you to the Monastery; surely such behaviour is acceptable.'

'Of course it is, Sister, and thank you.'

'And have you met our Mother Superior?' Louise hesitated. 'Your hesitation tells me you have.'

'She struck me as old and forgetful, needing to be prompted.'

'Doctor Alzheimer would confirm she has dementia and the older nuns have told Father Flory who I assume has told Bishop Vaine. She is like Marshall Pertain, a leader in name only. Because of the war, our religious leaders have chosen to wait and address Mother's condition once hostilities cease.'

Louise didn't know what to expect inside the monastery but a young, outspoken and erudite nun was not high on her list of expectations. 'You seem knowledgeable in these matters, Sister.'

'I know a little of church politics and even more of medicine. Before taking holy orders, I trained as a doctor.'

Louise wasn't sure how to respond. 'You must have experienced a strong calling to forsake your career in helping the sick.'

'Not really. I was in love with one of my university lecturers but he dumped me in favour of an heiress with large breasts. I was penniless with small breasts so unrequited love pushed me to become a nun.'

Louise's shock disappeared when she saw her colleague grinning. Her eyebrows lifted and fell. The shared grin became a shared chuckle, and Louise felt warm inside for the first time since jumping out a plane only a few hours ago. The older nun continued.

'I'm having trouble picking your accent, Sister. I'm from Paris but you, I'm not so sure.'

Louise encountered this question before when working for the SIS and during her training earlier this year. Then in Paris, when performing at the Folies Bergère, she was arrested on the false charge of murdering a playboy in Montmartre. A senior Parisian policeman asked Louise about her accent. "You say you are from Marseille, Mademoiselle but I cannot place your accent."

Louise gave the same answer to her new friend. 'I was educated by Italian nuns and their French was always a little off key.'

'I would say more than a little,' and they both smiled. 'So what can I tell you about your new life here at Lyon?'

'If the Mother Superior is unwell, how does the order operate?'

'The culture is longstanding, Sister. Continuity is all. The older nuns guide our leader, nobody comments, and life goes on.'

'And what do Father Flory and Bishop Vaine say about this?'

Sister Gabrielle mused. 'I think I will allow you to discover their response for yourself. Have you met His Excellency?'

'No.'

'We could visit the Cathedral if you have nothing better to do.'

Louise was confused. 'I'm sorry, Sister, but do you mean we could go into Lyon?'

'How else could we visit the Cathedral?'

'But we are enclosed, required to live within the Monastery.'

'True but there are exceptions for health and matters spiritual. Besides, the world is at war, and our bishop is a practical priest who likes all religious to serve the people.'

'Do I need permission?'

'Normally, yes, but if your reason for going involves Bishop Vaine, then you will have used the magic words; open sesame.'

'He must be important.'

'He is both important and unique. Some priests work assiduously to move closer to God. Some, like His Excellency, work assiduously to move closer to the Holy See. I do believe Bishop Vaine has Archbishop and Cardinal written on his CV in pencil.'

'Not Pope?'

Gabrielle laughed gently. Louise liked her and again worried she was falling on her feet. She wondered how being stuck in a monastery would allow her to examine the parish priest. Now, the combination of a senile Mother Superior and an unorthodox young nun may have given her an unlikely helping hand.'

Sister Gabrielle stood. 'Well we've missed Mass with Father Flory so going to Confession in the Cathedral sounds like a good fallback position. Shall we go?'

Louise liked the suggestion and they walked into the monastery. 'I'll meet you at the front door,' said Gabrielle and went to her room.

St John the Baptist Cathedral, Lyon France

Two nuns walking together attracted no attention. As they headed to the cathedral, Louise kept her head down but her eyes peeled.

Do I need to become familiar with these streets? What am I looking for? If I need to escape, where are the best hiding places?

They approached the building and Louise tried to hide her reaction. The striking facade grabbed her attention. She was a nun, not a tourist. But she failed the nun test when they entered the cathedral. Louise drew a sharp breath. Stunning would be one word to describe this house of God. The sheer size of the building with its massive stained glass windows, soaring ceiling, organs—plural, and unusual objects such as a giant horizontal clock were more than impressive. Despite a world war, people came and went. Tourists flocked to this cathedral in peace times and even now, people lit candles, prayed or simply stared in awe at the splendor of the structure.

'I'll show you around,' said Sister Gabrielle and led Louise towards the altar. They stopped at the front, knelt and crossed themselves. They were still kneeling when a voice caught their attention.

'Sisters, to what do we owe this visit?'

The nuns stood and turned to Bishop Marc Vaine. He was tall, slim, and almost handsome with piercing brown eyes and hair refusing to lie straight or go grey. Sister Gabrielle knelt and took his hand. He enjoyed having lesser mortals treat him with respect.

'Your Excellency,' she said then arose and indicated Louise. 'Today a new nun arrived at our monastery. May I present Sister Claudine?'

Louise reckoned copying the routine she just witnessed was the thing to do. The Bishop extended his hand.

She too knelt and held his hand but avoided eye contact and, with head bowed said, 'Your Excellency.'

He showed a genuine interest. 'Welcome, Sister. It is always pleasing to see a new face and especially one so young. Where did you train and when did you take your vows?'

Louise panicked internally. For weeks she rehearsed her back story. It was made deliberately vague or difficult to check but one slip and she could be exposed. She repeated her Italian nun situation story and gave the name of a Bishop in that region who recently died.

His Excellency seemed to accept her answer then went on another search. 'And are you like your fellow Sister, qualified in another field? You do know Sister Gabrielle is a medical doctor?'

'I do Your Excellency but alas I have no career other than my calling as a Carmelite nun.'

The pressure mounted. The questions probed her story. Before the next one arrived, two young men approached.

'Your Excellency,' said the enthusiastic Resistance fighter Jean Alpen. The spotlight on the nuns shifted. Jean made a show of greeting "his" bishop. 'Your Excellency, may I introduce my friend Remi. He has been fighting for France and not been to confession for some time.'

'Your Excellency,' said Remi and his only two words had a familiar accent. In speaking French, Remi sounded like Louise Wellesley.

'It would be a great honour, Excellency,' said Jean, 'if you could hear my friend's confession, especially as we are often away and in danger in this part of France.'

Louise glanced at the Bishop's face. Jean's confusion grew from the Bishop's lack of response. Hearing the words, "fighting for France" made Louise wonder if these young men were members of the Free French Resistance. *Or are they Communists?*

'Certainly,' said the Bishop. 'Come back in an hour.'

The young men departed and the Bishop addressed the nuns. 'I could do with some help on a special project, Sisters. If your Mother Superior asks, which is most unlikely, tell her you are acting under my orders. Report to me here tomorrow morning after Mass.'

'Yes, Excellency,' said Sister Gabrielle and Louise agreed.

'And there's no need to tell Father Flory about your work for me.' He made the sign of the cross, turned on his heel and left.

The nuns stared at one another. Sister Gabrielle spoke first. 'You've set a record, Sister.' Louise was puzzled. 'You've been here five minutes and already the Bishop has anointed you for higher honours.'

Louise was about to blurt her answer in French. 'What on Earth does that mean in English?' but stopped.

She died inside. Sister Gabrielle gave her a curious look and set off. Louise almost blundered and worse, to an intelligent woman.

Chapter 33

A forest near Lyon

Raoul was in another of his filthy moods. 'We need guns, ammunition and those explosives,' he fumed. 'Where are those SOE agents?'

His lieutenant, Barrack, shook his head. 'We don't know, Raoul and without a radio, we never will. Those agents have disappeared.'

'I bet de Gaulle's mob have guns.'

'If London has made a drop, de Gaulle's mob or even the Germans may have taken the supplies. Someone betrayed them in the forest.'

Raoul exploded with blasphemy decorating his tirade. 'How can we be expected to kill Germans without guns, or communicate without SOE agents without a radio? The war is lost!'

His men were used to Raoul ranting although lately he seemed unhinged. Barrack tried to talk him down.

'Raoul, there are new Resistance cells springing up all over France. We need to make contact with one or more.'

'They all hate Communists.'

'And Germans, which makes us comrades.' Raoul scoffed. 'Someone is sure to have a radio and know an SOE agent. And then there are civilians. The priest, Father Flory in Lyon; he has contact with the SOE. We should speak with him.'

'He hates me,' spat Raoul. 'We cannot trust anyone who is not sympathetic to our cause.'

'And what about the train rumour?'

'Has anyone checked?'

'Yes and it seems solid. There's a large troop movement passing through this area in the next two days. It will be near Lyon at night. We need to blow the bridge.'

'With what? Fire crackers? Baking soda? And you can forget the bridge. It will be guarded by half the German army. We need another site, one they won't expect us to destroy.'

His men despaired. His courage was beyond criticism, but his temper was explosive and scary. He stared at them and snapped.

'What is the matter with you cowards?'

That hit hard. His men were many things but never cowards.

Barrack believed in Communism and nobody wanted the Germans gone more than him. 'We could try again to contact the Free French and ask for some of their equipment.'

'Nah, once the Germans shelled them they will have moved and probably think we were the ones firing.'

'How did the Germans know they were there, that we were there?' asked Barrack. 'Someone betrayed us.'

'Of course someone betrayed us,' snapped the boss in anger and frustration. 'If I knew who, they'd be dead. But I want those explosives. I want to push the plunger when the train comes through here not expecting our ambush. I want those tanks and Nazis dead and buried.'

He stormed out of the cave desperate for an idea to make his plan work. He wanted to lead the most successful Resistance group in Southern France. Right now he believed he was a failure.

Carmelite Monastery, Lyon

Walking back to the monastery, Louise wanted to quiz Sister Gabrielle about the Bishop's job offer. Something told her to say nothing. As they reached the front door of the monastery, Father Flory, having finished Mass and Confession, came out and confronted Louise.

'Ah, caught in the act. Missing Mass is never wise but when it's your first day, Sister, you'll need to spend even more time meditating and certainly have a damn good explanation at Confession.'

'It's my fault, Father,' said Gabrielle. 'I wanted Sister Claudine to see the Cathedral and to meet Bishop Vaine.'

'Oh and that makes it all right, does it?' he scoffed. 'And did you meet His Excellency?'

Gabrielle answered for Louise. 'We did, Father, and I apologise for leading our new Sister astray.'

He asked Louise. 'So, what do you think of our new Bishop?' Louise genuinely didn't know what to say. 'Don't tell me. He told you he needed help on a special project to carry out the Lord's work and you are not to mention this extra work to Father Flory.'

Louise hesitated. *That's exactly what he said.*

'He did, Father,' said Sister Gabrielle taking the pressure off Louise. 'As you well know, that is exactly what happened.'

He grunted. 'I hope I don't have to remind you, Sisters, I am the parish priest for this monastery. You are required to attend every Mass I give and I alone will hear your Confession.'

He stormed off leaving the nuns to exchange glances.

SOE HQ, Baker Street, London

Several SOE officers discussed the latest reports from France. 'The Germans are moving troops and equipment by rail. All cable intercepts confirm the move is in the next 48 hours,' said the French SOE officer, Gabin.

'Who do we have in the area?' asked Parkinson.

'There's a priest, Father Flory just outside of Lyon.'

'Then we need to discover what the Resistance groups in the area are planning to do.'

'We can't,' said Buckmaster who'd been observing the discussion and shocked the others.

'Can't?' asked Gabin. 'This is a major opportunity to kick Fritz and delay any help they might give to Rommel in Africa.'

'We can't,' said Buckmaster. 'We've lost contact with our two agents in the area, and the priest is under suspicion of being a double agent.'

That rocked the others.

'Since when?' asked an angry Gabin. 'Why wasn't I told?'

'Because we're running a secret mission to see if the priest is still one of us. We have a new agent in Lyon right now doing exactly that.'

'Well contact him and get his report.'

Buckmaster sighed. He wanted Louise's assignment to be top secret eliminating any chance of a leak which might put her in danger and warn the possible double-agent, Father Flory. 'We can't contact him because he's a she and is not acting as a typical SOE agent.' He stunned the group. 'She's a nun living in an enclosed monastery.'

'She's a nun!' exploded Gabin.

Buckmaster had no choice but to tell all. 'She's an SOE agent pretending to be a nun. Her two tasks are to verify the priest's status and to check on the two Resistance cells.'

Murmurs took over and flattened the meeting. Gabin fumed.

'So we can't contact the priest or the Resistance groups?'

'Correct. Our two agents near Lyon are missing along with their radio. If the priest has been turned, he may have told the Gestapo who grabbed our agents. All we can do is wait for the nun to make contact.'

'Has she a radio or access to one?'

'We're not sure.'

The others were shocked. It was unusual to run a secret SOE agent and one where the agent seemed to have few if any resources. Why?

Parkinson summed up the situation. 'So we can try and contact the priest but if we do and he's been turned, we've blown the chance to hurt Jerry. And we can't contact this nun because she's isolated in a convent.'

'Monastery,' corrected Buckmaster.

Gabin groaned. 'Is this what you English call a dog's breakfast?'

A forest near Lyon

'I have a suggestion,' said Nic, a senior member of the cell. 'It's risky but with time running out, we have no choice.'

Raoul was desperate. He needed a plan, an idea. 'What?'

'We have to go back to the priest, Father Flory. He knows men in the Free France Resistance cell. He might be able to tell us where they are or how they can be contacted or he could be the go-between.'

Raoul only saw negatives. 'And even if he does know de Gaulle's men, are you saying we join forces with them? They hate us. They would kill Communists as quickly as they kill Germans.'

'It's worth a try, Raoul,' said Barrack. 'We are nothing without those explosives. The Free French may have some and they're our only hope. Even if Nic simply sniffs around, it's worth a punt.'

Raoul knew that. 'Okay. Check out the priest but don't get caught.'

Nic left. The other fighters wished him luck.

St Nicholas Church, near Lyon

Father Flory poured himself another glass of wine. His life was a mess and getting worse. He hated the war, his new bishop, and the fact his parents were ill, probably dying, and he couldn't travel to Paris to see them. His sister's letter begged him to return before one or both parents die. "It is your duty, not as a priest, but as a son," her letter screamed at him.

Flory's love hate relationship with the new bishop bothered the parish priest. It wasn't so much the Bishop's ambition and dictatorial attitude but rather his delight in seeing people suffer. Flory delayed asking for permission to leave because the bishop would enjoy saying no.

Turning to drink didn't help. His depression increased and was about to get much worse when someone banged loudly on his front door and shouted.

'Open the door, immediately!' None of his parishioners would speak those words or do so with a rich German accent.

Nic travelled into Lyon by foot. The Resistance had use of an old truck but driving into the mountains and the cave where they lived was impossible. It took him an hour to reach the roads where he waved down a farmer and hitched a ride.

He alighted near Father Flory's church and walked on the opposite side of the road. His only weapons were a 9mm pistol hidden in his jacket pocket and an old walking stick. His disguise was his age, he pretended to be old. He hobbled using the stick, bent over a little, not too much, and kept an eye on the church.

He froze when a black limousine came to a halt across the road and two Gestapo officers stepped out and attacked the front door.

A shaken Father Flory opened the door and Nic watched as the Gestapo agents piled inside.

'Forget that,' said Nic and hobbled away.

Chapter 34

St John the Baptist Cathedral, Lyon France

The bishop said Mass to a large congregation which included two Carmelite nuns, Sisters Gabrielle and Claudine; well, one real nun and one pretending. They remained in their pew after the Mass. Altar boys attended to their tasks as the Bishop moved to the robing room.

'What happens now?' whispered Louise.

'Patience, my child,' replied Gabrielle. Louise wanted guidance. Gabrielle winked and Louise breathed easier. 'When the worshippers are gone, we report to His Excellency and not before.'

Louise was kept in the dark and whispered her concerns. 'I've no idea about this special work for the Bishop. I hope I can do it.'

'You're impatient, Sister. Were you like this as a postulant?' Louise wondered if this was a trick question and tried to bluff her way out.

She whispered. 'I don't wish to fail the Bishop.'

'Fail the Bishop?' queried Gabrielle. 'You use quaint expressions, Sister Claudine.'

Louise sat taller and said nothing. Whatever she said seemed to reveal her true position. Not only was she possibly putting her foot in it, she was no closer to discovering Father Flory's status as an SOE contact and knew nothing about the Resistance groups in the area.

'Our turn,' whispered Gabrielle, 'follow me.' She headed towards the back of the altar where Louise discovered the cathedral's second organ. She admired it not realizing Gabrielle had disappeared. Louise saw a flight of stairs with a flash of Gabrielle's habit.

Down the stairs she followed and along a corridor. Louise caught up and stopped. Gabrielle spoke. 'Never come down here without the express permission of His Excellency.' Gabrielle paused. Louise realized she needed to agree.

'I understand,' she said.

Gabrielle headed into the vast crypt past a huge grave and into the darkest part of the underworld. The cathedral was an ancient building and took some 300 years to build. The pioneers prepared the crypt to bury important souls. Candles resting in mini recesses on the walls threw shafts of light giving a spooky feel to what was already an eerie place. The silence grabbed Louise and the next sound made her jump.

'Welcome Sisters,' said Bishop Vaine stepping out from behind a tomb. 'This way.'

The nuns followed him to a corner of the crypt. He stopped and spoke into the darkness. 'You can come out now.'

The trio watched as a child emerged then another and another. They were young, aged between 6 and 10. Two sisters were older and the third, their brother, the youngest.

'Just the usual, Sister Gabrielle, and afterwards, you Sister Claudine, what can you do?'

Louise clenched her fists. 'I don't understand, Your Excellency.'

The bishop addressed Gabrielle. 'Explain then give her something useful to do. Is she a teacher or an entertainer?'

Louise held her breath. *He thinks I'm an entertainer or does he know?* He stepped back into the darkness and disappeared.

Gabrielle moved to an area with more light in which was a chair and small table. She sat. 'Come here, children.' They followed her as did Louise. 'I am Sister Gabrielle and this is Sister Claudine. We are here to help. First I need to examine you.'

With a stethoscope and tiny torch, she examined the children. She listened to their heart and lungs, asked them to cough, peered in their mouth and ears and studied their eyes, ran her hand through their hair and asked them to bend their arms and legs. She thanked each one.

'Please wait here, children and we will return soon.' She led Louise aside and whispered. 'They are Jewish and being taken to a safe house to escape the Germans. I don't know when they will be collected. The Bishop doesn't want them to be left alone. If they have nothing to do, they will be more frightened than they are already. Can you teach them something, a song, a game, anything?'

Louise knew she could. 'Yes but for how long?'

'No-one knows. As soon as the people handling the escape think it is safe, they will be collected. This is the final move.'

'Why not move them at night?'

'Too risky. The policy is to hide in plain sight.' She paused. 'So, can you be an entertainer?' Louise glowed.

She moved to the children and taught them a simple folk song. She knew it in English but easily taught it in French. The children sang, learnt a simple dance and soon their fear grew weaker in this frightening place. Louise then introduced a new song and then a game. Gabrielle watched the performance, impressed. The children became so involved, they squealed with delight.

The older nun whispered. 'Shhhh, you must play quietly.'

'Indeed you must,' said Bishop Vaine stepping out of the shadows. Everyone stared at him. 'Sister Gabrielle, take the children out by the river door. The contact is waiting.' Nothing happened. 'Now please.'

Sister Gabrielle took hands and led the children away. They vanished and the sound of a door closing was heard in the distance.

'I'm impressed, Sister, very impressed.'

'Thank you, Excellency.'

'Where did you learn to be a performer?'

Louise's throat tightened. 'I didn't, Excellency.'

'Come now, Sister, you have a flair, a gift to be used on the stage.'

Louise went into her shell and chose not to speak.

'Come closer, Sister.' She moved and stood before him. 'Closer.' She took another step. He sniffed, staring at her. She made eye contact for a nanosecond then averted her gaze. With eyes downcast, her peripheral vision sensed a hand at either side of her head. She was alone. Even if she screamed, no-one would hear her. If they did, and came to investigate, what would or could they do? They were operating under Bishop Vaine's rules.

His hands were in under her headpiece. They touched her ears. She stopped breathing. She'd heard about nuns being abused by clergy. Just as she was about to step back preparing to deliver a blow to the Bishop's papal bulls, he removed her glasses and smiled.

'There, now what an improvement.' He examined the lens. 'These appear to offer little magnification, Sister. They might as well be for show. You are far more attractive without them.' He thought about throwing them away then changed his mind at the last moment. 'Your spectacles, Sister,' he said handing them to her.

'Thank you, Excellency.'

'Now run along. There's a good little Sister.'

She made her way back into the Cathedral and then to the nave. Despite the sizeable crowd, it was easy to spot a fellow nun. She moved to Sister Gabrielle.

'So you survived?' asked the older nun.

Louise's face said it all. 'What do you mean?'

Before Gabrielle could answer, young Jean Alpen approached. 'Hello, Sisters. I am looking for Bishop Vaine. Have you seen him?'

'Yes, only a few minutes ago,' said Gabrielle.

'My friend over there wants to have His Excellency hear his confession.'

'He won't be long.'

Jean was about to leave when Louise posed a question. 'Excuse me, young man, but can you help with a question?'

Gabrielle and Jean were intrigued.

'Of course, Sister, what would you like to know?'

'I have a small bet with Sister Gabrielle that your friend's accent is from Paris. I said it is.'

'Well I'm sorry, Sister, but you've lost your bet. My friend grew up in England.'

Louise made the appropriate expression. 'Oh well.' Jean smiled and prepared to leave. 'And good luck with your fighting for France.'

Jean's face showed pain and he moved closer to the nuns. 'Please Sister, do not say such things. If the wrong people overhear, I might be in danger.'

Louise stared at him and whispered. 'Your secret's safe with us.'

He went to leave, checked to see if anyone was watching then whispered, 'And stay away from Father Flory. I heard he was raided by the Gestapo this afternoon so you may soon need a new parish priest.' He forced a smile and joined his friend.

Sister Gabrielle studied Louise. 'For a nun, Sister, you'd make an excellent spy.'

Louise tried to make light of it and they returned to the monastery. Walking to their rooms, the Mother Superior came out of her office and stopped. She knew both nuns but couldn't remember their names. The nun assisting Mother Superior helped her out.

'This is the new arrival, Mother, Sister Claudine.'

The Mother's face beamed and she smiled at Gabrielle. 'Of course, welcome Sister Claudine.'

Mother and her minder moved off and the two remaining nuns spoke with their eyes. 'See you at prayers in the chapel,' said Gabrielle.

Louise retired after prayers, meditation and supper. She worried.

I know little about either of the Lyon Resistance cells, the SOE contact in Lyon was raided by the Gestapo, Sister Gabrielle may have seen through my disguise, and the Bishop, as creepy as he is, runs a scheme to save Jewish children from the Nazis. I need confirmation of information and a radio to contact London.

She lay on her bed and pondered her next move. She had to escape. She would learn little if anything in the monastery. Bishop Vaine had the power to destroy men in an instant. Father Flory not so but if the Gestapo raided him, I need to know why.

The monastery was a quiet place at any time. At midnight, it made a funeral parlour seem noisy. Even the clocks ticked softly. Louise added some hose to her toes as wearing sandals forever took a bit of getting used to and slipped on her shoes. She crept from her room, went to the garden door and slipped outside. The full moon struggled to peep through the massive cloud cover. For Louise, the darker the better.

It took longer to reach Father Flory's church because she used back streets and lanes. Twice she stepped into a doorway when a vehicle drove by, its headlights picking out anyone not obeying the curfew. The SOE sessions on following and hiding from people paid dividends.

She reached the church. Not a soul to be seen or heard. A dog barked. She tried the church door. It opened. She pushed it enough to allow her to squeeze through. It creaked. She stopped. Silence ruled. She crept inside and closed the creaking door. The church barely breathed. She tip toed to the priest's house and to Father Flory's office. *What am I looking for? Will he have a list of Abwehr contacts?*

She could hardly see so lit the candle on the desk. It was no sooner giving light when she heard voices and footsteps. Puff. She blew out the candle and dived under the desk.

'In here,' said the priest and two people entered. The candle, just extinguished was lit. Louise could see two pairs of feet. The priest's she recognized but not the other until they spoke.

'Thank God you're okay, Father,' said Jean. 'When I heard the Gestapo raided you I feared the worst.'

'Someone betrayed me.'

'What?' gasped the young Resistance worker, and Louise froze.

'They accused me of helping those two agents from London. They searched the place but found nothing. Who would know I'm helping the English? Who?'

Louise's mind raced. *Have I fulfilled my first task already?*

Jean worried. 'There are suspects everywhere, Father. The Germans and the Milice threaten and bribe. We cannot trust anyone, even the men in the Communist Resistance cell.'

Their breathing became heavy. 'What does your Resistance cell say about those two British agents?'

'They fear they're dead or in jail.'

'So who betrayed them?'

Louise cramped. She concentrated on slow breathing.

'Father, there's something else.'

'What?'

'We've heard reports of a large troop train passing through Lyon this week.'

'Well that's a job for you in the Resistance.' Louise lifted one knee ever so slightly to stop the pain. The floor creaked; or was it her knee? 'If I could contact those missing British agents, I would.'

The priest put a finger to his lips but waved his other hand to encourage Jean to keep talking. The young man was confused. The sudden silence scared Louise.

'Is there something wrong, Father?' asked Jean

Louise screamed in pain and fear as her ankles were grabbed and she was hauled out from her hiding place.

'You!' spat the priest. 'What the hell are you doing in my house?'

'Sister Claudine,' gasped Jean.

She made a pathetic figure in the flickering candlelight.

'May I get up, Father?'

He said nothing and Jean stepped forward to help her stand.

'Explain yourself, Sister,' ordered the priest.

Louise adjusted her habit playing for time. She could offer some pathetic excuse about having lost her rosary beads or being locked out of the monastery and needing shelter but having heard the conversation when in hiding, she decided to tell a version of the truth.

'Father, I want to help you in your fight for liberty; you too Jean. Vive le France.'

She paused. Jean was thrilled with Father Flory a non-believer.

'Liar,' he said. 'You are not even French. Your French is from a textbook and not from your mother's breast. And you are no more a Carmelite nun than I am the Pope. So who are you and this time let us have the truth?'

Louise knew the dictim, "Sign nothing and say nothing" but chose to ignore it. The priest saw through her disguise, her superb acting was no longer superb and, as she believed he remained a friend of the SOE, she came clean.

'Father, you are correct. I am English, not even a Catholic let alone a nun, and have been sent to see if the missing SOE agents are missing because their contact, Father Felix Flory, is a double agent.'

Jean was flabbergasted. 'What?'

Flory remained calm. 'So now you have the answer, what do you propose to do?'

Louise's heart rate slowed. 'Find a way to tell London you're still on our side and do what I can to find the missing agents.'

Jean struggled to keep up. He stared at a nun who sounded French. Most of the nuns he knew were older than Methuselah and wouldn't be able to hide under a table in a priest's office at any time let alone 2 am.

Flory decided she was telling the truth. Her behaviour impressed him. He got down to business. 'We have to assume they are dead or in jail which is the same thing.'

'Do you know which jail?' asked Louise.

'No but the Gestapo are using an old police station which suits them as it has cramped cells and thick concrete walls to hide the screams.'

Louise opened her hands. 'What are we waiting for?'

Chapter 35

Former Police Station, Lyon

She led the way. Flory knew which streets to avoid but Louise knew how to move from shadow to shadow. Jean followed, a bit like a puppy. Twice he stepped out of line or whispered too loud and copped a glare from the nun. He kept thinking. *Is she really a nun?*

They turned into a cobbled lane. 'Wait,' whispered Flory. 'There, across the road, the old white place.'

It was an attached double-storied building with one entrance. She assumed there would be a rear entrance. No lights showed.

'What do we do?' asked the priest who had accepted the nun as his leader. She spoke like a leader.

'Jean, you stay here out of sight. If we don't come out in twenty minutes, go and say nothing. Do you understand?' He nodded. 'Tell nobody, not even your friends; especially not your friends.'

She and Flory exchanged glances. He nodded. They crossed the road and stopped at the door. 'You do the talking,' she said. 'We've come to administer the last rites to prisoners.'

She knocked. Nothing. She knocked again, louder. From inside came grumbling. The visitors stood back. Keys rattled, the solid door opened, and a French official, a guard, half asleep, stood scratching his distended belly.

'What?'

The priest switched to humble mode. 'Pardon, Monsieur, but we are here to administer the last rites to the prisoners.'

The guard scoffed. 'Why? They're dead or will be in the morning.'

'But they are Catholic, Monsieur. Please, let us help them prepare for eternity.'

The guard was tired and bored. The prisoners were no trouble. He was alone and before him stood (and begged) a priest and a nun.

'Five minutes,' he said and waved them in. They waited as he closed and locked the door. He ambled along a corridor and stopped at a cell.

He unlocked and opened a door. The stench was overpowering. He turned and walked away, laughing. 'The last rites; ha ha ha ha ha.'

Two men were in the cell, one on the bed, the other slumped on the floor. A bucket, filled with waste, gave off vile fumes. A small barred window high up was the only source of daylight and air. The feeble light from the corridor crept into the cell.

'Are they our men?' asked Louise.

'Yes,' said Flory struggling in the poor light.

Louise gently shook the man on the bed. 'Wake up, it's time to go.' The man groaned.

Flory examined the man on the floor. 'This is Barney, he's dead.'

'So this is Alfie, the radio operator. Help me get him up.'

They struggled. The man, codenamed Alfie, suffered horrific torture. The bruises were hard to see in the dim light but his eyes were blackened and his fingers bloody where fingernails were removed with brute force.

He wanted to help his rescuers but pain and exhaustion dragged him down. They helped him to his feet with one of his arms around each of the religious. They turned to face the door when the room became even more dark, the light blocked by a large man.

'And what have we here?' asked the leather-coated, smug and malicious Rudolf Müller from the Lyon Gestapo.

Flory struggled and they lowered Alfie back to the bed. 'Father Flory, Officer, from St Nicholas church in Lyon. Sister Claudine has come to tend to the wounds of the prisoners and I to tend to their souls.'

'Get out,' spat the officer. The visitors hesitated. This infuriated the German who took a step into the cell, grabbed Flory's hair and dragged him into the corridor. He stumbled and fell. The guard was amused. The officer turned and stamped on Flory's hand. His cry of pain prompting another grin from the guard who pretended he was in ancient Rome witnessing the Christians being thrown to the lions.

Slumped on the corridor floor, Flory's head was in a perfect position, like a golf ball on a tee about to be whacked. Müller had murdered many but never a priest so welcomed this opportunity. He steadied himself, balanced on this left leg and began the kick at the coconut shy. As his boot began its bombing run, a pair of hands latched onto it and his foot was twisted sharply to the right. The sound of a kneecap being dislocated was almost as loud as his scream.

The guard, choking on his laughter, struggled to remove his pistol, and while he struggled, the foot attacker, dressed as a nun, stepped over the screaming Gestapo officer and plunged her knife into the guard's heart. He didn't make a sound other than his obese body collapsing as he died. Clattering on his colleague's shattered knee ramped up the Gestapo officer's pain adding a nice touch to the suffering of the perpetrators.

Father Flory witnessed the whole thing. 'Jesus, Mary and Joseph, Sister, you didn't learn that in a nunnery.'

'Come on,' said Louise heading back into the cell. Flory struggled to his feet, wringing his aching hand. Together they dragged Alfie, the radio operator, to his feet and stumbled their way into the corridor.

Stepping over the guard was relatively easy but the screaming Gestapo goon kept rolling clutching his leg and blocking their exit.

'Hold him,' said Louise, and Alfie collapsed against the priest.

The nun knelt behind the wailing Nazi, and all her unarmed combat training and silent killing experience in Scotland came in handy. This was no lipstick on a wooden dagger routine. Louise did as she was taught and slit the German's throat. If nothing else, it stopped his screaming. Flory gawped.

She wiped her dagger on the Gestapo coat—red and black were artistically acceptable—stood and supported her fellow religious as they helped Alfie to the door. 'Damn,' said Louise and passed him to Flory, dashing back for the keys. As she returned, she disrobed.

Now there's a first. Father Flory had witnessed many unusual sights but never a nun disrobing and certainly not in a Nazi jail in occupied France.

Louise wore a shirt, jumper and trousers under her clerical gear. She unlocked the door, helped Flory get the escapee into the street and whistled to the shadows. Jean sprinted towards them. She locked the door, heaved the key, and spread her habit on the road.

'Lie down,' she said and Alfie found a new snippet of strength.

'Where's the other agent?' asked a breathless Jean.

'Dead,' said Flory who too wondered what was happening.

Louise tied the ends of her habit around the feet of the patient. 'You take this end, Father. Jean, you and I take the head.' The nun was running the show. What began as a failed investigation in the priest's office, ended up a minor triumph as the badly beaten SOE radio operator was carried on an improvised stretcher through the darkened streets of Lyon and away to a safe house.

Getting the tortured man to safety was only part of the job. At the safe house, Louise examined Alfie's wounds. 'He needs a doctor,' she said.

'There's trouble there,' said Flory. 'We know two. We think one is a Nazi sympathizer, and the other too old to make house calls.'

Louise sighed and dressed as a nun. 'I'll see what I can do. Bathe his wounds and give him soup. I'll be back before dawn.'

She left and the residents of the safe house did as she ordered still in shock at the skill and determination of the bride of Christ. Jean stared at his parish priest. 'Tell me Father, am I dreaming?'

The monastery was locked and dark. Breaking out was far easier than breaking in. She climbed the back wall and ran across the lawn to beneath Sister Gabrielle's window on the first floor. Louise grabbed a handful of soil and threw a bit. She needed three throws before the nun appeared. In the darkness, Sister Gabrielle made out the beckoning of her fellow nun. Louise whispered her request. Shaking her head she made her way outside.

'Are you insane?' she whispered. 'What the hell are you doing?'

'Good morning, Sister, and please mind your language.'

'You *are* insane.'

'I really do need your medical services to help someone who has been tortured by the Nazis?'

Gabrielle shook her head. 'There *is* something not right about you.'

'Please?'

'Is it far?'

'Good girl,' said Louise and set off. 'This way.'

For any night-owls, it was an unusual sight. Here were two nuns with fluttering habits, hurrying through the suburbs of Lyon in the wee small hours, both on a mission of mercy. Just look out for the Gestapo.

The back door of the safe house opened and the occupants stared open-mouthed.

'This is Sister Gabrielle,' said Louise. 'She is a doctor as well as a nun.'

The radio operator was examined and, despite the lack of equipment, Sister Gabrielle cleaned and dressed his wounds as best she could, bandaging those which needed stitches. The lady of the house produced ingredients purported to help with ancient cures, with one said to guarantee a pregnancy. Alfie would have preferred his radio to a baby.

'Can you obtain medical supplies?' asked Gabrielle. The husband in the safe house knew a sympathetic pharmacist. Gabrielle wrote a list. She announced. 'I will try and return tomorrow night.'

Father Flory followed the nuns to the rear of the safe house.

'Thank you, Sisters, and if there's a problem at the monastery, please refer Mother Superior to me. I will explain all.'

All three knew the Mother Superior's mental capacity would make this incident a non-issue. Not so with the Bishop. None of them knew how he would react and didn't intend to ask.

Heading home, Sister Gabrielle chatted. 'As soon as I met you, I doubted your calling. I bet your life was fascinating before you became a pretend nun.'

'You can talk,' replied Louise, 'Doctor Small Breasts.'

The older nun liked her colleague's humour but pressed home her point. 'I'm sure your heart's in the right place, Sister Whatever-Your-Real-Name-Is. But seriously, fighting Germans is dangerous and unlike you, I'm not blessed with bravery.'

'I don't believe you,' said Louise, 'and is there a simple way into the monastery?'

'There's a door at the back of the kitchen which is never locked.'

'Good girl,' said Louise, 'and you're right about my interesting life before I became a nun with one exception.' They continued walking.

'Which is?'

'I'm not even a Catholic let alone a nun.'

Gabrielle smiled. 'I thought so, but you're a bloody good actress.'

Louise enjoyed the first-rate review.

They climbed over the rear wall and crept through the garden to the rear of the kitchen. Sure enough the door was unlocked and they silently tip-toed into the building. Through the darkened kitchen and dining room they went, and then to the main corridor leading to their rooms. They were close to their destinations when the corridor flooded with light and two nuns, in their appropriate night attire, stood there like statues.

'And what is the meaning of this outrage?' hissed the senior nun.

'It's all my fault, Sister,' said Louise. 'A good Catholic was injured and I begged Sister Gabrielle to use her training to try and save the man's life.'

Her statement was partly true but the problem was Mother Superior's poor mental health. Her senior offsider, the one leading the interrogation, reckoned the order needed a serious serve of discipline and approached Louise.

'Just look at the state of your habit.' She pointed. 'What is that?'

Everyone, including Louise, examined her clothes. 'I believe it's blood, Sister.' The other senior nun recoiled. 'We have dedicated our lives to prayer and contemplation, and you leave the monastery without permission and mingle with men who have broken the law.'

'Not all were lawbreakers, Sister. Father Flory was with us.'

That was unexpected and again, having truth, gave it credence.

'Go to your rooms. I will report your behaviour to Reverend Mother who will deal with you in the morning.' The recalcitrant nuns departed with the senior calling after them. 'And do not be late for Mass.'

As Louise reached her door she whispered. 'Good night, Doctor Tiny Tits.'

Sister Gabrielle hurried to enter her room so her stifled giggle would not be heard by the bosses.

Chapter 36

Forest camp, near Lyon

Raoul stewed. With no radio, no SOE agent, no contact with London, no explosives, and his botched plan to "borrow" supplies from a rival Resistance group ending in disaster, he was ropeable. Someone betrayed the De Gaulle fighters to the Germans and Raoul and his men were lucky to escape the ambush. Life stank.

His mood improved a little when news of the death of a Gestapo officer in Lyon filtered out, and even better was the rescue of an SOE agent. But where is he and where is his radio?

Then Raoul's luck changed. Jacques, one of his fighters, went south to a family wedding, met a true believer in the Marxist cause who knew where to obtain explosives. Jacques paid over the odds but now, overnight, Raoul and his boys packed fire power. Life was on the up.

When confirmation of the German troop train's timetable arrived, plans were made. Raoul became human. His excitement infected his fighters. Destroying such a train would be fantastic. It would deal a mighty blow to the Bosch and give Raoul one over the Free France Resistance cell. He called in his men.

'There's a chance to smash the troop train tomorrow night. Now we have the explosives, we need the ideal location, somewhere the Germans will never expect.'

He was buzzing then nearly died when told the news.

'Raoul, we might have the explosives but Henri has gone home to help with the harvest.' Henri was the electrician, the one who set the wiring for the explosives.

Raoul explored apoplexy. 'What is it with you men? Our country's conquered. The Bosch has their jackboot on our throat and we go home to see Mummy and Daddy How can we kill Germans and make France a Communist paradise if we're part-time Resistance fighters?'

'I can handle wiring,' said a quiet electrician from Chaponost.

Raoul's rage stalled. 'What? You've set explosives before?'

The man hesitated. 'I'm an electrician.'

Raoul faced two options—pull out or risk it. 'Right, we strike tomorrow night.'

'Do we blow the bridge?' asked a keen but dim fighter.

'Oh for Christ's sake,' snapped Raoul. 'The bridge is guarded night and day and they'll have the place awash with Krauts.'

'So where do we attack the train?' asked Barrack.

Raoul looked at them then made the announcement. 'We blow up the line at the Valine Bend.' His words struck terror. His men reacted, their murmur full of fear. The brave ones argued.

'Are you mad? We'll have to abseil 50 metres to even reach the line, and to escape climb down the mountain to the river.' Others agreed

He spat back. 'And the Bosch will never think we'll do that. We can plant the charges, blow the line and slide down the mountain.'

'But we'll need time to escape and if we blow the track well before the train, it'll stop and not derail.'

The mood was tense. Raoul's men knew he was mad and would willingly die to achieve his goal. Not them; in 20 years' time they preferred to be able to tell their grandchildren they were victorious.

Raoul knew they were right but still argued his case. 'Because of that location it will take them days to repair the track and they'll need troops to protect the workers. Delays will help them lose the war.'

He spoke the truth but his men hated the risks. He pushed them.

'Our attack will prove Communists are the ones to kick the Krauts.'

Raoul failed to convince. He wanted glory and political victory. The others wanted to survive. This looked like a suicide mission.

The area to blow the line was half way down a steep mountain. To reach the track was dangerous; to escape even more so. They would abseil to the track then slide or scramble to the raging river a hundred metres below. If the Germans arrived early, it would be like shooting fish in a barrel.

'Check your supplies then check them again,' shouted Raoul. 'Tomorrow night, we kill those Krauts.'

The Carmelite Monastery, Lyon

During Mass next morning, nothing was said about the escapades. When Louise received the sacrament from Father Flory, she tried to make eye contact but he avoided her glance. As he passed her a wafer, she saw his bruised hand was a deep purple. At least his attacker's boot-stomping days were no more.

The priest remained for Confession and Louise lined up awaiting her turn. She held back wanting to be last in line and avoid the angry sisters who confronted her and Sister Gabrielle at 4 am.

Finally Louise knelt before the seated priest. 'Bless me Father for I have sinned.'

'Yes, all right, I think we can dispense with the pantomime.'

That word made Louise think about a certain performance in a castle, and a certain family with a kidnapped daughter.

'I'm in trouble here, Father.'

'Are you pretending to confess or is this real?'

'When we came back last night, two of the senior nuns were waiting and threatened us; well, me in particular.'

'Do they know you're not a nun?'

'No and I'd prefer to keep it that way.' He grunted. 'And I'm afraid I mentioned your name in passing.'

'It's not the nuns who're a problem. By the way, what *is* your name?'

'Plum.'

He thought he misheard. 'Plum?'

'Yes.'

He shook his head. They stared at one another. 'The one to watch is His Excellency in the Cathedral.'

She paused wondering what he meant. 'I'm keen to find the SOE radio and I hope Sister Gabrielle can continue her medical services.'

He understood. She paused. Neither knew what to say. He was still in awe and shock at the person kneeling before him. He whispered.

'I will be at the safe house around midnight.'

'Thank you, Father.' She hesitated. 'What penance do you require?'

He sniffed. 'Three Hail Mary's and a dozen dead Nazis.'

She wanted to laugh but he was up and gone. She gathered herself and stepped into the corridor to be confronted by the two senior nuns who had become the Carmelite cops. They were waiting.

'Come with us, Sister Claudette.'

One set off and Louise followed. The second nun slipped in behind the prisoner. The trio headed to the office of the Mother Superior. Louise relaxed. *How can this dear old woman even understand let alone rule on my situation? And what can she do anyway?*

All three entered an empty room. Louise worried. The door closed. Sister Grumpy turned and faced Louise. Sister Grumpy 2 joined her colleague. Having recently confronted and killed an evil Gestapo agent and a Nazi-sympathizing guard, facing two elderly nuns who couldn't jump over a jam tin, didn't exactly fill Louise with dread.

'We know all about you, Sister Claudette,' snapped the senior Sister. 'You may have fooled Mother Superior but not us.'

'Exactly,' sneered her sidekick, 'you can't fool us.'

Louise was surprised; disappointed her acting was not up to snuff but genuinely surprised they'd seen through her disguise. But her surprise turned to shock when the senior nun continued.

'We know you're secretly working for the Germans.'

Louise froze. She became the actress who dried.

'We've known all along,' added Sister Grumpy 2.

What the hell do I say? thought Louise.

Before she could speak, the two nuns smiled, stepped forward and either squeezed her arm or shook her hand.

'Congratulations, Sister, we are so proud of you,' they said in unison.

Louise continued thinking. *What the hell do I say?*

'Bishop Vaine knew the moment you arrived in Lyon,' said Sister Grumpy with a smile.

'He knows everything,' added her partner in crime.

Louise thought it better to say something rather than play the role of a mute. 'Bishop Vaine is a wonderful man of God.'

The Sisters were delighted with their new friend's response.

'We want you to continue your good work, Sister Claudette, and anything we can do to help, please ask.'

'I will, Sisters, and thank you.' She paused. 'May I go now?'

'Of course, and God bless you, Sister.'

She gave a half smile, a head bow, and headed for the door. She stopped when Sister Grumpy spoke.

'Do be careful, Sister, and stay well away from Father Flory. He can never be trusted.'

Louise left. Internally she was a mix of glee and horror.

Chapter 37

The streets of Lyon, midnight

The two unenclosed nuns hurried towards the safe house. 'I don't understand,' said Sister Gabrielle. 'Not only are we not in trouble, they've turned a blind eye to us escaping the monastery.'

'If I told the truth, you wouldn't believe me,' said Louise. 'Now I promised Father Flory we'd be at the safe house ten minutes ago.'

They ducked up a lane and entered the back yard. The husband was waiting and led them inside. Father Flory breathed easier.

'Any trouble?' he asked.

Sister Gabrielle attended to the radio operator who looked better mainly because he now harboured hope of survival.

Louise led the priest into the kitchen and spoke in hushed tones. 'The senior nuns think I'm working for the Germans.'

'What?' hissed Flory.

Louise shushed him. 'And worse, they warned me off contacting you. I think they're getting advice from our favourite Bishop.'

'Bastard,' spat Flory. 'He's getting intelligence from a traitor, but who? The Resistance groups were attacked in the forest by the Germans. How would they know where to find them?'

'Is it Jean? He's a big fan of the Bishop.'

Flory shook his head. 'No, he's simple but no fool.'

'Meaning?'

'He knows things. A German troop train is passing near Lyon in about an hour. Jean said the Communists are going to blow the tracks.'

'So who told Jean?'

Flory shook his head. 'Good question and why would anyone tell him at all? He's not important in the Resistance.'

Louise had an idea. 'And if the Resistance fighters are ambushed, the blame will fall on Jean and the de Gaulle Resistance cell.'

Flory understood. 'Someone's using him. It's a trap. The men at the Valine Bend will be slaughtered and London will never trust the de

Gaulle cell again. Two Resistance cells wrecked and your SOE is dealt a double blow.'

'We have to call off the attack.'

'Oh,' mocked Flory, 'just like that.'

'How far away is this Valine Bend?'

'Two miles, more, and what can you do?' He mocked her. "Hello boys, the Bosch are coming". He squirmed seeing her determination.

'Where is it?'

Flory hesitated. Louise went to the lounge and called the husband. 'Monsieur.' He entered the kitchen.

'You are mad,' said Flory.

She addressed the husband. 'Monsieur, I need to reach the Valine Bend in less than an hour. Can you tell me the quickest way?'

He looked at the priest who nodded. The husband grabbed a notebook to draw and explain. Flory left the room.

'It's two miles, Sister,' said the husband. 'You will have to run if you want to make it in time.'

'And I can't go through the forest?'

'You could but it is dark and obviously there are no sign posts.'

'Stick to the roads,' said Flory wheeling in an old bicycle. 'May she borrow this Henri?'

'Yes, of course,' said the husband.

Flory pushed the bike through the house. Gabrielle stopped her medical work. 'What's happening?'

Louise approached her. 'I'm off for a bit of fresh air, Sister. I'll be back as soon as I can.'

The real nun watched as the fake nun disappeared. This was not what Sister Gabrielle expected when she took her vows.

Trainspotting in a French forest

The bicycle never made it to the Tour de France. Louise scrunched her habit under her crotch leaving her legs free to pedal. She cursed the fact she didn't pay more attention to map-reading during her SOE training. At least she was heading out of Lyon and the rural roads were empty. If a vehicle approached, the sound would give enough warning to hide in the forest. Arriving at a fork in the road, she took the road to the left. *Come on Plum, pedal faster.*

She'd been told to abandon her vehicular transport once she reached the crest of a long hill. Then head due west into the forest and you will reach the top of the Valine Bend. The railway is directly below.

She was tired from all the activity she'd tackled since landing in France. She craved a hot bath, a slap up meal and some uninterrupted sleep; lots of it. Then a bloody big hill reared up.

The moon let its hair down and the white clay glowed in the dark. Then pain arrived. The bicycle sans gears became a torture machine. The pain bit her calves then added extra agony by sticking pins in her thighs. She couldn't ride in a straight line so began a switchback routine going from one side of the road to the other. She couldn't look up. On and on she went choosing prayer as a way to keep going.

Dear God, I know I'm only a pretend nun but could you please whip up a tail wind?

In excruciating pain, she gave up, pushing the bike off the road into the forest. She sucked chunks of French air, lifted her head and couldn't believe the sight; the night sky. She'd reached the summit so stumbled into the dark forest.

Branches whacked her and fallen twigs were stood on with one foot only to trip her with the other one. Then she saw an opening, well, the end of the forest. She pushed on and broke free of the trees. Steady, Louise. The tree line ended just a few feet from the edge of the mountain. She crept forward and peered down at the Valine Bend.

The Resistance Communists were scattered on the railway line. They had little space and were hard up against the cliff face. Beyond the line was the steep drop, the remainder of the mountain.

She'd thought about her approach. *Get it wrong and I'm dead.* Moving beside a huge tree, she cupped her hands and yelled.

'Bonjour!'

Her voice sailed out into the valley. The men on the track dived for cover, grabbed their weapons and scanned the forest above them.

Their fear was allayed as the Germans never gave a warning before firing, and the pitch of the voice sounded decidedly feminine.

Raoul hissed. 'It's a woman.'

'Where is she?' queried Barrack.

The female continued. 'I am a friend. You are in great danger. The Germans know you are here and are coming now to ambush you.'

Silence from below. 'Show yourself,' called Raoul.

'What? So you can shoot me?'

'Raise your hands and we will not shoot.'

Louise decided to bite the bullet wishing that thought hadn't entered her brain. At the edge of the cliff she stepped out and raised her hands. In the moonlight the Resistance fighters, their guns aimed at the target above, blinked.

'She's a nun,' gasped Barrack.

'You have been betrayed,' cried Louise. 'You must destroy the track and flee—*now.*'

Raoul yelled. 'Come down so we can see if you are lying.' Other men would have said, "if you are telling the truth" but not Raoul.

The cliff face was steep and sans vegetation. 'How?' she yelled.

Barrack pointed. 'There's a rope ten metres to your left.'

She moved, found the rope, pulled it hard to test it, turned her back to the fighters and abseiled. 'Cover her,' snapped Raoul.

They watched her bounce down the cliff like a professional soldier staring in amazement at her skill. So impressed with the nun were the fighters, their guns dropped. She landed and overbalanced. Two fighters reached out to help her. Raoul stepped forward.

'I'm impressed, Sister. What do you do for an encore?'

She didn't waste time. 'I've been sent by Father Flory. There is a German spy in the Resistance cells in Lyon, possibly yours.' Murmurs began. 'You've been set up. You need to blow the track and flee.'

No-one moved. She couldn't believe their lack of action.

'What? You think an unarmed nun rides through the forest to warn you because I'm some sort of Nazi spy?' It was a good question. Raoul hesitated and Louise lost it. The SOE would take a big hit if this went wrong, not to mention Resistance fighters being slaughtered along with one pretend nun.

'For God's sake, if you stay here, the Krauts will slaughter you.'

They heard a sound. It came from the cutting before the bend. Footsteps got louder as a member of the Resistance cell raced towards them, yelling as he ran. 'The train is coming.'

Minds concentrated. 'The nun is right,' yelled Barrack.

'Right,' spat Raoul, 'blow the track. The rest of you, go now!'

Men scattered. Their plan was to slide down the cliff, enter the trees by the river below and disperse into the forest. Someone screamed.

'Wait!' They stopped because the person doing the screaming was the nun who knelt beside the explosives.

Raoul confronted her. 'If you're a German, you're dead.'

'The wiring is wrong. You won't blow the line like that.'

Raoul worried. His chance to stick it to the Bosch was on a knife edge. If the train sailed through he would die of shame. *Who is this nun who knows about explosives? Is she trying to wreck our plan?*

Before anyone could speak, the far off sound of an approaching locomotive filled the night air. It was working hard.

Raoul looked at the electrician who prepared the explosives. 'Are you sure?' he thundered. The man quivered. He thought he knew.

Without hesitating, Louise knelt and began adjusting wires. The train sounds were close. Raoul didn't know what to do.

Someone looked up and saw movement on the cliff top. 'Germans,' he screamed and opened fire.

Panic began. Raoul crouched beside Louise firing at the enemy. The Resistance members fired pining down the Germans. The locomotive's whistle screamed above the din of the gunfire.

'Now,' yelled Louise and slid down the mountain clutching the firing mechanism, the wires trailing behind. She flattened herself against the stones, looked at Raoul who lay beside her. She turned the switch. Nothing. Raoul was about to hurl abuse when an almighty bang sounded and ballast and dirt showered from the heavens.

Raoul didn't hesitate. His men were already scrambling towards the trees and the raging river. Louise followed. Above, the Germans opened fire with anger. Bullets pinged and whizzed around them.

The locomotive crawled and stopped before the wrecked rails, giving cover to the Resistance and helping the escapees.

They were in the trees. Louise was with them. They kept running. Orders were screamed from the railway track. 'Schiessen! Schiessen!' But at what? The enemy disappeared. And for the Germans, sliding down the slope with what they reckoned might be a hidden enemy lying in wait, killed the idea of a chase.

In the forest, the Resistance fighters re-grouped.

'Take her,' shouted Raoul as two fighters each grabbed one of Louise's arms and she fled with the men into the forest.

Resistance 1, Nazis 0, but the night was far from over.

Chapter 38

The forest near Lyon, France

Louise hoped her handlers knew where they were going. Dodging trees while running flat out was a new game for Miss Wellesley. Trunks and branches loomed out of the darkness and just as she expected to crash into one, her fellow runners veered slightly, kept going and took her along for the ride. To make running even more difficult, the ground sloped and they were heading down.

'How much further?' she gasped after a good ten minutes of this scary activity.

'Drop,' yelled one of the men and she found herself on her bottom as the three of them tried a form of tobogganing down a steep slope. Pine needles and soft earth cushioned the ride. They hit the bottom. A narrow stream trickled over Louise's shoes.

The men stood and each gave Louise a hand up. 'Welcome to our home, Sister,' said the first Resistance fighter.

'Sorry about the transport,' said the other. 'Please come this way.'

They climbed but not far. The undergrowth was thick and if you were choosing a secure hiding place, this was it. Resistance fighters knew the forest better than the Germans who were reluctant to venture deep into this terrain. Wide-open plains and roads were the preferred settings for the invaders.

It was pointless sending out aircraft by day or night. From the sky, nothing could be seen and small fires were inside the caves.

Louise and her pals walked the last few steep metres and reached the camp. One took her arm. 'Soon you can have a hot bath, Sister, and a superb meal.'

Other men laughed and made gestures for her to move inside their cave. From the ground level, it was vast. From the sky or elsewhere in the forest, it was invisible.

Raoul came forward his hand extended. 'You are welcome, Sister. My men owe you a huge debt of gratitude. Vive la France.'

They shook hands and the other men applauded.

'Vive le France,' said Louise and moved inside where a fire and cooking pots were on the go. Two men, who had been guarding the hideout, came forward to see what all the fuss was about.

Raoul dragged forward a chair of sorts. ''For you, Sister, this is our special seat for important visitors.'

'Merci,' she said and sat.

Someone handed her a cup. 'And here, our finest wine, Sister.'

Louise raised the cup in a toast to the men who surrounded her. 'Vive le France,' she said and sipped then coughed as the rough red burnt her throat. The men laughed.

'We do not even know your name, Sister or where you are from,' said Raoul.

'Or how you knew where we were,' added Nic.

'Or who taught you to use explosives,' added Barrack.

A plate with bread, cheese and ham was offered. 'Am I to eat alone, gentlemen?'

They appreciated her consideration. Food was distributed and the fighters sat on the ground surrounding the nun. She ate. They waited for her to speak. She kept eating giving her a reason to remain silent. She was in an unknown location with men she didn't know and, in certain quarters, her bridges were well and truly burnt.

I need to escape, find a radio, contact London and then decide what next to do. Surely I'm safe here having helped blow the railway track and halt the German troops. Oh, and I saved the lives of this ragtag Resistance cell.

Now, staring at the faces staring at her, pulses raced. She worried. Lust was in the air. Forget the fact she was a nun, she was a female.

The meal finished and the men enjoyed the wine. Louise answered their questions in as vague a manner as possible. She played a straight bat. Her father was a WW1 veteran and taught her how to fire a rifle. Her uncle worked on the railways and used dynamite to blast soil and rock to lay a new line. The war made her want to do something for France. She was posted to Lyon where Father Flory became her parish priest. She heard how the Gestapo raided his home. She wanted to help. Father Flory rescued a British agent, a radio operator. They got word from the other Resistance group about the Germans attacking the fighters at the train. Father Flory sent her to warn the Communists and, 'Here I am!'

The men applauded. Raoul and those listening seemed satisfied although Raoul had doubts. He reckoned there were more holes in her story than the Swiss cheese they ate for supper. Mind you, he was suspicious of everyone.

It was late. For now, they would let her rest. Tomorrow the examination would begin in earnest and new plans made. Nic asked her to come with him. He led her into the cave. Candles sat on small ledges giving a flickering, eerie light to the space reminding Louise of the crypt in the basement of Lyon's cathedral. The cave became lower and turned a corner. Nic lit another candle and stopped in the main "bedroom". There was a palliasse and a bucket.

'I apologise, Sister, this is not the Ritz but it is the best we have.'

'Thank you, I will sleep like a log.'

'At least you can see it is an en suite.' She forced a smile. He kissed her hand. 'Good night, Sister,' he said and left. The candle flickered in the breeze made by his departure.

Louise surveyed the walls and roof. *What terrifying creatures share my suite?* Ferocious Nazis were child's play alongside creepy crawlies. They would keep her awake all night and the thought of a rat nibbling her toes meant she slept in everything she currently wore, shoes included. The thoughts of rats and bats kept her awake.

She heard the footsteps. They were creeping, trying to be quiet. It was pitch black. She smelt him before she saw the outline of his body. It was an hour or more since she retired. The sound of the drinking fighters faded. The cave produced its own brand of silence. The insects were the noisy ones. But now human sounds kicked in.

The human coughed, stumbled and swore. Louise was wide awake and what she thought might happen, did. *My kingdom for a torch and a Sten gun,* she thought. She felt for her knife. It was missing. *Shit! All that cycling, abseiling and running must have dislodged it.*

'Sister,' whispered a voice and Louise knew who it was.

'Go away,' she hissed with as much a threat as she could muster.

'I have come to see if you are safe and comfortable.'

'You might be the leader but you are not welcome. Now go away or I shall scream and your men will attack you.'

Raoul chuckled. 'Attack me? But it was they who suggested I visit.'

'Go away.'

He lit a candle with difficulty and held it aloft. Only Louise's eyes were visible and they shone with anger. There was fear there too and he saw the fear more than the rage.

'I want to give you a present, Sister. You will enjoy this gift. When it comes to making love, I am an expert. A hundred women agree.'

'This is how you repay the person who saved your life, the lives of your men and destroyed the railway to stop the Germans.'

He raised a finger to make a point of order and stumbled. The wine was in full swing.

'Not destroyed, Sister, only damaged. Now, do you want me to seduce you in the dark or would you like a candle so you can see my magnificent manhood?'

'I am a bride of Christ and you will suffer damnation unless you stop right now and *go away.*' She couldn't be any clearer.

Her heart was racing as was his although she endured fear while he was bursting with excitement and anticipation. He undid his trousers and let them fall. He dropped his belt. He placed the candle on the ground and knelt beside her. His shadow danced on the wall of the cave and Louise's greatest fear screamed in her mind because if he succeeded in raping her, every other man would arrive for their turn.

A tear ran down her cheek. She thought of family and particularly brother Edmund. Wounded and damaged be damned. If he were here now, he'd be out of his wheelchair in a flash thrashing the blaggard.

Raoul bent to kiss her taking her head in his hands. She twisted her face away making him angry. He locked her head so she couldn't twist her face from his. As he moved closer, the stench of his breath now proved stronger than his body odour. His mouth leered and as it was about to kiss her mouth, she spat.

She frightened and annoyed him. He slapped her face. It stung and sent her fear level rocketing.

He put one hand on her throat, dragged back the blanket and threw his left leg across her body and straddled her. He was strong and way too powerful to push away. The fear she might be strangled was overpowering.

He struggled to pull down his underwear then struggled again to drag up her habit. Despite the effort, he loved it. For a breather, he collapsed on top of her and belched; his idea of foreplay.

Was being raped by a sweet-smelling, freshly bathed and shaved gentleman any better than by a filthy stinking piece of shit?

'And now my darling, you are about to have the time of your secluded little life.'

He scrambled to pull down her trousers and rip her underwear, and Louise knew she had to fight back. She feared for her life but had to try. Her left hand patted the ground, touching dirt and pebbles. A rock would have been handy. She touched his belt and dragged it closer. Then something solid attached to the belt. He tore away her underwear. His hand moved roughly on her inner thigh trying to force apart her legs.

She touched the sheath and then the knife handle. Using one hand to release the knife was tricky. Time was running out.

'Now my beauty, try this on for size.' He prepared to thrust into her then let out an enormous scream. Louise had loosened the knife and, and using her non-preferred left hand, stabbed Raoul in his right buttock, a seriously tender part of the anatomy.

He fell off yelling and screaming. Down the cave, his fellow fighters laughed at his success thinking the latest notch on his belt was a nun. Men who bet against him handed over their money.

Louise was up, rearranging her clothes. She grabbed her bag and saw the Resistance leader writhing in agony. He couldn't lie on his back because of what was stuck fast in his arse. He lay on his side trying to reach the knife. She saw his open mouth, screaming. He fell silent when her shoe made a brutal connection with his teeth. By attempting to rape her he'd put his foot in it; she returned the favour.

Heading to the front of the cave, a couple of men made crude comments. Most were drunk, counting their winnings or asleep. She reached the mouth of the cave, paused then ran.

Now her fear rocketed. Not so much because her attack on the boss would have his followers chasing her hell bent on revenge, but rather because her current location and desired destination were unknown.

Where the hell am I? Where the hell am I going?

The moon was on its lunchbreak, it was pitch black, the forest was a scary place and she tried to remember her training with the SOE.

Where is Lyon? Where is the moon? Where is my sanity?

Chapter 39

A forest near Lyon, France

She heard the Resistance fighters crashing through the forest, shouting at one another telling one another where to look. Some used torches and their beams flashed from tree to tree. She collapsed. Her energy fled. If she ran again, someone would hear or see her. She picked up two chunky rocks and slipped them into her bag. Not the best weapons but something.

She stood and hit her head on an overhanging branch. Running was out, climbing was in. Those obstacle courses in Inverness-shire did the trick. Up the tree she went until she was several limbs above the ground. In the darkness, she couldn't see the ground and hoped her pursuers couldn't see her.

Voices came and went. She heard two talking about Raoul. 'You know the nun stabbed him in the arse.'

The other man cringed. 'Christ, I bet that hurt.'

'Whoever heard of an abseiling nun knowing about explosives and stabbing a Resistance leader?'

They moved on and Louise didn't. When the loudest sound in the mostly silent forest was the trickle of a stream and an animal or bird scratching or calling, she climbed down and set off.

She needed to return to the monastery or to Father Flory. The number of new enemies kept climbing. The Wehrmacht soldiers from the train, the Gestapo from the jail, the furious Resistance fighters, and whoever the traitor or traitors were in and around Lyon. Oh and not forgetting a couple of Nazi-supporting nuns in the monastery.

The Gestapo would be ropeable because the SOE agent escaped and their leading bully had his throat slashed. This was not a good time to be alone behind enemy lines in war-torn France.

Louise wondered who knew her true identity. If it was the traitor or traitors, the price on her head would be a king's ransom. Was now the time to lose the costume? Its benefit allowed her to hide her few unusual weapons. The pockets on her trousers would have to do.

Dressed as a nun, she stood out in a crowd. If her enemies spread the word—find that nun—she was asking to be caught. She decided to play a second character and stripped. She removed the cyanide pill from the rosary bead and dropped it into her shirt pocket. SOE training kicked in as she buried her clothing and kicked the habit.

The compass in her pen told her the general direction of Lyon and off she went. Dawn was an hour or two away and the darkness in the city would be her friend.

Standing on a ridge she saw a clearing; a woodcutters' camp with the men still in bed. She crept closer. A dog barked and a man berated the animal. These chaps were not early risers.

A battered old truck snored and Louise reckoned as it was facing the wrong way, her chances of even starting it let alone escaping were zero. But in the tray lay a bicycle. Her thighs and calves began immediately to protest. She lifted the bike out of the truck, crept away from the camp, hopped aboard and set sail. It was slightly downhill to start which helped her aching limbs. The rough track threw everything at her but she kept moving. Her bottom begged for mercy.

When the track met the road her speed increased. Her senses pinged at the slightest man-made sound. The forest thinned and the first signs of civilization appeared. She approached the outskirts of Lyon alas from the wrong direction. The monastery and Father Flory's church were on the other side of the city. Damn.

The outlying villages gave way to the outlying suburbs. She saw a river and hoped it was the one behind the cathedral. She kept pedalling as the first rays of sunshine struggled to climb above the horizon.

The city of Lyon

The city with its shops and commercial buildings meant early risers were out and about. Some people stared at a young woman cycling through town at the crack of dawn. Shopkeepers were not a problem but a truck full of German soldiers was another matter.

She saw them swing out of a road ahead of her but drive in the same direction. She took an immediate left turn. Too late as soldiers seated in the rear of the truck saw her and shouted. The yelling increased. Louise turned into a road with a steep incline. Damn. The bicycle groaned although not as loudly as Louise's legs.

She could hear the truck sounds getting louder. It was in pursuit. It turned the corner. She slipped off the bicycle and wheeled it into a greengrocer's shop.

'Hey!' yelled a startled owner.

'Bonjour Monsieur,' she smiled, resting the bicycle against a stall of oranges all the way from Spain. She picked up an orange. 'I pay one bicycle for one orange,' she said skipping to the back of the shop.

German soldiers were running along the pavement trying to locate the woman. Their instructions were simple. Find and arrest a young woman who is pretending to be a nun. Find her. She is a British spy.

A German burst into the shop. 'Where is the woman?'

'Pardon Monsieur?'

The bicycle waved at the German who exploded. He pointed. 'She was on that bicycle!'

The greengrocer was a terrible actor. 'Oh *that* woman. I think she ran out the back, Monsieur.'

The soldier ran into the street and yelled. 'She's in here.' He ran back into the shop as others followed. They crashed through the room at the rear scaring the life out of Mrs Greengrocer. 'Where is she?'

The woman pointed to the open back door. The soldiers poured out to the yard past crates and boxes of vegetables. There was a lane at the rear for deliveries with the back gate open. Some soldiers burst into the lane while others searched the yard. Their cries of frustration and anger grew louder. The ones in the lane came back into the yard and then all of them re-entered the house and shop.

Threats were made. The greengrocer and his wife pleaded. They did not know the woman. The threat of a visit from the Gestapo made no difference and the Germans left in a rage.

The couple went outside. They knew the nooks and crannies of their property. No sign of the mystery woman until the wife pointed.

There was an area against the fence with two wooden sides where all their spoilt fruit and vegetables were thrown ready for the pig farmers. The stinking material moved. Not a lot, just enough to attract attention. The couple moved close to the putrid pile.

'Mademoiselle?' asked the confused husband.

After a pause, a voice spoke from within. 'Have they gone?'

'Oui.'

She pushed at the rotten and rotting material and emerged. She was not dressed for the debutant ball at Buck House.

The wife took her in hand walking to the pump in the yard. The husband produced the water and the former pretend nun endured today's pig food being plucked from her hair and clothes while her exposed skin was washed in damn cold water.

'Merci,' she said over and over. Who said the SOE lacked glamour?

The towel needed washing but Louise gladly dried her hands and face. The wife disappeared.

'Please Monsieur; I need to know the way to the Cathedral.'

He wondered why but explained. His wife appeared with an old work coat and put it on the visitor. This French couple saw up close how the Germans abducted people from the street, took them away never to be seen again. Anyone being chased by the bâtard invaders was worthy of their help.

The husband walked Louise to the back gate, checked the lane, kissed her hand and pointed.

Louise waved and said Merci as if on a broken record. She jogged along the lane and reached the street at the end. She put her hands in the coat pockets and discovered apples. She smiled. The street was clear of Germans.

She crossed the street with a limp. Lanes and small streets led her to the square in front of the cathedral.

Being so early there were few people about. *Is the cathedral even open?* Of her three choices—the monastery, Father Flory's house or the cathedral—she decided this was the safest. Why? It was big with plenty of possible hiding places.

Can I call on, count on the bishop? Not according to Father Flory.

She went to the rear of the cathedral seeking doors. She came to a flight of steps leading down and took them. She met a locked door. So back up the stairs she went and around the side of the cathedral to the front where she was exposed. She saw no-one. Straight to the closest front door, she opened a wicket gate, and stepped into the cathedral.

The Cathedral, Lyon

It was empty and the quiet seemed loud. The sound of her footsteps dominated. She hurried along the side, moved behind the altar and took the stairs down to the crypt. Her only plan was to avoid being caught. *At least I have apples for breakfast.*

In the crypt she stopped, slumped on the floor breathing slowly and deeply. The smell of rotten fruit wafted from her hair and clothes. *My kingdom for a radio* she thought, or was she praying?

It must have been the latter because she heard something. She strained to hear. It sounded like someone tapping. She stood and moved on tip-toe deeper into the crypt. Darkness dominated. The sound grew louder. Yes, it was tapping as in Morse code.

The operator was close, behind the massive monument upon which stretched the outline of a long dead saint. She hoped like hell she could remember her training in Morse.

She craved a pen and notepad. Interpreting was one thing; remembering the words another. She concentrated. The audio was clear, and because of the darkness in the crypt, the flashing lights on the radio gave off a kind of glow.

Letter by letter, word by word she understood the conversation. Seconds ticked by. She believed the sender was an enemy of Britain. She or he must be. The SOE radio operator was recovering in a safe house somewhere in Lyon. This was his radio. So who was sending?

And what is the message being sent here in the crypt? And why here? Then the penny dropped. The shock hit Louise so hard she almost gasped aloud. The receiver is not the Gestapo, Abwehr, Milice or Wehrmacht in Lyon, Paris, Vichy or Berlin. The receiver is in London! The person in this cathedral crypt is talking to the SOE. Why? *Why don't I know this person?*

Then the full penny dropped. Louise's stomach kicked. The person receiving in London, in the SOE is not a loyal officer of the King but a fifth columnist, a spy, a double agent.

My God, there's a mole in London, in Baker Street, in the heart of the SOE. Her heart beat so loudly she was sure she'd be discovered.

With their next message, whoever was sending and receiving messages put a nail in Louise's coffin.

We are closing in on the nun.

Her mind raced. *If I attack before they sign off, the traitor in London will know their traitor in Lyon has been unmasked.* Desperate to know who sat a few feet away, she removed her pen and crouched ready to spring.

The Morse finished. The radio was switched off. Gripping her pen, she crept to the edge of the tomb. She planned to spring out, land safely, feet apart and balanced, then stab the neck or eye of the enemy. She paused then sprang. A piece of rotten fruit, hidden inside her shoe, popped out when Louise crouched. Pushing off to launch herself, Louise stood on the slimy bit of plum—how's that for irony?—and her foot slid back. She didn't spring; she sprawled and clattered on the floor.

The Morse sender panicked, grabbed a torch and a gun and confronted the prostrate former nun speaking perfect English with a Home Counties accent.

'Ah Sister Claudine,' said the voice as the gun was cocked. 'Or should I say Miss Louise Wellesley?'

It was difficult to see with a torch shining in her face but Louise knew the voice and the accent. It was Remi, friend of Jean, Resistance fighter and now revealed as a double agent in bed with the Germans and, what was really frightening, with someone in the SOE in London.

He stepped forward and stomped on her hand holding the pen. That hurt. 'Let it go,' said the arrogant Quisling. Louise had little choice and the pen was kicked into the darkness.

He grinned and mocked her. 'I'm annoyed with you, Miss Wellesley. I've just told London we're closing in on you when in fact you're captured and will shortly be dead.'

Louise surveyed what seemed a hopeless situation. 'So who's your contact in London?'

He laughed. 'Ha, nice try.' He mulled over the request. 'Actually I might as well tell you because, as the saying goes, dead nuns tell no tales.' He stepped back. 'Get up.' She took her time but stood. 'Sit.'

Her thinking was simple. *Keep him talking, delay the execution for as long as possible, and grab any chance to strike back.*

She sat on the chair beside the radio, the one belonging to Alfie, the SOE agent tortured by the Gestapo and rescued by Louise, and the same chair used by Gabrielle when examining the Jewish children.

'You've made a name for yourself, Sister. Murder, jailbreak, train delay, impersonation, you name it; pity it's all over.'

'May I smoke?'

He ignored her. 'Bringing Resistance groups together; you've done it all.'

'I need a match.'

He kept the gun pointed at her but pushed a candle forward. She produced a cigarette from a pocket. 'You should thank me, you bitch. I could turn you over to the Gestapo.'

'Why don't you?'

He scoffed. 'Too much trouble.'

'You're too scared.' He sneered, although she couldn't see him behind the torch blasting light in her eyes.

'So what's your real name? I bet it's not Remi.'

'Roger, if you must know, *Plum*.' The last word was delivered with scorn. 'You even smell like a rotten plum.'

'I bet the free France Resistance cell don't know you're a Nazi.'

'Cells plural, if you don't mind.'

Wow. He shocked Louise. Here was another piece of the jigsaw. Roger from Romford was doing Louise's job; working with, or rather betraying, both Resistance groups and liaising with London. Problem being his SOE contact in Baker Street was on the wrong side.

Surviving was clearly Louise's goal but identifying the SOE mole was all. She formulated a plan. Capture Roger and torture him for the name. She reached for the candle to light her cigarette.

She knew goading him was risky but persisted.

'You know your Morse is not up to scratch.'

He moved towards her, raging that she should taunt him when he was the one with gun. When he was about two metres away she fired.

The cigarette gun possessed only one bullet and accuracy was not its best feature. The bullet entered his right shoulder. He was as much in shock as pain. He dropped to his knees. Louise was at him snatching his gun. His torch fell on the floor creating shadows in the darkness. He slumped on the floor. She put the gun on the table by the radio and knelt beside him. He was losing blood and consciousness.

'Tell me,' begged Louise. 'Who's the London traitor?' He gasped. 'You're dying. No-one can save or hurt you now. What is their name?'

He tried to speak. His lips formed the word. Louise put her ear to his mouth. She heard something but didn't understand. He started to speak again when the gun fired.

Chapter 40

The final act, Lyon, France

The bullet grazed Louise's scalp on its way into Roger's brain. He certainly didn't divulge anything ever again.

Louise fell back in fright and in the shadowy light saw the assassin holding Roger's gun, the one she placed by the radio. The words of one of her SOE instructors boomed inside her head. 'Always know where your weapon is at *all* times.'

Roger's torch cast an even more eerie light in the crypt. It took an age for the gunshot's echo to finally fade.

'Bonjour, Sister.'

'Bonjour, Excellency.'

'I do believe you're in need of a long session in the Confessional.'

She gave a wry smile. 'I don't understand, Bishop. You could have let your colleague give up the name of the SOE mole. Before I told others, you could have done to me as you did to him.'

'Kill you, Sister? Shoot you in cold blood? I am shocked you would even *think* such a wicked thought.'

'You're not going to kill me?' She was genuinely surprised.

'Oh that would be far too kind. No, no, no and besides, what would the Church think of a Bishop who bumped off a nun?'

'It might blight your career.'

'And we can't have that now, can we? No, Sister, I'm going to deliver you into the arms of the Devil, better known as the Gestapo. They'll love you. Did your training cover tin snips and nipples, or bottles in orifices?' He saw her visibly wince. 'Never mind, it's something for you to look forward to.' He picked up the torch and she was in full light.

She bowed her head and gently pressed a hand against her shirt's breast pocket. The tiny lump was there. This was the cyanide pill all SOE agents carried. She'd taken hers from a rosary bead now buried in the forest and needed to extract the pill without attracting attention. He stared at her.

'Right, Sister, this is what will happen. You will walk in front at a steady pace, into and out of the cathedral via the main front door. Once outside, we will hail a policeman, soldier or Gestapo officer and you will be arrested. Failure to obey my orders will leave me no choice other than to shoot. But I will not kill you; that would be the easy way out. Rather, I will send a bullet or two to your buttocks.' He smirked. 'Now you've discarded your disguise, I can appreciate that superb part of your anatomy, and shooting you there will be a payback for what you did to Raoul of the Resistance, n'est-ce pas?'

Fear flooded her body. *Bad news travels fast.* He continued.

'Then, once you recover, your holiday with the Gestapo will begin. Are we clear?' She said nothing. He spat the words. 'Are we clear?'

She spoke in a soft voice. 'Clear.'

'Right, move.' He indicated with the gun and she set off for the stairs out of the crypt. Shining the torch, she was lit as if under a spot while on stage at the Theatre Royal, Drury Lane.

She kept a steady pace. With the light and the bishop behind her, she placed her right hand under her borrowed coat and jumper and felt for her breast pocket. She touched the cyanide pill. A finger and a thumb worked their way into the pocket. She gently squeezed the pill to ensure her grip, and prepared to remove it.

Vaine barked an order. 'Show me your hands.' She wanted to withdraw the pill. 'Now or I shoot your arse.'

She withdrew her empty hand and showed both hands.

'Keep them there.'

They climbed the stairs from the crypt and reached the empty cathedral. He ordered her to walk down the nave. The altar was ignored. They passed over the crossing. The front façade drew closer. The pews ended and they reached the open space leading to the main doors.

Louise knew being killed was a distinct possibility for every SOE agent. But she'd seen the torture endured by two SOE agents—she rescued one—and just didn't think she could remain silent if that type and amount of barbarity was metered out to her. Shame washed over her believing she would yield to the Gestapo.

Then, appropriately, in the house of God, a miracle of sorts happened.

'Excellency,' cried a voice and a young man moved towards the Bishop. It was Jean, genuinely seeking counsel and a blessing from his favourite cleric. As the young man approached, he didn't recognize the former nun, thinking she was another parishioner like him.

Vaine hid the gun but panicked. 'Go away,' he cried and Jean stopped dead. He stared at the Bishop and then the woman. He thought he recognized her but what she was wearing threw him.

'I need to confess, Excellency,' he said and walked towards the cleric who produced his gun. Jean froze. *The bishop has a gun!*

'Go away,' screamed Vaine and the young man lost it. He raised his hands in confusion then took a step towards the cleric who fired. Louise watched all of this waiting for her chance to escape.

Jean screamed and collapsed. Louise ran. Vaine pointed the gun at the fleeing nun and fired. He missed. She raced out of the cathedral interior and up the stairs leading to the gallery. Vaine went after her. His climb up the ecclesiastical ladder was at risk. If this pretend nun escapes, I'm dead. No problem with the Vichy government or Gestapo but possibly massive problems with the Vatican.

Louise knew nothing of the layout of the upper echelons of the cathedral. She flew up the stairs, opened the only door and stepped onto the balcony, a narrow walkway along the side of the cathedral. There wasn't time to examine the massive stain glass window now almost within touching distance. To flee was her only instinct. The walkway was built with a low fence or barrier on her right as she ran. She could hear footsteps and knew His Excellency was in pursuit.

Then horror struck. The gallery stopped; was interrupted by some monumental piece of architecture. Could she leap at this, cling on then slide to the cathedral floor?

Could she simply jump from the gallery? Could she remember her parachute training and avoid broken limbs. Footsteps grew louder.

Vaine's problem was again discharging the gun. The sound could bring anyone, and he rather fancied no witnesses at this time. Then a bullet hole through a priceless stain glass window would need some clever explaining. He would become Vaine the Vandal. His best result would be to have the bitch fall.

He knew the interior of the cathedral and made his move.

Louise crouched expecting a bullet or three at any time. Above her was another door leading out of the gallery. Where it led was immaterial; any port in a storm. She looked back and Vaine appeared. He saw her crouched and smiled. There was evil in his grin.

'Bonjour, Sister' he said, stepping towards her.

Decision time loomed for Louise. Stay where she was and be shot. Jump and break one or both ankles and probably her neck or make a dash for the door above. Her breathing was loud getting louder. Twenty metres away, Vaine moved steadily, his gun pointing at the terrified actress. He stopped, aiming at her lower body.

'Go on, see if you can fly, bitch.'

She hated being forced to die like this and froze in fear. Her failure to respond drove him mad with rage. He decided to shoot when a cry filled the cathedral.

Young Jean had collapsed more in shock than pain when a bullet smacked into his thigh. He lay there, mute, trying to grab a handkerchief to stop the bleeding. Being shot was shocking. Being shot in a house of God for this faithful Catholic was incredible. But being shot by his favourite man of God was beyond belief. The shock wore off and the pain took over. Jean yelled. 'Help! Help!' He continued calling.

His cries flew to the vaulted ceiling. They bounced about and Louise wanted to thank God for this distraction but concentrated on surviving. She knew the sounds would upset her attacker but needed to move. The second door above was only a few feet away. She swiveled on her toes, her thighs in pain and prepared to take off. Jean continued to scream and his cries meant she didn't hear Vaine hurry to her.

He didn't want to miss.

She pushed her foot against the balcony to give herself a fast start, up to the second door, but froze when Vaine threatened.

'Stop, Sister, or the first shot will make you a cripple.'

Louise couldn't move. Jean fell silent. It was time to surrender.

She raised her hands. What could she do? Jump seemed her only option but if the fall didn't kill her, the bullet in her spine would follow.

'I want you to do exactly as I say or I shoot.' He paused. 'Stand, face the altar and move forward to the railing.'

He's going to push me over the edge, she thought. *What do I do?* She thought of her mother and brothers. The tears were lining up and her chest pain kicked in.

'Put your hands behind your head.' She paused. 'Now!' he hissed.

Slowly, she did as instructed. She heard him moving, heard him come closer. Her mind whipped up a horrible memory of a hot air balloon over a Lancashire field, and a murderous Flight Sergeant. She'd been pushed before but this time wore no parachute. *My habit might have saved me.* This time she couldn't kick back at her enemy; there was no room to move.

He was behind her. 'Keep facing into the cathedral.' She did.

It was easy to tremble. How do we react when facing certain death? Then it happened. His hand pressed on her neck and his gun pressed the back of her head. He couldn't afford a dead nun with a bullet hole in her head but a suicidal Sister is just fine.

The hand on her neck stiffened as he applied more pressure. It was no sudden push, just a gradual push, push, push and you're gone. Sadism was listed on his CV.

On the cathedral floor, Jean's pain kicked in and again he screamed for help. The bishop knew he needed resolution. Absolution would follow. He ramped up the pressure and as he gave the final push, Louise squatted. Her aching thighs roared and the bishop's hand slid forward into space. Goodbye balance. His forward movement saw him lurch towards the edge. Louise lifted her head and their eyes met.

He pointed the gun at her and went to pull the trigger. Gravity took over his thinking as he toppled off the balcony and fell with windmill histrionics to the cathedral floor. It was many years since this bishop sat in a pew but now he embraced one.

Louise peered over the edge. His Excellency wasn't moving, his prostrate position was incorrect in terms of canon law, and nearby, Jean lay there thinking how his life had changed forever.

Did I just get shot by the Bishop then see him fall from the balcony of the cathedral?

Louise ran back along the balcony, down the stairs and to the wounded Resistance fighter. His trousers turned red as his thigh oozed blood. Jean's face was a portrait of incredulity having been shot in a holy place by a bishop while being helped by a nun who dressed like a Resistance fighter and stank to the heavens. He pressed his hand to the wound. She produced a handkerchief and made a simple tourniquet. She tried to comfort him and explain the events.

'You're not dreaming, Jean. His Excellency is helping the Germans. I'm not a nun but a British agent. Your friend Remi betrayed us all.'

Jean couldn't speak. The physical pain was bad enough but then to be told his friend betrayed him heaped pain upon suffering. 'It's true and now we have to take you to hospital. Are you okay to walk or even limp?' He nodded. She struggled to get him upright, put one of his arms around her and they set off for the front door.

Jean's blood would disappear but the cleaners would struggle with the others. His Excellency made a right religious mess, as did the dead Englishman turned German sympathizer spread eagled in the crypt.

Supporting Jean, Louise surveyed the Cathedral square. The less impressive forecourt didn't match the grandeur of the building. There were buildings close by and Louise, giving Jean plenty of warning, helped him move.

They crossed to the nearest building with a covered entrance over steps leading to its door. They made it and Louise helped Jean sit. His blood loss was a worry. How could she carry out her plan?

A hospital was the logical place to save Jean's leg or life. But did the Germans check on new patients? Was there someone on the hospital payroll, even a porter, to report anything unusual? If so, she would be taking Jean to harm not help, and almost certainly putting herself in danger. The nun at the railway explosion was a wanted person.

'We need a safe house, Jean. Any ideas?'

He explained. It was the same house the radio operator, Alfie used for sanctuary. It was a good fifteen minute walk away for a fit person; longer going along side streets and lanes to avoid the Germans. That task was too difficult and too dangerous.

Louise was stumped. The radio was inside the cathedral. Forget the dead bodies. She must help Jean then grab the radio.

Tackling these problems stumped her. Then, coming out of a street on the other side of the forecourt was a man and a cart; not any man and not any cart. It was the greengrocer with a load of rotten fruit some of which still clung to the young woman from Farnham.

'Stay here,' said Louise and set off. She expected anyone supporting the Vichy government, any German, to spot her and call out. She moved trying not to be noticed. The greengrocer saw her and stopped.

'Bonjour Monsieur,' she said smiling.

He smiled. 'I see you have found the cathedral, Mademoiselle.'

'I have but I need your help again, please.'

'Of course, Mademoiselle; anything to fight those bastards.'

'Over here,' she said and set off to Jean.

With the cart in front of him, the young Resistance fighter didn't hesitate when asked to disappear beneath the foul-smelling material. Louise gave the driver directions, thanked him then slipped away.

She ran, heading to the monastery. Despite at least two of the nuns thinking she was a closet German, with Louise's track record as an uncontrollable nun, and now dressed as a headstrong female Resistance fighter, knocking on the front door didn't appeal.

She climbed the rear wall of the monastery, dropped to the garden and jogged to the side door she'd used when escaping. It opened. She crept inside and gently tapped on Sister Gabrielle's door. The nun's face would have won a photographic prize.

'You again. Are you breaking in or out this time?'

Louise explained and Gabrielle agreed without hesitation to support her fellow Sister now in mufti. It wasn't so much the Hippocratic Oath persuading Gabrielle to leave the monastery but rather the chance to be part of what sounded like a cracking adventure with this mad fake nun of whom she'd become so fond.

As they hurried along the main corridor, a nun appeared and thought the war had landed in the monastery. She looked for the pursuing soldiers.

The duo escaped and reached the safe house. Alfie was much better but Jean gave off a certain aroma. He lay on a single bed attended by Father Flory and the wife of the household. How the homeowners would ever remove the rotten fruit smell was anyone's guess.

Sister Gabrielle set to work on Jean, and Louise led Father Flory to the kitchen. As she explained the cathedral saga, Flory interrupted.

'I believed Jean when he told me he was shot by Bishop Vaine. But not that Vaine tried to kill you and in so doing fell to his death inside the cathedral. I thought Jean was dreaming.'

'No dream, Father, and the missing SOE radio is in the crypt.'

'It's not important.'

Louise was shocked. 'Oh yes it is.'

'Vaine is dead and I want today declared a public holiday.'

'Ha, ha; look we have to go back and retrieve the radio.'

'We? I'm going nowhere with you dressed as Sister Sabotage.'

'I can fix that. Wait here.'

Louise grabbed the wife of the household, borrowed a dress then asked Sister Gabrielle to leave her medical activity for a minute. She refused until she finished the most she could do for the patient. Despite his stench, Jean managed to smile.

Thank you, Sister,' he called. 'God bless you, Sister.'

'What?' asked Gabrielle when she and Louise were alone.

'I need your habit.'

'What?' Gabrielle was confused even angry. 'Why?'

Louise held up the dress provided by the woman in the safe house. 'Please, let's do a swap.' Gabrielle hesitated. 'Sister, you've trusted me before. Have I ever let you down?'

'Constantly,' said Gabrielle removing her uniform.

'You're a saint,' said Louise putting on the habit over her clothes.

'I'm an idiot.'

'You'll be saving many lives, Doctor.'

And so Gabrielle dressed as a Lyon doctor and Louise as a Lyon nun. The women embraced. Louise went to Father Flory who shook his head.

'You and your costume changes; are you sure you're not an actress?'

Louise pondered answering, didn't, and instead led the way to the cathedral wondering about the two dead bodies.

It was a bright new day and the crowd outside the cathedral was big getting bigger. The bishop's mangled body was huge news. The problems for Louise and Father Flory were getting into the crypt then escaping with the radio undetected.

They reached the crowd and when people saw them, opened up for those they thought should be inside. Words of sympathy were heard. The priest and nun moved through the crowd to be stopped at the front door by police.

They were denied entrance; a ruling from the mayor trying to keep a lid on this major scandal. Father Flory demanded admission and his behaviour challenged the police who relented. Surely a priest and nun should be allowed to enter and pray for their Bishop. No-one knew the priest hated the Bishop or the Bishop died trying to murder the nun. Flory and Louise went inside. A Gestapo officer observed them. An unknown, unnamed nun was on their most wanted list.

Despair and disbelief hovered around the Bishop's body. A young priest sobbed, two nuns knelt and prayed. Police, government officials and medical officers stood around examining, gesticulating and arguing. This was no ordinary death. The Bishop's dead hand held a gun. Flory led Louise to the other side of the cathedral and around behind the altar. At a distance, the Gestapo officer followed.

Down to the crypt went Flory with Louise following. The faint smell of bad fruit lingered, the darkness broken only by the odd flickering candle. Once inside, Louise led the way, around the large tomb and straight to the body of Remi a.k.a. Roger the rat.

'Dear God,' said Flory. Louise was already packing the radio. Flory knelt beside the body and administered the teachings of his calling.

'Come on, she said. 'I know a way.'

'Wait,' said Flory and finished his religious routine.

The Gestapo officer crept down the stairs to the crypt. He heard them. Louise removed a rat from her trouser pocket and placed it by the body. With radio in hand, she left. Flory hesitated which was his downfall. As he stood to follow her, the gun-brandishing Gestapo officer appeared and fired. Flory staggered away.

Louise turned in fear and saw the shape of the gunman. Barely visible in the darkness, he moved forward to shoot her, and stood on the rat. It exploded and the sound caused panic upstairs. When the explosion was followed by hideous screams—Gestapo fiends don't handle pain well—people rushed to the crypt.

Louise dragged Flory to his feet. His upper arm was hit with a flesh wound. He bled and it hurt. 'I know a secret exit.' She helped him out via the way Sister Gabrielle once took the Jewish children.

His wounded arm didn't impede his legs. Up the stairs they ran and reached the back of the cathedral devoid of people.

'Give me the radio,' said Flory. Louise argued.

'No, Father, I can carry it.'

'Not to Spain you can't.' She thought him mad.

'Spain?'

'You've killed Gestapo agents; you blew up a railway, exposed a traitor, and finished off a high-ranking Nazi sympathizer. There is a price on your head, Sister.' He stopped. 'I feel foolish calling you Sister Claudine when you're no more a nun than I'm the Pope. Am I right?' She nodded. 'So what is your real name?'

'I told you, Father, it's Plum.'

'Plum,' he scoffed, 'as in rotten fruit?'

'As in plum jam.'

'You'll have everyone after your blood. The forest, safe houses, here and the Monastery will be searched and searched again. Go. Flee. Return to England. You can't fight the Nazis if you're dead.'

She saw his passion for her safety and admired him for it.

'Thank you, Father.' She looked and felt helpless.

'Give me your habit ... now.' She disrobed becoming a Resistance warrior again. He gave her directions to a hut in the forest. 'No-one but me knows it's there and now our two traitors are dead, no-one will know. I'll send a guide who'll take you to the Freedom Trail.'

She wanted to argue. She wanted to stay. She alone knew a secret so powerful it could destroy the SOE in France. She stared at him. 'Father, you must get the radio to Alfie, and have him send one message to London.' She paused.

'What message?'

'Plum is missing and is presumed dead.'

'But ...' He stopped when she raised a hand.

'Nothing more; just those words. Repeat them please.' He did.

Her fierce expression sealed the deal. He shook his head. She was young and brave and a woman. He trusted her but wanted her gone if only for her own safety.

'I will do as you say, Sister Plum.'

They embraced; neither expected to ever see the other again. Both knew they could be dead by nightfall. He repeated the directions. They looked at one another then turned and walked in opposite directions.

Louise headed out of Lyon wondering if her plan would work. If the SOE thought her dead, and the mole in Baker Street did not know Roger and Bishop Vaine had been exposed, she stood a chance.

Return to London, tell no-one her secret, and discover the traitor in their midst. Easy. As she reached the forest, she thought of an ancient Chinese proverb.

A journey of a thousand miles begins with a single step.

The Detective Joanna Best Mysteries

www.cenfoxbooks.com

Joanna Best is the youngest homicide detective in town. Smart, feisty and gorgeous, she's brilliant at cracking cases and rubbing people up the wrong way. Some jealous colleagues are desperate to undermine her. Certain criminals want her dead. Juggling a career with Victoria Police, having three men madly in love with her, and a strange family,

Jo Best's adventures will drag you in. Her second banana is an Australian born Chinese IT guru who makes computers sing. Her best pal is a female 60ish police surgeon, a forensic genius and chocoholic.

I could not put this series down. The characters, plots, settings, kept me reading. I really liked the word comedy phrasing. A couple of characters I wanted to smack. **Amazon**